Montagu

20 Avenue A

Turners Falls, MA 01376

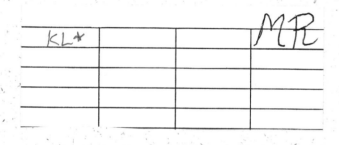

The
Days When
Birds Come
Back

The
Days When
Birds Come
Back

DEBORAH
REED

Houghton Mifflin Harcourt

Boston • New York

2018

For information about permission to reproduce selections
from this book, write to trade.permissions@hmhco.com or to
Permissions, Houghton Mifflin Harcourt Publishing Company,
3 Park Avenue, 19th Floor, New York, New York 10016.

www.hmhco.com

Library of Congress Cataloging-in-Publication Data
Names: Reed, Deborah, author.
Title: The days when birds come back / Deborah Reed.
Description: Boston : Houghton Mifflin Harcourt, 2018.
Identifiers: LCCN 2017044910 (print) | LCCN 2017047824 (ebook) |
ISBN 978-0-544-81740-1 (ebook) | ISBN 978-0-544-81735-7 (hardcover)
Subjects: LCSH: Man-woman relationships—Fiction. | Divorced women—Fiction.
| BISAC: FICTION / Literary. | FICTION / Family Life. | FICTION /
Contemporary Women. | GSAFD: Love stories.
Classification: LCC PS3602.R3885 (ebook) | LCC PS3602.R3885 D39 2018 (print)
| DDC 813/.6—dc23
LC record available at https://lccn.loc.gov/2017044910

Book design by Chrissy Kurpeski

Printed in the United States of America
DOC 10 9 8 7 6 5 4 3 2 1

The author is grateful for permission to quote lines from *The Poems
of Emily Dickinson,* edited by Thomas H. Johnson (Cambridge,
Mass.: The Belknap Press of Harvard University Press),
copyright © 1951, 1955 by the President and Fellows of Harvard
College. Copyright © renewed 1979, 1983 by the President and
Fellows of Harvard College. Copyright © 1914, 1918, 1919, 1924, 1929,
1930, 1932, 1935, 1937, 1942 by Martha Dickinson Bianchi.
Copyright © 1952, 1957, 1958, 1963, 1965 by Mary L. Hampson.

For
Robert Kelleher

These are the days when birds come back,
A very few, a bird or two,
To take a backward look.

These are the days when skies put on
The old, old sophistries of June,
A blue and gold mistake.

— EMILY DICKINSON

A thundering boom, the house went dark, and June pulled her knees to her chest and clutched her robe. She thought of the glass of chocolate milk on the table that day, the swirl of cocoa and fresh, toothy-yellow milk, that offering, that swallow of tangy and bitter and sweet, that moment of waiting to be told her father was gone forever. *Too-ra-loo-ra-loo-ral.* Her skin felt bristly, as if infested with mites, and she scratched her arms and legs and backed up on the sofa, turned sideways and dug her heels into the cushions. And now she held her fists to her eyes and screamed to drown out the sounds inside her head, to drive away the images that followed.

PART ONE

1

It was nearly noon on the Oregon coast, the day already hot when June Byrne shook out her father's old camp blanket on the backyard lawn, removed her T-shirt, and lay with bare breasts to the sun.

She had phoned the contractor again and, like last week and the week before, hung up at the sound of his voice. Except today a woman answered, and pleaded, gently, with June: *Why do you keep calling? What is it you want?* June was drawn to the warmth of her tone, and hesitated before disconnecting the call.

Aside from the golf course beyond the edge of the property, June's yard was relatively private, bordered by birch trees and evergreens and ferns. She lay squeezing her eyes shut, trying to exchange the world inside herself for the one out around her — the foul sea breeze slicing the air, the chickadees' singing at the feeders. Every now and then she heard the *thwack* of a short iron hitting a glassy little ball. But the salty sweat on June's upper lip made her think of margaritas on the beach, and June was one month sober, and yes, it was not quite noon.

Thirty-five years old — nearly thirty-six — and at night with the windows open, June could smell her own skin, and she smelled different without the drinking. She *was* different, or perhaps she was something of a snake, having shed one skin to live inside another.

The contractor came highly recommended, though the phone number she'd been given was no longer in service. She had only his name and that of the small town where he'd moved in recent years. Information gave a listing for a landline. When June hung up on him the first time, she stared at the phone, surprised at what she'd done, and expected he might dial her number in return. He didn't. Not even after the second and third calls she'd placed the following week. Perhaps his phone didn't have caller ID. Perhaps he didn't want to know who she was. Perhaps he believed she was someone he knew and never wished to hear from again.

June pressed the heels of her hands into her eyes and drew a long breath. The rot still drifted on the wind.

It would take most of the summer to restore all the woodwork and period detail in the bungalow next door — the plumber had already come and gone and this had been his best guess. The electrician, too, his initial phase of rewiring behind the walls finished so quickly — a week? June had been drinking then, and writing, too, so it was hard to say. "At least the whole summer," the electrician said. "Like having a roommate." He laughed. "Right there every single day. A cousin coming for the summer like when you were a kid. You ever have a cousin come stay like that when you were a kid?"

June was an only child of an only child. She shook her head no.

Seven weeks ago she was high above the earth, drinking Manhattans on a plane from Ireland, her adopted country for the past twelve years. She'd come home to America, to the carriage house where she was raised, a place her Irish immigrant grandfather built from a mail-order kit nearly a century ago, a man whose presence June still felt in every piece of molding and plank of creaky fir. He'd built the bungalow next door at nearly the same time, and when her grandparents died three years ago, their absence had the quality of a dream, a tale someone told that couldn't possibly be true, not here atop the ridge that had once been a logging road, not here where all of June's life her grandparents shaped this place, in the same way they had forever shaped June.

Both homes faced the ocean, and waves could be heard day and night, a rhythmic crash that helped settle the chatter in the corners of June's mind. Settled her the way the bungalow always had, with its hollyhock garden and stained-glass windows and rooms that once smelled of piecrust and furniture polish and Granddad's musky lard soap. The bungalow was one of June's most favored places on earth. She and Niall Sullivan married there, surrounded by the colors and smells of the Pacific Northwest — rosemary, mint, and salty sea. The properties stood side by side on a square of land amid eight acres of old-growth conifers. Shady, untouched forest flanked the houses to the north and south. Elk, foxes, and bobcats wandered the soft pads of pine needles and emerald-colored moss, downy woodpeckers rattled the trees, and during summer, when the sun set late and rose early, the sharp cries of coyotes cut across the small meadow at the darkest hour of night. The *entire outfit*, as Granddad called it, had belonged to him and Grandmam, and now it belonged to June. By fall she would own less, when she sold the bungalow and the lot on which it stood. She needed to get hold of the contractor. She needed to not hang up.

Both front porches offered a panorama of ocean sunsets and rainstorms and the chalky lighthouse with the red roof when the sky was china blue, like today. Visitors — in the unlikely event June were to have any — needed to be mindful, especially during downpours, not to pull their cars too close to the edge or slip on the footpath across the road and plummet down what Granddad had called *the gorge*, a sharp, hundred-foot tumble over a rocky cliff to the sea.

The fetid breeze June smelled was death, lifting off *by-the-wind sailors*, gelatinous sea creatures that had washed ashore by the thousands over the past three days. Several could fit in her palm, and resembled dinghies made of sapphire glass, with a clear fin like a crystal sail along the spine. As gorgeous and unearthly as a glassblower might have wrought, though they'd turned quickly in the heat, and the blue streak now faded for miles down the beach. The stench lessened only when the wind shifted west, bringing mouthfuls of pinesap and lilacs and forest peat down the side of Neahkahnie Mountain.

"That's Forest Pete," June's father used to say, and for years she believed a giant man of that name lived on Neahkahnie and reeked of the earth.

Her father had bequeathed her the camp blanket when she was seven years old, placing it at the foot of her bed before walking out of the house and into the bungalow, and from the bungalow outside to his death. The last time June saw him alive was a slivered view from across the expanse of both yards — his flannel sleeve rolled above his elbow as he entered the back door of the bungalow. And then nothing but a slant of sun pulling steam off rosemary sprigs, wet tree leaves dangling in sparkles. It was an image June seemed to have stared at for hours, though that couldn't be true. Either way, it was then that her father had walked out of her grandparents' front door, stepped off the long pine porch, and crossed the road. Whether or not he cried out when he dove into the sunset, June did not hear a thing.

Native people on this native land believed the direction of endings was west. "And here we are," Granddad once said to little June from his wraparound porch, facing the whitecaps and charcoal sky, his small field notebook returned to his jacket pocket with a pat. He'd read the journals of Lewis and Clark, and kept detailed notes of the natural world around him, as if his life, too, were an expedition. "It's the troubled moods of the one," Grandmam pointed out, "that he most admires," referring to Meriwether Lewis's depression.

Her grandparents had meant to raise a large family, though

there had only been June's father, Finn, and after he was gone, there was only June. Her grandparents seemed to have been everything that June and her father were not — adventurous and surefooted, moving through the world with ease. Maeve and Cronin Byrne, with their beautiful mess of fair hair, their hearty confidence when they said goodbye to County Carlow at the start of World War II. Granddad had sold his portion of the family dairy farm, and Grandmam saved her bookkeeper's pay for four years while living at home, and together it was enough to mail-order two houses from a Sears, Roebuck & Co. catalog in America, plus a small down payment on a rugged piece of land. June imagined them standing in the fresh clearing with raw hands and mouths gaping in joyous disbelief as everything they needed was delivered in tidy boxes and crates.

But the contractor. This morning when the woman answered, June had listened to the patience in her voice. June could be a little anxious, a little shy, and, according to Niall, a little off-putting to people who didn't know her — didn't *understand* her, he'd corrected. That woman, though, had conveyed kindness in only a couple of words.

June crossed her ankles, spread her arms, and lay as if crucified to the ground. She burrowed her shoulders into the wool and released the fustiness of winter — the funk of rubber boots and sludge and months of thin, dark rain. It must be eighty-five degrees now, June glistening everywhere with sweat, recalling her childhood days on the beach, lying on the camp blanket in the cove of a dune to read a book. Entire afternoons were lost this way; even when the weather was cool and the wind strong, June wrapped the camp blanket around her shoulders until the rain chased her away. At night the illuminated bonfires down the shore, the fishing boats, and the lighthouse all mirrored the stars and planets above, and June would stand on her front porch in her nightgown in the dark with her arms out to the sides, feeling as if she were floating, untethered, in the sky.

Summers had changed since then, the season beginning early and hanging on until the middle of October. Tourists arrived during those bright weeks, with kites and a determination to swim in the Pacific's frigid waters. The village had three restaurants, and they bustled with the sandy and sun-crisped, with loud children intoxicated by fresh, ionized air. When June had returned it was spring, and she was greeted on this continent on that April day by the Irish sky she'd left behind, thick and pewter and honking with geese. Only the dogwood and cherry blossoms sprouted color, a radiant pink, and the beach had barely a human print in the sand.

Now the camp blanket, the summer sun, the distant smack of golf, memories trailing like flares behind the bright orange sun on June's lids. When she was very young, milk still arrived twice a week in glass bottles on the porch, as if it were the 1950s instead of decades later, and the jangle of jugs against the metal carrier would wake her before dawn. If her father happened to be up and making breakfast, he spooned the cream off the top and gave it to June.

After his death June often sat on the beach in the same spot where she believed his life had come to an end, and she did not think this morbid then, and she did not think it now. Grandmam would send her off with a cheese and butter sandwich and a molasses cookie. "Watch yourself, love," she'd say with a gentle tug of her chin. Those days belonged to June.

She had always been tall, with slender fingers like her grandmother's, her thoughts flittering like her father's, like frantic flies in a jar. When she gave up drinking a month ago she discovered the next day that she could not write, and writing had proved to be the single most important constant of June's life for the past ten years. *You don't know what you don't know until you know it,* her father used to say. He said plenty of things, but on this June could agree. She wrote emails now instead of finishing her fifth novel, and of her emails, nothing stretched the imagination, just a flood of dry inquiries concerning her missing belongings from

Ireland. She'd shipped sixteen parcels to herself before she departed, and at some point while crossing the Atlantic, the last remnants of her life with Niall had disappeared. "Did the liner sink?" she asked. "Was it pillaged by pirates?" Victory International Shipping emailed back that they did not joke about such things, and offered assurances that her belongings would certainly turn up very soon. "Like jetsam?" she replied, but heard nothing in return.

The spate of rain from both continents was behind her now, and that was something. For the past thirty-one days she hadn't had a drink either, and that was *really* something. She'd made it further this time than at any time before, and she had accomplished it without help — all the trembling, vomiting, sweat-soaked sheets, the certainty that she was going to die. She did not die. But she could not write. Could not perform the single act she believed had saved her long ago.

She ought to feel proud. She ought to feel safe here. When the sprinklers kicked on at midnight across the golf course, the spray on leaves and bark and shrubs sounded like fabric being torn, a rip-ripping with an eerie silence in between. June closed her windows until the sprinklers shut off. Afterward she opened them, and the smell of cool wet grass made her miss everyone she'd ever loved or had tried to love for as long as she could remember.

June missed her pillow. She missed her stoneware coffee mug with the white speckles, and she missed being able to caress Niall's soft sleeves between her fingers. She missed burying her face in the shirts he'd worn, breathing as deeply as her lungs would allow. Within two months of his leaving, his scent had vanished from the clothes he'd left behind. Gone, like her vodka, her wine, and her confident way of moving through the world. June missed thinking of herself as funny and uncomplicated. She missed believing that all of those other things were her real life, and being frightened by sprinklers was not.

She didn't need much. The carriage house appeared nearly the same as when she was a child — simple and spare, with *books and lamps and drawers full of maps*, as her father used to say, absent of mementos or kitsch. The only artwork was her mother's botanical drawings and paintings in golden frames, a few in raw birch that had darkened over time. Myrtle, fig, eucalyptus — *Myrtus communis, Ficus carica, Eucalyptus cinerea*, written below each illustration in her mother's cursive hand. Upstairs, the two small rooms at either end of the steps mirrored each other, with single iron bedsteads next to the windows — her father's frame painted light gray, June's white, and each room accompanied by knotty-pine five-drawer dressers built by Granddad. Down in the living room there remained the same nailhead-trimmed leather chairs, soft and cracked and angled toward the hearth. In the small square kitchen at the back of the house stood the small square Quaker table that her father had built using alder from the northernmost acre of the property. June had often sat in the chair facing the multipane window that wrapped the corner, with a full view of the white birch trees at the edge of the backyard, and beyond them to a slice of the bright green golf course, and above that, acres of Douglas firs all the way up to the craggy tip of the mountain. Her grandparents' house was to the left, and it was here at this table where June had sat when she caught the final glimpse of her father while she was coloring or reading or imitating her mother's penmanship. She was no longer sure. She'd glanced up, saw his hand, saw the rosemary and leaves. At some point she'd taken a sip of chocolate milk but had no idea who'd given it to her, no memory of ever having been given it again.

It was also at this table where, on a good day, her father had prepped her for spelling tests, often pausing to say she surely knew the words already, and most times she did — *aggregate, catkin, deciduous, habitat*. Grandmam had taught June to read when she was four, using circulars and illustrated feed catalogs that came in the mail. Sometimes her father made oatmeal with cream, or BLTs using Grandmam's homemade dill mayonnaise, and they sat across from each other with an even split of Coke. Sometimes, too, her father set his glass down and glanced up from his plate with raised eyebrows at the sight of June, as if surprised to find her there, surprised by her very existence. Other times his lids remained closed while he spoke in a whisper, as if through the fog of a headache, though he never complained of one. Maybe he was searching for the right thing to say. Maybe he was drawing on his thin supply of patience needed to make it through another hour with June.

He wasn't always so unreachable. There were days, too, when the house rattled to life in the form of maps — artful copies of hand-painted pines and snowy slopes and roads from long ago, spread out in a series across the living room rug. Towns circled in red were places her father and mother had visited; others, circled in green, were places her father promised to take June. His eyes were electric then, open and aflame, the way Granddad spoke of the rockroses bursting on the patio. The washing machine churned all afternoon with laundry, while a pot on the stove bubbled Jonagold and McIntosh apples, and the house had the feel of a mother and a father, everything working, cinnamon and butter, the tart-sweet scent of homemade applesauce filling every room. On those days her father called her *Buttercup Byrne,* and June collected primroses or daffodils, whatever was in season, and placed them in a jam jar on the table, the way she imagined her mother might have done.

June closed her eyes every time she spoke to Victory International Shipping.

Last week Niall called for the first time in a year, and June closed her eyes and listened to what he had to say.

2

Evening arrived on their high-desert acres in eastern Oregon without a chance for Jameson and Sarah Anne Winters to settle into lamplight, have a meal, and watch the news.

At first they'd held off preparing dinner, thinking the boy would wake at any moment, but three hours passed and he was still facedown on the sofa where he'd cried himself to sleep. He hadn't had lunch or been cleaned up in any way — his feet, hands, and face were smeared red and black from tripping in the strawberry patch at the side of the house after he'd hit the ground running. He'd sat in the damp soil and cried while bees floated near his sweaty face and hair. He dug his heels into the patch and shrieked when Jameson tried to come near.

Their confidence was slipping. Soon it would be bedtime. Should they carry him to his room in this shape and tuck him in for the night? He clearly needed rest, they said, gazing from the living room doorway. The poor boy, they said. On this they solidly agreed.

His sixteen-year-old mother, Melinda, had been shooting heroin in a convenience store bathroom at the start of her labor, and the clerk, an eighteen-year-old boy who'd graduated from the same high school Melinda had dropped out of, tired of waiting for her to come out, and busted in. Then he tired of waiting on an ambulance, and locked the glass entry doors and drove Melinda fourteen miles to the ER. She named her baby Ernest, because the boy had a book by Ernest Hemingway on the dashboard of his car, and she held it in her hand as he drove, and was holding it still when the nurses wheeled her in. She called the baby Ernie, like a stuffed toy one could leave on a bed for days. Now he was two, and for the past twelve months he'd been in foster care with Jameson and Sarah Anne. After all this time they should have a feel for what to do. After all this time they shouldn't have days like they had today.

Not true, Sarah Anne said. She called that wishful thinking, said no one was going to be served by that, and could Jameson please pass her the broom?

A short while earlier Jameson had imagined fever in the boy's bright cheeks while he slept, but his forehead felt cool and moist and soft. The child was simply worn out, and his face, coated with the sticky sheen of dried tears, held a beauty that occupied Jameson, a strange blessing that had stalled him, crouched and staring at the small mouth and swollen eyelids and the tiny spiral of his ear.

"Maybe the smell of hash browns will wake him," Sarah Anne had whispered, and Jameson tilted his head as if listening for some other voice, but he took the hint. Hash browns were a household favorite. And dinner needed to be made.

"It'll be ready in about forty-five minutes," he said, walking past her, and it sounded as if he were giving *her* a hint, implying that she figure this thing out by the time he put food on the table. And then he guessed that that *was* what he meant, but wished he hadn't meant it, so he stepped back and kissed her on the cheek to soften what he'd said and how he'd said it, but he could see she knew all about that kiss, and barely raised her face to meet his lips. When he began cooking up their breakfast for dinner, he no longer cared for the idea, and was pretty sure Sarah Anne didn't either.

They'd received another crank call this morning on the kitchen phone. People who knew them didn't call that phone, and of course they wouldn't hang up if they did. Jameson's best guess was Melinda. Maybe she was trying to scare them. Maybe she had something to say but kept losing her nerve. This morning Sarah Anne heard breathing on the line.

Shadows had sloped across the cabinets and oven where earlier in the evening Jameson had leaned into his hip; the crooked feel of his bones, especially his left leg, added to the distraction. He'd been lost in thought with a cold egg in his hand, the desert air drifting through the screen and chilling the back of his neck. If the boy was dreaming, what might those dreams turn out to be? Maybe that first year of his life had vanished from memory. Maybe it continued to haunt him in his sleep.

Jameson knew how the past could rise up inside the walls of a dream and fill the body with an urgent confusion, with all the markings of a real and merciless now. How could a child be expected to understand that what he saw wasn't happening again when a grown man with logic and defenses could be jerked from sleep by his own screams? Three years after the worst days of his life, Jameson's feet still might swing to the floor in the middle of the night, eyes wide and hands pressed forward in the dark, until Sarah Anne's touch went from a threat on his shoulder to a woman's fingers guiding him back beneath the sheets, a woman slowly shifting from a stranger into the shape of his wife, someone he had loved for the better part of twelve years.

The boy was slight for his age; his arm dangled above the floor as he slept. His fist twitched near his soft blanket, tucked and hanging from beneath his neck. Every now and then he slugged the sofa cushion.

Jameson cooked hash browns and cheddar omelets and ready-bake biscuits with Sarah Anne's homemade strawberry jam while Sarah Anne picked up the mess of the day throughout the house, sweeping the dried grass and dust trailed in on Jameson's work boots, for which he apologized and she waved off, saying the whoosh and scratch of the broom calmed her nerves.

When dinner was ready they took quiet care scooping it onto plates and into bowls, the melted cheddar escaping the folds of each omelet, stringing cheese from dish to dish. They placed the boy's empty plate in front of his equally empty snap-on highchair, just in case, and his small fork and spoon there, too. Steam rose from the food at the center of the table, and Sarah Anne reached for Jameson's hand, laid hers on top of his, and each offered the other a small, defeated smile, like a prayer before lifting their forks. They ate, setting silverware gently against stoneware, swallowing slowly as if the sound of their throats might wake the boy, though they wanted more than anything to wake him.

We look feeble, Jameson thought. Thin and sapped and frail as fifty years from now. They were thirty-five years old, with spring birthdays two months apart. They ate what they could and then they cleared the table and began washing dishes, taking turns peeking into the living room.

Jameson leaned next to Sarah Anne at the sink and asked if it wasn't better to keep soap off the iron skillet she was washing. She blinked as if coming to, set down the bottle of dish soap, and thanked him for noticing. He reached for the skillet, and with it, her hand. He said, "You can go rest in there with him if you want."

"I don't think I could," she said. "Rest, I mean." She slid her fingers from beneath his. "But you can wash the skillet if you want."

His mind had wandered while cooking the hash browns, trailing the many things that had gone wrong by midday. He'd stared at the woolly sunflowers across the meadow, the sway of yellow petals still bright in the dusk, while thin strings of potato burned along the edge of the skillet, encrusted so deeply it appeared to have been soldered to the iron. Now he was scouring with the arm of a man capable of rebuilding a house, and still the black scabs remained.

He eyed the dish soap, let it be, and then eyed it again, wanting only to accomplish this one simple thing.

When Sarah Anne turned to open the fridge, Jameson squirted a shot of blue soap onto the edge of the skillet. He went at it with the steel brush, and this time the flakes broke free.

She was teaching the boy that it was all right to sleep and eat and play when he wanted those things. She was teaching him to perceive his own needs. It was all right to leave him on the sofa like that. It was.

Jameson and Sarah Anne only ever called the boy Ernest. They liked to say, "Why so serious, Ernest?" because it made them smile, just enough, while greeting sorrow head-on. But Jameson continued to think of him as *the boy,* a changeling who'd come to live with them, a substitute for the real child who'd lost his place in their home. *This* boy could sleep for long hours in the daytime. *This* boy's deeply red mouth was often puckered in quiet, like an old man gathering answers from the corners of his mind. *This* boy was unnaturally angelic, round-faced, with immense brown eyes. *This* boy was slightly lovelier in looks than Jameson's own children had been, and he hated himself for thinking such things.

He and Sarah Anne had stood over him wondering what to do today, but it wasn't like they didn't know how to parent. Parenting wasn't new. Until three years ago Jameson and Sarah Anne understood just what to do with a child, with two children, with twins. "Oh, they're twins!" everyone said, especially in summer on the beach, surrounded by tourists who didn't know them. "Boy and girl *twins!*" they'd say, like a joyous discovery. For the entirety of their short lives, seven years to be exact, Piper and Nate had remained polite about being on curious display. They were courteous when told how identically they resembled each other. Said thank you and smiled as if they'd never heard it before, grinned as if it were a compliment, and in truth, it was. There were times when it had pained Jameson to see the love the twins had for each other; to look directly at it was like looking into a fiercely bright light not meant for the eyes. The soft sound of their voices in the next room, the giggling they sparked in each other, was like listening to a beautiful piece of music with the volume turned way too high. That undercurrent of blazing affection was not of this world, and he could never say this to anyone, especially not now — certainly he could never say this to Sarah Anne.

3

JUNE'S CUTOFFS WERE SHORT, very short, practically underwear, the only strip of clothing that marked her skin when she woke twenty minutes later in the sun. She peeled back the waistband to see the burnished tan line across her belly. She was becoming browner by the day.

"What if I was wrong?" Niall had asked on the phone last week. June almost didn't answer when she saw who was calling. "And what if you were wrong, too?" he said.

This morning June filled the bird feeders in the front and back of the house, with millet for the chickadees and sunflower seeds for the nuthatches, and even with her eyes closed she knew which birds had arrived by their songs. Granddad had taught her to pay attention.

Aside from the houses, June had kept very little of her family's belongings. She was trying to make her life her own, shaving off pieces of the past in exchange for the larger whole of the present. She'd kept the braided living room rug in the carriage house, soft wool and the greenish white of spindrift, its oval shape like a pond in the center of the room. She added a charcoal-colored loveseat to the two leather chairs, and the furniture appeared to float along the edge of water when the glow of summer sun saturated the walls by late afternoon. As a child June often anchored herself to the spiral at the center of the rug and read a book, the same small swirl where her father spread out the maps. Several nights ago she sat there while reading Granddad's field notes.

Thirty elk arrived today, and took refuge in the post office parking lot, causing a stir for the locals and their dogs. The bluebells rose to the sun on this third day in March, 1971, a glory that has lightened the mood.

Overcast, and the last of the Canada geese are headed south, their final calls echoing from sky-high arrows that broke my heart until Maeve set the house to smelling of roast and garlic stew.

"Pay attention," Granddad used to tell her. "The trees and the birds and the orb weaver know as much as we do about this world, if not more."

When she'd hung up with Niall, the desire to jump into her father's old truck and head to the liquor store in Wheeler was difficult to calm. Reading Granddad's notes had only made it worse. She could practically hear her grandparents' *Sláinte*, and see their tumblers of beautiful brown whiskey on the porch during long summer evenings, and by the fire during winter when the sun set early and the days were unbearably short.

"I'm sober," June had said to Niall. "Nearly a month. What do you make of that?"

"That's grand, June. You sound wonderful, brilliant. Are you happy? You sound quite happy."

June opened her eyes to the yard, shielded the sun with her hand as the sudden, frenetic flood of golden-crowned kinglets rushed in like small leaves scattering through the Douglas fir. It was that time of day, the air filling with their thin, boisterous song as they picked the cones clean. June's father had mastered their cheeps, calling them into the yard, within a foot of June if she and her father remained still. Tiny bright crowns lifted off their heads like flames. Whether the song imitated calls for mating or declared a territorial war, June couldn't remember, or perhaps had never known. *The goal of every living thing is to stay alive,* her father once said.

Mornings June drank coffee from one of Grandmam's rose and white teacups, displayed on her open kitchen shelves above the woodblock counter. Grandmam's peacock-blue linen apron, a little threadbare, hung on the copper hook near June's stove. Granddad's field notes lined the bottom bookshelf in her living room. Her grandparents couldn't possibly have gone.

Granddad had traced the height of the hazel tree until it finally stopped growing, having sprouted like a miracle from the pocketful of hazelnuts he'd brought with him from Ireland. Hazel was one of the seven noble trees of the Celts, and he encouraged June to climb it, this lanky shrub of a tree that somehow stood nearly fifteen feet tall. It brought wisdom and inspiration, he said with genuine seriousness. Her grandparents spoke Irish when they were alone, and their melodic voices sifting from the next room caused a knot in June's chest, something felt but not understood, at least not then, not until twelve years ago when she decided to study Irish literature in Ireland, met Niall, became a writer, and made a life for herself in the very county her grandparents left behind so long ago. All those details in Granddad's little books an example of what it was to be a pupil of life itself, devoted to making sense of the world, and beyond making sense, to no purpose at all, except to sit with the wonder of it. "Write it down," he used to tell her. "Then you'll know what it means."

June had grown bored with her fictional characters, Leigh and Cordelia, spindle-legged sisters with not enough trouble in their lives. Perhaps this was the real problem and not June's lack of drink. She'd abandoned the twenty-somethings just after they had zipped themselves tightly into elegant dresses and slid their feet into matching champagne-colored heels.

Niall had been June's editor in Ireland. When they separated, he went to work for another publishing house, in Australia, something he'd been considering for years. Lately it had crossed her mind to call him and ask for advice, to see if he could talk her through the puzzling out of plot, the ways in which she might fit it all back together.

The camp blanket was one of the first things June unpacked from the airtight cellar that Granddad built to the right of the carriage house's back door. The blanket was of 1960s vintage, with a fleecy pattern of pink, green, and orange diamonds on one side, a solid canvas-green on the other, and if June had to choose what she loved most of the things she'd kept, she'd say the blanket. She'd say the notebooks. She'd say her mother's artwork. She'd say that nothing quite compared to the bungalow. Its three bedrooms and large dining room with the heavy pocket doors sliding out of the living room wall, the large French doors opening onto the garden and the spread of white trees, had always been enchanting and dreamy, especially compared to the moody, complicated rooms of the carriage house.

A week before her father died, a flurry of life took over the carriage house, a chaos of cleaning and making plans. Her father purchased a Polaroid camera for June and took her on the only trip they would ever take from their map of circles, though it ended the second day in the high desert when her father began speaking to her with eyes closed while driving. The truck lurched into a ditch and the axle snapped in two. June's top front baby teeth, already loose, were knocked out when her mouth collided with the dash. Granddad and Grandmam arrived hours later and got the truck fixed. They wrapped June in the camp blanket and everyone was quiet, speaking only of the axle, nothing of the cash Granddad handed to the tow driver and mechanic, nothing of June's bloody lip and missing teeth. On the way home June rode with Granddad in his truck, Grandmam drove her father behind them in his, and June glimpsed their dulled faces in the side mirror when the light was right. They didn't appear to speak in all the hours it took to get home. Up front with Granddad the conversation ranged from desert rabbits and birds of prey to the way Americans cut their food with the side of their fork. Granddad lisped his brogue in a show of solidarity with June's missing teeth, and June laughed against the golden sunset, her Polaroid beside her, while eating cup after cup of vanilla pudding from the Shop and Go, where they'd filled both trucks with gas.

A few months before June returned from Ireland, she'd hired a crew to clean and repair the carriage house. Windows washed, yard landscaped, the daphne and violet thistle and lamb's ear coming up nicely around the front porch, the rockrose a peach-red arch over the back patio door. Every room was coated in fresh white paint, and the cedar shingle siding was layered with chestnut stain. June had wanted to avoid the distraction and awkward discomfort of strangers coming and going at all hours of the day. It turned out that the roof needed to be replaced; there'd been a leak, some dry rot, and the ancient sewer line from both houses, made of clay, was strangled by twisted roots and busted every few feet. Months ago when June footed the bill, American dollars were worth far less than the euro, and the money seemed abstract and distant, like the life waiting for her on this coast. Even now the extreme tidiness had the feel of a movie set, her life playing out like the part of a young widow living in a small holding on a hill.

Of course Niall wasn't dead, though there was a time she'd wished him dead, wished herself a widow to be pitied, but Niall was alive, living with an Aussie named Angie in a white Queen Anne with a green-tiled roof in Melbourne, with Angie's ten-year-old son, all of which June had discovered before tearing herself away from social media. When Niall told her about his new life on the phone last week, she pretended not to know.

It helped to think about other things.

The bungalow was twice the size of the carriage house and severely neglected, the life eaten out of it during its abandonment, though it could have been much worse if Grandmam and Grand-dad hadn't taken such excellent care of it for decades. They'd taken care of everything, including each other, until the last moments of their lives. They died two hours apart, in their sleep, and there had been no real explanation. "Natural causes" was written on both death certificates, but June imagined Granddad waking in the dark to find Grandmam had slipped away, and he continued to lie beside her, holding her hand, willing himself to join her before the sun had a chance to fill the house with unbearable cruelty.

Months before they died, at the age of ninety-eight, Grand-dad had continued to drive, and Grandmam still walked ramrod straight. It wasn't until Granddad wrecked the Pontiac on Highway 101 that things began to deteriorate. Neither was injured beyond bruises, yet soon they were dead. Something had been set in motion the day of their accident, and for weeks Grandmam left June long voicemail messages about people June didn't know — they were not in the accident; no, it was not their fault, hers and Granddad's, was it? It couldn't be their fault, she'd say, mixing Irish and English, of which June was pretty sure she was unaware. June could not pick up or call back, could not bear the weight and confusion of Grandmam's suffering while June's own life had fractured into sharp, revolting pieces that were getting harder to mend. The drunken fights, the lies overlapping into braided ropes, which June had used to hang them both. Two months after the accident her grandparents were dead, and one year later, in a scene so ugly June was grateful she could not recall it in its entirety, Niall was gone.

June had entered the bungalow twice now — once to make sure the windows were closed, once to open them again. She'd disrupted the moths, caught her hair in the orb weaver's web, swiped dead house flies from the windowsills as the windows went up, and again when they came down. She stood face-to-face with a chipmunk on the kitchen counter who looked at her and flicked his tail in a gesture of defiance. "I am a thousand times your size, little man," June said, sounding like Grandmam. The tiny creature scurried down the cupboard and along the baseboard into the living room. "Enjoy the run of the place," June said. "You'll be thrown from the manor soon enough."

She had smelled the decay, looked up at the blackened trim, a leak, she assumed, after a massive storm two years ago had ripped an ancient spruce from it roots and sent it flying toward the house. By some measure of grace the tree landed within feet of the dining room windows, and only the gutter was torn away. But even in its current state of disrepair, the house was still worth a small fortune. June hated thinking of it this way, but her finances were dwindling, her backlist of books fading from popularity, the dollar her only currency now, and no telling when she would finally finish her novel.

You'll be dead in a year if you don't stop drinking, her doctor had told her two years ago, but that wasn't enough. If the goal of every living thing was to stay alive, it had seemed that June was no longer a living thing. Some part of her had undergone a dull demise, and it took her sideswiping a child on his bicycle with her car a year later, in the middle of an afternoon in County Carlow to shake June back to life. It took the terror in a boy's glassy blue eyes, his bleeding elbow and torn jeans as he lay beneath the twisted spokes and cracked frame, looking up at June, for her to finally feel the hot jolt of resurrection. "I was in the lane," the boy said, shivering, stuffing back tears as she reached for him. "I didn't do anything wrong," he repeatedly told her, and June understood that when he got home he'd face a scolding for being careless and unworthy of the gift he'd been given by disciplined and long-suffering parents. "You're not broken," she said, though what she'd meant was to ask if anything was broken. He shook his head no. She trembled, handing him all the money in her wallet — 230 euros. "You're a good lad," she said, or wanted to say, but couldn't get the words to leave her mouth. "You've done nothing wrong," she said, for certain, and told him to go buy himself a new bike and clothes. It was then he began to cry, hard and silent with his chin to his chest, eyes closed over the notes in his hand, and June curled his fingers to keep the cash from being carried off in the wind. She stepped back and apologized again as she returned to her car, apologizing still as she watched the boy in her mirror, slowly pushing his bike down the sidewalk, his tears breaking with a freedom she knew he would reel in once he rounded the corner to home.

Rather than driving off a cliff—accidentally or with determined calculation, no matter—June had somehow arrived home and gathered up Niall's clothes for charity. She remained awake all night, piling her own things into boxes to be shipped. West was the direction of endings, and though she did not feel the shape of an actual plan, the image of the carriage house and its cedar scent, the familiar feel of its temperamental spaces, was drawing her home.

Now June had landed back in the place where she began, alone and wishing someone would show up, stay just long enough to agree with her about how wondrous the heat felt on cheekbones, knees, and breasts, a simple nod would do, and then he—she would like it to be a he—could hand her a glass of ice water, sit beside her on the lawn without getting in the way, and speak a line or two—some small, smart thing, like how it wouldn't be long now, not at all, he'd say. In a little while this hurt will hurt no more.

"How is it, then, being there without your grandparents?" Niall had asked on the phone.

"It doesn't quite seem real."

"What's in bloom?" he'd asked, which made everything seem real, and she told him about the iris and foxglove and yarrow she'd seen along the forest shore, and he said he could picture it perfectly. He said how fine it was for her to be there at the start of summer. Like the day they were married in the backyard, and the golfers had agreed to remain quiet during the ceremony. "Do you remember?" he asked.

"I do," she'd said, and they shared a small laugh.

The belongings she'd taken such care to hold on to were now missing, thanks to Victory International Shipping, and yet she knew exactly where Niall's had gone. When he departed, he took only what he could fit in one suitcase, and this stung as much as anything he might have come up with to punish her, though she did not think he was trying to. Even so, she understood enough to know that everyone was capable of grievous, despicable acts given the right circumstances. What he said was that he didn't want any of the possessions that had made up their life together, and she did not restrain herself from hurling insults at his back while his steps crunched the gravel driveway with an amplified sound. When she'd dropped off Niall's shirts, pants, and shoes at the Goodwill shop, it occurred to her that in time people would be walking the streets wearing his clothes, and if she remained in Ireland much longer, she'd have seen Niall everywhere she went, which might have been enough to drive her fully round the bend, off a cliff, or falling-down drunk on the kitchen floor.

How did widows find the wherewithal to march their stalwart bodies to the charities and deliver the cottons and polyesters and denims that contained the scent and sweat and stains of their beloved men, only to come across them another day on the backs of strangers? An act of altruism, that was how June thought of it, how she struggled to think of it, even as her own husband had left at her request, a man still alive and well, making love to someone else the way he'd made love to her — or not: perhaps he was discovering new and better ways of lovemaking in someone else's bed, surely he must be doing that, the kind of thing that would keep a man from going back to his wife. It had taken a sort of courage to let fall his things from her arms, because to stand up straight and turn her back had the feel of being trapped inside an airless room, lungs gasping for oxygen.

Where's my lionheart? What happened to my lionhearted lassie? Her father's rubber boots had remained in the mudroom for twenty-one days after his death, his razor and comb in the medicine cabinet for seventeen.

Niall spoke of belongings as possessions; he was the first to say that word choice was no accident. Possessions, as if these things had owned *him,* as if he'd been bewitched and bound to the place against his will. It was excruciating to hear when he said it, excruciating to recall his flat tone of voice, its quality of pure disdain. It took all she had to keep from shouting like a drunk that it didn't matter anyway because she knew she deserved to be left, until she did shout, and shout and shout and shout. It was confusing. June was confused. She had had five martinis in the course of the previous hour when things escalated. She threw her boot at his head on his way out the door and missed. She didn't say how relieved she was to see him go, but she was. When his car neared the road at the end of the drive, June shouted that she hoped he would live long enough to regret what he had done. She crouched as his taillights disappeared in the rain, wept quietly as vodka and bile rose in her throat. She remembered being on her hands and knees, and then lying on the wet gravel, where she woke several hours later in the cold rain.

She had woken late the following day on the sofa, her cheek still marked by the gravel, so deeply she could feel the grooves with her fingertips, feel a bruise there, too. The same with her knees. After that, she passed out. When she woke the following morning, she did not realize what day it was until it began to get dark and she was trembling with fever. Vomit had dried on the front of her shirt. She glanced around moving only her eyes, saw the lamp and books and a framed photo of herself and Niall knocked to the floor. The sofa cushions had been tossed wildly about, and she lay half covered beneath them. She had done all of this in a fit of delirium after not having had a drink in, what, thirty, forty hours?

She'd risen very slowly, placed her feet gently on the floor. Her legs shook, all of her shook, her tongue was glued to the roof of her mouth, and she was soaked through with sweat. She had wet herself. She had shat herself. The stench alone was enough to make her sick. She could not stop shaking. She lowered her body to the floor and crawled in the direction of the shower. Each movement seemed like that of a crippled cat, every step forced and calculated against the corresponding throb of agony.

She finally made it to the liquor cabinet, where she sat on her knees and caught her breath. This was not the time to quit drinking, not like this. She couldn't do it this way even if she wanted to, so she leaned her head against the wall and swallowed straight from the bottle, breathing harder through her nose as the liquid drenched her throat, her hand shaking so badly she repeatedly missed her mouth, and the bottle slipped and vodka poured down her legs and into the cuts on her knees. She snatched it up with a tempered rage, her mind slowly rousing as the drink set her system back to its fragile stasis. By the time the bottle was empty, she recalled with perfect clarity that the last thing she had said to Niall, that thing about hoping he'd live to regret what he had done, was the very last thing June's father had said to her.

4

It was true to say that their children had been easy to parent, which was partly why Sarah Anne had come up with the idea that she and Jameson could foster a child, surely a single child. But fostering was something else. Every decision seemed in need of approval, every move watched over as if the state had put cameras in the house. It wasn't true, it wasn't like that, the caseworker didn't come around that much, but the shadow of a higher power seemed cast, at least for Jameson. Ever since the boy arrived, Jameson worried that one wrong move could take him away, especially from Sarah Anne, have him packed up like a parcel and delivered to another couple where the father figure had a solid laugh and a grade-A frame of mind that everyone had reason to depend on. The child hadn't eaten since breakfast. And why was his breakfast always nothing more than a few bites of Cheerios and vanilla yogurt? That wasn't right by anyone's standard.

He only ever ate small bites — pecking, Sarah Anne called it, throughout the day — and yet he wanted food nearby, just in case. Especially at night, even if it meant only a single swallow of applesauce. Sarah Anne said why not. She said we're looking at the big picture here. You can't ruin a child raised on violence and starvation by setting a jar of applesauce near his bed.

Too many things had gone wrong today, beginning with Er-

nest's forced visit with Melinda at her court-mandated reha-
bilitation center. Afterward, Ernest walked out holding hands
with the caseworker, the laces of his bright white sneakers dou-
ble-knotted by Sarah Anne, and the sight of the child's faltering
steps caused Jameson's heart to clench. He flashed on the video
he and Sarah Anne had been required to watch on neonatal ab-
stinence syndrome — the shuddering newborns, fish mouths
gasping for air, wails of agony that Jameson had to excuse himself from and get to the bathroom, where he let go of the vomit
rising to his throat.

When Ernest saw Sarah Anne, he darted and dove upward into
her arms. She lifted him to her hip, mouthing, *What happened?* to
the caseworker. Before the woman could answer, Sarah Anne felt
Ernest's diaper and whisked him off to change it. The caseworker
took Jameson aside and explained how Melinda had checked
her phone nonstop while Ernest stared at her. Neither of them
touched or even moved within two feet of each other. Their only
real interaction had been Melinda's waving a plastic truck in his
direction as an invitation to play.

"It's not as if anyone ever played with *her* as a child, you understand," the caseworker said. "She's a product of the system too,
and it failed her in unspeakable ways."

Unspeakable ways.

Jameson wondered why she insisted on talking like this. He
found it distracting, a performance of some kind.

They'd understood that Melinda wanted to hold on to Ernest,
however threadbare the tie would turn out to be. It was her way of
gaining control over a system that had abused her, and she'd said
as much in the court filings. *You can take him, but you can't have
him.* Even so, they'd hoped that as time went by she would change
her mind and let them adopt, something Sarah Anne began suggesting within weeks of bringing the boy home. Two months earlier, on the night they heard that Ernest's father had died from an
overdose, Sarah Anne woke from a dream in which Melinda had

died too — at Sarah Anne's feet — clawing her ankles, convulsing across the floor. "It was horrible, Jay," Sarah Anne said. She called him Jay when she was saying one thing and meaning another. "It was too *real*."

He'd held her hand in the dark while she held a fist to her heart, but he couldn't find a single set of words to comfort her. He couldn't find an honest way around the fact that Melinda's death would be the most straightforward solution to adoption, and he knew Sarah Anne was thinking the same. In three months the state could force Melinda to give up her rights. Ernest would have been living with Jameson and Sarah Anne for well over a year by then. But what if the state didn't enforce it? What if Melinda convinced them she was rehabilitated and prepared to be a mother? What if she truly *was*?

Jameson worried daily about Sarah Anne and Ernest in equal measure. He also liked to imagine a happy ending to this story. But which story would that turn out to be? The one where a child returns to his mother after more than a year away? He would give his own life if it meant Nate and Piper would be returned to their mother.

He couldn't remember the caseworker's name, and didn't feel right about asking so long after the fact, especially when she kept calling him Jameson. She smiled often, had certainly worn braces as a kid, though her appearance was plain, so nondescript that the pink, satiny gloss on her lips came across as a poorly chosen add-on that didn't go with her coloring and clothes. He thought of her as a house he was hired to renovate. It wasn't right, and he knew it wasn't right. But his life's work was to return things to the way they were meant to be, to the original state in which they'd shined, and this girl, this young woman, was simply out of sorts. She couldn't have graduated from college more than a year ago, and spoke like a pedagogue, her exaggerated manner like someone who'd recently become acquainted with the jargon and big ideas of her field. New concepts were still unfolding in her brain, and Jameson thought how far removed he was from such a thing, how nothing could surprise him, nothing could take a sudden turn toward discovery, ever again.

This caseworker was the third assigned to Ernest in less than a year, and she explained to Jameson how things got a little hairy when Ernest showed no interest in the truck. Melinda had tossed it back into the toy box, and the startling crack of plastic hitting plastic made his bottom lip quiver, and for the final few minutes he chewed the blue satin edge of his blanket. Melinda didn't look at him after that. She got up to leave, saying "OK, kid. OK, little dude. You keep being cute," and Ernest didn't exactly cry. "He roared," the caseworker said. "Like some vicious howl of a protest."

Jameson glanced toward the bathroom door. Ernest didn't like trucks. He liked a Wiffle ball he could wear on his fingers. He liked to stand back and cover his ears while Jameson ran his tools, smiling through his fear of loud noises. The only thing he ever threw were rocks in the creek behind their house.

"Could you hear it in the waiting room?" she asked.

Jameson crossed his arms. "No," he said. "No, we couldn't," though his ears were not what they used to be after years of using power tools. The way she was describing the scene, he imagined an unleashing, a child possessed, curtains sucked outward through windows, a water glass shattered on a table. She demonstrated how Melinda had cupped her ears against the screaming, saying "Jesus!" on her way out the door.

The image of that small boy in that room under those circumstances, without Jameson or Sarah Anne to comfort him, caused a helplessness to rise and snag in Jameson's throat. They were the only true caretakers Ernest had ever known, and they had brought him here for this. Left him in there while his lip quivered and he cried like the day he was born, a cry so awful they should have been able to hear it in the waiting room but did not.

Jameson filled his chest with air, drawing as hard as he could manage without appearing troubled. It was important to appear untroubled. Their fate rested in the hands of this young woman who could not have been much older than Melinda, and their lives already so fragile and dangling, held together as loosely as a mobile shifting at the slightest touch. This person, with the scratch of a pen, had the power to send the entirety of their days swinging.

"I think she's been calling us and hanging up," he said.

The caseworker narrowed her eyes. "Melinda?"

Jameson nodded at his feet.

"How do you know it's her?"

"We don't."

"OK."

Jameson should have kept his mouth shut.

"I can ask her about it if you like," the woman said.

"No. Forget it. We've got enough . . . we just want to focus on Ernest."

After a moment she went on to tell him she would not recommend returning Ernest to his mother's custody. Not yet. Then she reminded him that the courts do shoot for that, for rehabilitating the birth parents. The state's objective was to safely extract the children from the system and return them to their homes. She made air quotes around the word *homes*. It was impossible to tell whose side she was on, if anyone's. *Extract,* like ticks, Jameson thought, like parasites, though he tried to cut her some slack. Maybe she was just trying out the word.

Sarah Anne exited the bathroom looking as stunned and voiceless as Ernest. The caseworker walked them out. She took hold of Jameson's arm in the parking lot and faced him. "This is a great thing you two are doing here," she said. "I mean, after all you've been through." She sighed. "I really admire you."

"Thank you for your time today," Jameson said, hoping she

was trying to be kind. Surely her heart was in the right place. He stepped away to open the car door for Sarah Anne, then he took Ernest and strapped him into his seat in the back.

When Jameson started the engine, the boy's eyes appeared larger than usual in the rearview mirror, vacant and ancient, his body limp as if resigned to some terrible, inevitable fate.

"Why so serious, Ernest?" Jameson whispered to Sarah Anne, and his attempt at humor was met with a shake of her head at her window. By the time they pulled out onto the road, Sarah Anne blindly reached for Jameson's hand and gave it a squeeze.

5

SOMETIMES A DIFFERENT KIND of chatter sifted through the yard toward June — one of unseen golfers, spitting and cursing, their anger spiking at the game. The men's banter seemed to be born of the sport, and often was laced with homoerotic jabs. Perhaps this was the case with all sports. June did not claim to know or understand. *Get it in there! You went soft two holes ago!* The rain was a bitch, the green could suck their dicks, but what really got their backs up was the elk taking over the fairways with their half-ton bodies and mounds of dung left in their wake. Elk arrived when they felt like it and stayed until it suited them to leave. *I swear, if I had a rifle. And the goddamn dues we pay.* There was no shortage of growls and grunts at the sky, at the gods of indifference as the beasts shambled like languid camels, taking their time to chew and rest on the manicured greens. Chunks of grass flew from their hooves when they stood, and again when they trotted off toward the meadows between the forests. They ignored the men and their clubs, paid no mind to the groundsman and his oversized mower, which he sometimes gunned straight for the herd, as if this, too, were a sport. But the groundsman was forced to veer off at the last second as the elk stood their ground. The man must have known what would happen, even as he went after them, must have known after the very first time that elk did not seem to know fear.

"You need to face yourself," Niall said before he left her. "Face your fears for both of our sakes."

One month ago June had taken her final drink, in what she hoped would be the final series of final drinks, the same day a herd of elk wandered up the road, through the woods south of the house, and onto the golf course. She'd watched from the kitchen through binoculars as their leisurely bodies roamed the fairway, the morning dew beneath them a silver blanket in the sun. Puffs of warm breath clouded their faces in the chilled air. June set the binoculars down and held her coffee cup to her lips, still watching, while behind her the fire she'd made first thing was beginning to heat the rooms, the sounds of crackling, spitting wood already a comfort to her bones. The elk were a good omen, Granddad used to say. They understood when to come round and when to carry on, and the compass that guided them could be trusted and known. Like birds and their north-south journeys, the flowers and bears returning after lying low, every living thing, he told her — aside from human beings — could be trusted and known.

"Face *myself*?" she'd said.

"I mean face what happened to you," Niall said. "If you could see..."

"What happened to *me*?" June laughed. "Nothing happened to *me*, Niall."

"You see, that right there, that's what I'm talking about. You have this idea that the things you did and didn't do were of your own making, within your power or something. You were a *child*. A seven-year-old kid."

"You don't know anything."

"I know everything, June. That's the problem."

"What did you just say?"

"I know *everything*, and that means you've got nowhere to hide."

June had lowered herself to the edge of the bed, hardly able to find gravity. She felt too light, so airy, floating up and away while an imposter appeared to be acting out her scene below. "I know everything about you, too, Niall," she said. "I'm not stupid. I want you to leave."

"Don't say it if you don't mean it."

June had stood and made herself another drink.

Now she was slick with a healthy kind of sweat on the camp blanket, her skin tight from so much sun.

She caught a whiff of something rank that had not come from the sea, and lifted her arm and sniffed. A shower was in order. It had been in order yesterday, yet somehow she hadn't seen to it. She didn't care to undress in the bathroom. Her thin, angular reflection in the long mirror made her uneasy, made her feel as if she had to force another change, or at least take better care of herself. Just the idea of the effort exhausted her. Years of drinking, the last three in particular, seemed to have accelerated a decline in her looks, she thought they had, but there was no way to be certain, because she had, realistically, gotten older too. Her parents didn't live long enough for her to know their middle-aged faces, and to discover who'd given her what looks and lines, or lack thereof. Were the parenthetical creases around her mouth inherited from one or the other family member, like her first gray hair two years ago? Would her mother have aged the way June was aging if she had lived? June had only her grandparents to go on, and it seemed they had been old her entire life.

It wasn't until June returned to Oregon that she fully understood why Niall had left nearly everything behind. It had taken her a while to come to it, but by the time she was ready to leave Ireland, she'd felt like burning down the house, scorching every last possession that could be measured against the pain of its memory. Should her parcels ever arrive, she might just drop them off at the town dump, even her mug and her pillow.

Six months after they had separated, June received a large envelope that contained a handwritten letter from Niall.

Dear June,

Please be so kind as to forward my ties (see address below) and my expensive black leather shoes with the reissued heels. Enclosed you will find a letter from my attorney, who has drawn up the documents for the divorce. I should hope that by now you've considered everything yours, including the house, of course, as it was never really mine to begin with.

Sincerely,
Niall

Never really his to begin with? She liked to think he'd meant that the house in County Carlow had been more her project than his, and that it wasn't just about the fact that the advances from her publisher had paid for nearly all of it. Back then they had shared everything, including the belief that they would remain together for the rest of their lives. But the once-hallowed rectory they'd purchased as a couple, where monks had lived and died for centuries, many buried on the edge of the grounds at the base of the hill, this project they had thrown everything they had into making a home, would soon belong to some other family with plans and dreams still viable. Meanwhile, June was waiting for the market to pick up.

How arrogant for Niall to assume she had held on to his things for so long. And how humiliated she was that she had, in fact, done just that, left everything in place, like a shrine to the life they'd once shared.

An archaic law meant they had to wait to file for divorce until after a year of separation, giving both parties time for reconciliation, for the possibility that their ways might be mended and the sanctity of marriage saved from collapse. June thought it absurd, even as a part of her had begun to think that Niall would change his mind within a year, because twelve months without her should have been enough to make it all clear. She didn't think he'd move on so quickly, that he was capable of a freedom she did not possess, one that allowed him to start a life with someone new, to live free of the existence of what had once been a very full and mostly happy life, June had believed it was, a life that he had sworn to live out with her. Then again, he had taken liberties during their marriage, and now he had called her, and June was certain that Angie — his Aussie Angie — remained unaware.

She did not send the ties or the shoes. She did not ask why he wanted those things and nothing else. She did not reply at all, except to his lawyer, to say that yes, it was all agreed, everything so civil and cordial and sane.

June's own clothes were nowhere, or somewhere, but not here. She'd had the foresight to bring a few summer things with her, along with jeans and a jacket and her old robe for the mornings and late at night. Her father's custard-yellow cardigan hung in the living room closet. She'd rotated what she did have, sometimes in a single hour, layering and peeling off repeatedly as the weather shifted and shifted again. But for the past week the sun shone sudden and hot, and was apparently here to stay. June needed few, if any, clothes at all.

She lay on the camp blanket, allowing herself one last thought about Niall — recalling the casual, tossed-off nature of his clothes around the house, laundry appearing in various rooms in those early days of his departure like ghosts shocking her to her knees upon entering a room. His jeans and underwear on the back of the bedroom chair, shoes piled clumsily near the front door, everything vexing her, their purpose beyond her understanding. The laundered shirt she'd come across a good two weeks after he left, dangling from the hook on the bathroom door, smelled of lavender fabric softener, nothing at all like Niall, and June lost her mind. She grabbed the barber scissors from the drawer and made of the shirt twenty jagged pieces, which she threw in the bathroom wastebasket, and then she yanked the basket out and dumped its contents — including several cotton swabs with dots of orange wax from Niall's ears, which caused a screech of horrible laughter to rise in her throat — into the kitchen bin, and then she emptied that into the larger bin near the road. It was there that she saw the cuts on her left palm, three slick red openings, triangular points not severe enough to suture, she didn't think. Ravens squabbled behind her, the sound rising as more piled on, until there was no other sound in the world but the shouting match of these creatures. The stone rectory had been built in 1702, and the ravens had been there from the start, mentioned in the monks' records, and here, on this day, the cawing seemed to echo throughout the countryside, over the river and against the dairy cows dotting the hills of County Carlow. And then it stopped abruptly, and June found herself standing inside the front door, her arm dangling, blood dappling the wide oak planks, dribbling the side of her bare foot. Her pulse turned hot, the bones in the back of her hand heavy, so alive was she, standing for as long as it took her open skin to thicken and dry.

Niall had walked out the door wearing June's favorite shirt: soft blue linen and bright white buttons, a tiny hole near the bottom where he'd once caught it in his zipper, a hole made larger the time June snagged it while pulling down his jeans one Saturday afternoon.

God, don't let her think about any of that.

Let her think about Leigh and Cordelia in their pretty bridesmaid dresses, and about their problems, which June would need to make a whole lot worse before she could make anything better. And finish the damn novel at last.

A sudden hunger sneaked up on her as she lay naked from the waist up, lost in a kind of uneasy, savage heaven. She thought of steak, something she had not eaten, it seemed, in years. She wasn't eating well since she stopped drinking. Wasn't it supposed to be the other way around? She'd gone from three decent meals a day to finding herself sucking a spoonful of peanut butter at the sink, staring at her grandparents' house, those No Trespassing signs tacked on the front door and gate.

If she were still a child, she'd be afraid of that abandoned house and its orange cautionary signs. She was somewhat afraid of it anyway, staring through the window as she sometimes did while eating an apple at the sink, or throwing back a handful of grapes, maybe a slice of toast and butter if she remembered with her morning coffee. And pistachios. This morning she'd walked barefoot across nutshells that had somehow fallen to the kitchen floor. She'd cleaned them up and then stepped on others near the back door. Her clothes didn't quite fit. Her only pair of shorts slipped down around her hips.

Aside from the plumber and electrician, and of course the woman's voice on the phone this morning, June had barely spoken to anyone in the weeks before Niall phoned. Only Helen at Helen's Bakery and Grahame at the Little Grocer, and only then about bread, coffee, and Honeycrisp apples, and to ask if someone had the name of a roofer and a good contractor. The man who'd worked on the carriage house had since injured his back and was now lost in a fog of Percocet, gone to live with his sister in Phoenix. Grahame gave June the name of a guy who knew a guy. Then, as was always the case with coasties, Grahame talked about rain, lamenting the bright summer sky, the tourists and their SUVs lining the only road into town. Others in the store chimed in about missing the rain too, and June asked, "Even when it swells the walls of your house and loosens the roof tiles and grows toadstools and mildew in the corners and sends trees sliding down the mountain?" They thought she was funny, and told her she sure could talk, and Grahame said she reminded him of her grandfather. Six hundred people lived in the village and on the side of the hill, and June was one of them now, a coastie again for better or worse. She'd nodded in some kind of agreement with Grahame and the others, but she didn't miss the rain, not at all, and this was further proof that she did not know where she belonged.

Now the sounds of steel clubs jostling in someone's leather bag, a golfer settling near the ninth hole. He was close to her trees, and the jangling, high-pitched rattle of his clubs reminded June of the old milk jugs delivered before dawn.

It was impossible to return to this house without recalling the way her father had closed himself off inside his bedroom, days spent sleeping, June guessed, because by night she often woke to the sound of his transistor radio on low and the click-clicking of his typewriter filling pages with words he later burned in the fireplace. Sometimes she found snippets that remained in the hearth, sentences that June later understood were like those of a sportswriter. Her father had been summarizing the baseball and basketball games he listened to on the radio. She could hear him stand and stretch and slip around in the dark to use the bathroom, or tiptoe down the creaky stairs into the kitchen for something to eat. Drawers clattered and the refrigerator snapped open and shut, and then the smell of a grilled cheese sandwich might drift up to June's room at three a.m. Grandmam always said that the clock was off in her son's head, but Granddad gave a look that said it was much more than that. June would have liked a grilled cheese too, to go downstairs and say to her father that the smell of warm cheese and butter made her hungry. But she was five or six years old, and she remained beneath her quilt, pretending sleep. A single word from her mouth, the mere sight of her in the dark, might frighten her father. It had happened before, and Grandmam was the only person who could calm him. So June learned to be invisible, to breathe in the scent of the cinnamon-ginger tea and a peeled tangerine that her father carried up the stairs to his room, and to not make a sound. Lying low, holding back, was a form of love and charity, June believed, though she was beginning to understand that it had not served her well with anyone else in her life, and had in fact worked against her in the most dire ways.

Those mornings with the milk jugs clanging, June might have had only several hours of sleep. She'd wake and drift in and out to the noise that started with the bottles on the porch and then connected to Grandmam, who'd come over to make June oatmeal and toast before school. "Cinnamon-ginger tea again, love?" she'd ask June, draped in her blue apron and pale green house dress, her blunt bob, gone from red to silver, swinging at her chin. June would nod through a fog, slumped at the square table, and even if she was running late, even if it burned her mouth, she would drink all of the tea. She would run her tongue against the raw roof of her mouth while she waited at the corner for the bus, and again as she sat in the back of the classroom, where she read quietly, waiting for permission to pee, lying low in the best interest of others.

"Oh, fuck me!" a voice yelled, and June startled, sat up on the blanket, and glanced toward the course. A whiz cut the air, slicing through leaves, and then a *thunk* in the yard not far from where she lay. In all these years she'd only ever found three golf balls back here. Most people knew better than to swing too fiercely near the trees. Even if someone were to swing hard from a distance, the angle of the course usually sent the balls flying east, and if not, the branches and trunks blocked them from landing in the yard.

A man in a white polo shirt with an upturned collar and khaki shorts was suddenly fumbling through the trees toward her, stepping over the thin creek that deepened in winter.

"Hey!" she called out. "What do you think you're doing?"

The trees had always been the only demarcation of the property, a line everyone had understood not to cross. The man stopped, grabbed hold of a nearby branch, and held his other hand to his chest. She couldn't read his eyes behind sunglasses, but his mouth hung open, and he turned his head side to side as if searching for anything to set his sights on apart from June.

June stood. What possessed her to walk toward him? The world felt uneven, so far out of sorts it might never right itself again, and this stranger approaching her yard, invading her privacy, tilted her still further off-kilter. Her breasts weren't very large, so they swung only slightly in the open air. Her hair tumbled free of its tie, releasing grass and pine needles onto her shoulders. "You should watch your language," she said.

The man took a step back and clamped his mouth shut. June picked up the golf ball and tossed it toward him. Her breasts swung a little more with that. He was nearly twenty feet away, and the ball dropped at his feet. "You should learn to behave," she said.

It was as if she were practicing for a part, a role bolder than any she'd ever played in her life. And why not? No one knew her here. Not really. Not the *real* June. And the ones who did remember, who gave her any thought, would have known and loved her grandparents, and those who knew enough surely would have said, *After everything that happened, you'd be peculiar too.* There were rumors and there were truths, and she could never know who had gotten hold of what. Of course she was different than she might have been. Even more peculiar than before she went away that first time, to Salem. Who wouldn't be?

The man nodded, bent for the ball, nodded once more, and seemed to measure his steps when he turned, so as not to give the impression that he was running away.

6

EARLIER, AFTER THEY'D ARRIVED HOME from the meeting with Melinda, Ernest had darted from room to room, agitated, ferreting under beds and blankets in search of something, or maybe to be sure that whatever he didn't want to find, he would not. He didn't speak much to begin with, but now he denied them a single word, and he ran until they stopped pursuing, until his frustration peaked in the middle of the living room, where he plopped cross-legged to the floor. When they approached he elbowed the air, his cries evolving into screams, the worst they'd ever heard, and the house felt as if it were rising off its foundation in a state of panic.

Jameson walked out of the living room, then walked right back, questioning, as he had so many times, if he was cut out for this. His skin felt thin, no protection against the hot bundles of nerves firing underneath.

Sarah Anne sat on her heels several feet from Ernest, not asking anything of him, not trying to do anything. Jameson didn't feel it was enough, though clearly it was more than he could think to do. His entire body tingled with nervous sweat. This child's anguish was doing him in.

He tried to settle on the sofa, but immediately got up. He looked to Sarah Anne, but she frowned as if to say that *he* was the one who needed to cool off. There appeared no end to what felt like an inferno reaching the ten-foot ceilings, with Jameson disintegrating into ash and embers. "Sarah Anne," he finally said, hearing the crackle of dread in his own voice. "I can't keep . . . this is not . . . I've got work to do."

It was well past noon, and a whole checklist of things had to be loaded onto his truck — table saw, gloves, cords, toolboxes; other supplies he still needed to pick up from the lumberyard. He was to leave early the next morning to restore an old farmhouse in eastern Washington, and if his looming departure had been the only thing on their minds today, it would have been strain enough.

When he walked past Sarah Anne his mouth went dry and he started blinking. She didn't say a word. She didn't have to. Her upward glare did the talking. *A crying child is not the worst thing in the world. A crying child is a child alive, and you of all people should know that.*

Her eyes were not saying those things. This was what he told himself as he crossed the yard, kicking up grass already parched and splintered in June. She was not thinking those things about him, was she? He sat on the stool in his workshop, the door closed and the windows open. Jameson was thirty-five years old, but how could that be? It did not seem possible to have lived through all that he had lived in only three and a half decades.

He breathed in the smell of sagebrush and dirt, and he breathed in the potter's wheel stored lopsidedly in the corner. Its clay-encrusted scent somehow cut through a workspace full of sawdust and metal and turpentine. The wheel evoked his entire past with Sarah Anne, and he resisted the urge to drag it outside and fling it to the ground like a drunk thrown from a bar after everyone had simply had enough. Sarah Anne had not gone near it in the three years since they moved there, in the three years since the children had died. She said that in time she'd get back to it — she planned to get back to it. But now there was Ernest, and she was a different woman. Just as Jameson, even when surrounded by the tools of his trade, was a different man.

He leaned his elbows on the bench and listened to the clear and steady voices of public radio on the old transistor, as his father did in another era, and he thought of how heavy the start of each workday had become as his red knuckles disappeared inside cold leather gloves. And here, too, fatigued in the warm afternoon, bombarded by news of drought and forest fires and technology messing with the minds of the young.

His mother had lived and died by the belief that luck came in threes, though the bad got most of her attention. "Black marks on the day," she called them, superstitious to the core, the way her own mother had been. All she needed was one ruinous thing to start and she would set about preparing for the inevitability of a second and third. A bruised toe or a neighbor's dead cat could count, as could a cousin's lost job or the headline of a murder close to home. By day's end she would tell Jameson and his father to laugh if they liked, but there it was. Her proof of three black marks laid bare.

And so it was his mother who came to mind when Jameson's cell phone rang with an out-of-state number. He turned down the radio and thought, *Here comes the second black mark.* The man on the other end owned the farmhouse where Jameson was headed in the morning, and he apologized for not getting in touch sooner, said he'd had other things on his mind, mainly a diagnosis he'd been given for the pain in his upper left side. He was placing a courtesy call, politely implying that his approaching death was inconvenient. "I'm so sorry," he said. "But I've got to cancel the job."

A dull daze took hold of Jameson, seeped and set into his bones, a stupefied loss of feeling that would return throughout the evening, throughout the silent dinner with Sarah Anne. But before that, right here, a man was dying, and Jameson wanted only to get off the phone.

Voices hummed in the background and glassware chinked as if the man were calling from a restaurant. As soon as his wife got on the phone, Jameson knew what was coming. He told her before she had to ask that he would refund the deposit, of course he would, even as he was wondering how.

As soon as Jameson hung up, Ernest ran into the yard and fell down in the patch of strawberries. Jameson went after him, but Jameson was not the person whom the boy turned to for comfort, and the boy cried harder and scrambled away as Jameson approached. Ernest dug his heels into the dirt, his legs and feet and cheeks smeared with bright red juice while this grown man stood helpless, breathless as the child before him. Sarah Anne appeared as if from nowhere, and Jameson stepped to the side while she lifted Ernest to her chest, her hand on the back of his head. Ernest gave in to her quickly, tucking his face against the side of her neck, his arms up and over her shoulders.

Hours later, with the two black marks behind them, Jameson was washing dishes in the kitchen with Sarah Anne, the sun dipping orange behind the jagged white Cascades, the only sounds the running faucet and, from the yard, a set of collared doves cawing their final bids on the day. Don Marshall up the road once mentioned that it was legal to shoot the birds year-round, an invasive species, he said, worse than pigeons. Jameson had made a point to say that they cooed just like mourning doves, mostly they cooed all along like that without the cawing, and Marshall said he didn't give a rat's ass if they knew how to whistle the Lord's Prayer, they didn't belong here, and he tilted his head and asked did Jameson not understand the way a *system of life* worked? "A system of life?" Sarah Anne had asked when Jameson told her about it later. "That's what he called it," Jameson said, and they acted like they didn't know what the neighbor meant, like he was just a funny old-timer, but they knew, and they knew they knew, and each was thinking of the system of life they'd set in place, where they did not speak about the past, and they did not express petty complaints, though every complaint was now petty because nothing was worse than the death of one's children. This system of life got them out of bed, propped their bodies into upright positions, set their feet moving in the direction of the coffeemaker, still alive, the children still gone, not still, *again,* gone again with every sunrise.

Sarah Anne placed the covered leftovers in the fridge, and Jameson stopped himself from telling her not to bother. It wasn't likely they'd go near any of it, but Sarah Anne would not throw food in the trash unless it had gone bad, and there was no harm in letting her have this gesture of goodwill, a ritual that made one thing a little bit easier.

Everyone was tender and quiet now, Ernest resting on the sofa, everything put away, wiped clean and in place. Jameson dried the skillet, hung it on the hook near the stove, and looked around at the tidy solace of the kitchen, the orchestrated order that would greet them come morning when they would try again.

7

EVENINGS FELL LIKE A THICK black cloud ever since June gave up drinking, and tonight was no exception. The pressure on her skull weighed in fast. Dusk was the hardest part of the day, sidling up like a friendly drunk offering rounds. Just one beer, so refreshing on a summer evening, watching as the sun slipped into the sea.

Granddad used to say that *no matter how long the day, the evening comes.* In June's case, evening was the thing that did her in.

She was teaching herself to step aside at the worst of it, to focus on the things that happened earlier in the day, which wasn't easy when all she was doing was lying in the sun. She'd kept lounging after the golfer ran off, stayed right there where the clothesline used to hang, allowing memories to break open inside her until she found herself sucking in a breath to keep tears from building in the corners of her eyes. The tears escaped regardless, and pooled in the curves of her ears.

The clothesline. Her grandparents. Her father. Back, back, back before she'd ever known the taste of spirits in her throat, before she'd felt the soft sway of drink inside her limbs and achy heart. Back to hearing her father emerge from his bedroom, to the way she could be certain that when he finally did appear, in the kitchen or the yard or on the front porch, looking out at the rain on the white tips of the ocean, he would be dressed in his custard cardigan and crisp white shirt, faded jeans and black boots, like a uniform. The first words out of his mouth would be "What's the news, buttercup?" and June might startle from her reading on the braided rug, or doing homework at the kitchen table, or crouched throwing logs onto the fire, but she would feel herself unfold and warm up and brighten when she said, "You're here!" To which her father would reply, "Here and there and everywhere!" and within the hour the washing machine was churning.

Her father had an oval, lightly freckled face and fair, reddish blond hair that wisped around his ears. Women stared at him for seconds too long; mothers of June's classmates pinched and prodded their own hair and smiled broadly at him when he accompanied June to the bus stop. When Heather Atkinson's mother handed him a piece of pink paper torn from Heather's notebook, June pretended not to see. She looked at Heather, and Heather looked at June, and both turned in the direction of the bus, even though it hadn't yet arrived. That evening June spotted the crumpled pink paper in the kitchen wastebasket, and she saw it again the next day, its creases evened out on her father's desk in the living room, on it a phone number written in blue pencil.

For the rest of June's life the thump of a washing machine would have a way of lifting a dark mood, of peeling off a layer or two of grief, and reclaiming the day in a way that nothing else ever quite could. There had never been room in the carriage house for a dryer before June purchased the stackable set in there now. Back then they'd use Grandmam's dryer in winter, and in summer they hung everything on the backyard line. Basket after basket, it had felt so good to bear such a weight in her puny little arms, so good to be useful and praised. June's grandmother watched without watching from next door, her presence as solid and everlasting as the trees. "She thinks we don't notice," June's father once said. "But we know exactly how she looks after us." June would often glance up to see Grandmam working in the garden or rocking on the front porch, snapping green beans into a bowl. She seemed to sense June looking, and if her father was nearby, Grandmam went easy on the wave, offering a half-hidden one near her ribs and a tempered smile that remained after her hand went down. If June's father had lived into old age, he would have looked an awful lot like Grandmam; he'd looked a lot like her then. June had waved in the same secretive way, understanding how to model rules that no one spoke. Like the way June never mentioned her mother. No one mentioned her mother. Her father never returned a wave or a smile to Grandmam. He'd shake out the wet laundry in the air before fastening it on the line, and June helped by hugging the cloth sack of wooden pins to her chest behind him, handing them up as needed. "Next, next, next," her father would say, until the air was transformed into a billowing swell of T-shirts, sheets, and towels. Sunlight filtered through the bright fabrics and onto the blood-red peonies until the petals glowed with a velvety sheen that June's father once declared had looked delicious enough to eat, right before he plucked a petal, put it in his mouth, and chewed.

That poor golfer coming through the trees — what was June thinking? She wasn't thinking. Maybe she was.

She was thinking on her front porch at dusk, watching the sunset, determined that tomorrow she would sit at her father's old desk and not leave the chair until she'd written at least one paragraph. Thinking about tomorrow was as helpful as thinking about earlier in the day, or yesterday, or twenty years ago, other people, characters, anyone real or made up, other than June having to think about herself sitting here on this porch without a drink. One paragraph. How hard could that be?

Earlier today June had lolled her head to the side and opened her eyes to the thin blades of grass, to several black ants crawling inches from her face. They carried what appeared to be crumbs from the toast she'd eaten earlier on the patio, and she watched their microscopic feet, the flicker of each grass strand snapping and releasing from their weight. Then came that smack of the short iron and June's hands balled into fists. She knew what it was. Nothing else felt quite the same as old anger throwing its weight around. It was Heather Atkinson. All these years later and June had yet to figure out how to lessen the impact of those memories. The ferocity never failed to take her by surprise.

She dropped her chin and scratched her scalp and let out something of a growl. She sucked in a deep breath and then followed the rhythm of the waves. Venus glowed like a bulb in the sky.

"You smell that, June?" her father used to say, standing near the clothesline, looking out from beneath the brim of his straw hat, bearing a striking resemblance to Vincent van Gogh. June would smile at the breezy cocktail of sea salt, bleach, and lavender. Nights when they forgot to bring in the laundry, which was often, June lay listening to the shirtsleeves and bed linens thumping in the wind. Looking back, she thought she should have been frightened by the sounds. Surely most children would have thought of ghosts when they saw the rippling shapes in the dark, but when June got out of bed and looked down from her window, what she saw in the blue light of the Milky Way and the moon was a day when laundry had been washed and hung out to dry, her father having strolled through the yard and kitchen, to the bubbling pots on the stove, and when that happened, what June had felt, looking down in the night, was that the house, even if she didn't have the words for it yet, had been relieved of melancholia and despair.

This afternoon she'd rolled onto her stomach and immediately felt the pointed wings of her shoulders and the backs of her legs filling with heat, and she'd thought about how her skin, more than anything else, set her apart from her father and grandparents, who were a pale, Easter pink, too tender for the sun from May through October. June's mother had gifted her this easy season of summer — an undisputed fact, and one of very few of which June could be certain. Isadora Swan was the mother's name on June's birth certificate. According to her father, everyone had called her Izzy, and she had been an art student in San Francisco, where she and Finn Byrne met. Izzy Swan died of eclampsia shortly after June's birth. Izzy had a seizure, slipped into a coma, and died within the hour. "Her brain was bleeding," her father once said, after waking seven-year-old June in the night to see the cold, shiny stars. He named them off in a rushing stream, pointing with his entire arm while June shivered in her nightgown, her toes going stiff in the damp grass of April. "You're lucky to have me," he told her between Hydra the sea serpent and the Big Bear. "Your mother was an orphan. When she died there was no one to mourn her but me."

There was June, of course. June mourned her mother who had been an orphan, and now June was an orphan, and once June was gone there'd be no one left to mourn, and the idea floated toward her as calmly as a bright yellow leaf. Years ago in college, June had traced her mother's family online. There was no one left to find. Her search turned up nothing but death certificates, and two living cousins so distant that June didn't feel right bothering them.

When Grandmam took June to the grocery store downriver to find the freshest produce, strangers glanced from one to the other as if wondering where this creamy-pale woman with freckles and light eyes had found such a girl. A reservation? Mexico? The first day of kindergarten, June's teacher, Miss Louise, asked June if English was spoken at home. June was as dark as she'd ever been after a long hot summer. "Not the King's," Grandmam had said when June told her later that day, and Grandmam laughed at herself while removing her apron at the sink.

Tomorrow, yes, June would turn this ship around. Maybe her lack of drink had nothing to do with her inability to write. Perhaps she'd just written herself into a corner, taken a false turn, and arrived at a place that could not be reached from the horizon she had set her sights on. Perhaps what she needed to do was go against the grain, pull back, take everything in the opposite direction without hesitation, like the way she'd told Niall to leave.

The sun took a final bow, but the legendary green flare June had watched for her entire life was not to be seen. The night her father died she'd looked for it. Several days later, when Grandmam attacked the clothesline with a hatchet, June looked for it while Granddad gripped June to his chest, the crook of his elbow shielding her ear from Grandmam's awful cries, and said, "Shush now," into the top of June's head, "she can do as she needs." The sun was sinking and sinking and then nearly gone, and then it *was* gone, and June continued to watch for the green.

Now she studied her hands in the twilight, wringing them, flexing them, knowing how important it was to give them something to do. Her hands were Grandmam's hands, long, slender fingers fitting for a person of measurable height. Maybe her mother had been tall, too. Maybe her father had closed his eyes when he spoke to June because she looked like Izzy Swan. June had only a single photograph of her mother, though it was grainy and taken from a distance, a street scene with people her parents' age in what appeared to be San Francisco. Izzy is looking at June's father, and he is looking at Izzy, while everyone else smiles for the camera.

Izzy had a nose that resembled June's, though June liked it better on her mother's face. If June were to assign that nose to one of her characters, she might call it *hearty:* a nose of proper proportion, not large, but with a bridge that had a slightly high stature when seen from the side. It was the kind of nose that saved a nice face from looking plain, adding interest to the eyes, even if they were already pretty.

"Why do you keep staring at me?" June once asked Niall.

"I'm not staring."

"You are."

"I'm trying to understand your face."

"What on earth?"

"It's beautiful, but I don't know exactly how."

June had thought of Izzy Swan.

"The longer I stare, the more it takes me by surprise. It's arresting. You *arrest* me, June," he'd said, and June felt as if he were talking about her mother in a way that drew a direct line to June.

Someone once said that adulthood was like losing your mother in the grocery store every day of your life. Yes, well, never mind about that. Two months after Grandmam tore down the clothesline June was sent to a boarding school for "vexed and agitated girls," as Mr. Thornton called it. He was the thin-haired, ruddy-faced director of the school, who'd come all the way from Scotland to take this job, and he spoke to June and her grandparents from behind an oversized mahogany desk. "A long way from home," Granddad had said to Mr. Thornton in a tone that sounded like a question to June. "Aren't we all?" Mr. Thornton had replied. Salem, Oregon, where the air smelled faintly of a dairy farm down the road. For nine months June lived with girls of all ages who cut themselves with razor blades or plucked out their eyelashes, who cried long into the night or never spoke a word, who refused to eat or ate too much. Nine months before Granddad busted in and took June home, in exactly the way she had imagined every night of her captivity — arriving in a fit of strength and anger, shoving people to the side, taking June by the hand as they walked out the front doors, daring anyone to try and stop them. But while waiting for that to happen, June shut out the nighttime shrieks and sobs of the other girls by creating a list of seven comforts that she hid inside her imagination like sweets she could reach for when no one was looking.

All these years later, those seven comforts still held up. June could turn to them, though they embarrassed her. She felt eccentric in the privacy of her own mind. Niall was the only living soul she'd ever told about these things, and how good was he, becoming even more enamored with her. Hot sun on her skin was number three. The scent of horse sweat was number five, especially when tracing the air after a good pat of wool mitten against its neck on a chilly afternoon. This made her sound like an aristocrat, and she was anything but — raised on oatmeal and tea and her Irish Labour Party grandfather's sense of humor. June would learn later in life that Grandmam, who'd kept the books for several of the shops in Nestucca Beach, had asked each for a loan to help pay June's board at the home for vexed and agitated girls. June came to call the place the Infirmary of Innocents, and had written a school very much like it into one of her novels, including its old horse, an ancient pony with an arched spine that June had refused to ride, wanting only to pet the poor creature like a dog. Niall once referred to June as a "bit of a lower-class cock up," someone pretending to be who she was not. It was meant as a compliment, as a way to say that she was fine and good just the way she was — but of course that was before she could no longer pretend to be fine and good. Niall was in no way correct about everything, of course, but he was in the right about her wanting to be someone she was not. It was difficult to remember if there had been a time in her life when some part of her had not been missing. "You're a bit of a graveyard," Niall had once said of her, too.

Montgomery Clift came in at number six after June saw the scene of the crippling phone call he makes to his mother in *The Misfits*. "Ma, Ma, are you proud?" She watched the film for the first time in the days after her father died and before she was sent to Salem. While her grandparents whispered in fierce bouts of Irish in the kitchen, as if afraid June might suddenly understand what they were saying, June sat on the braided rug in the living room, watching the black-and-white film on their small TV, and it was then she began kneading the blue velvet hem of her favorite skirt between her finger and thumb. Kneading blue velvet was strange, she knew. Odd for a child to caress her clothing like a toddler fixated on the satin trim of her baby blanket, but it became a habit, a refuge ever since. It was number seven on her list. To have six and seven at the same time deserved a number all its own, like six and a half. When June turned thirty Niall bought her a robe with blue velvet trim. She'd packed it with the things she brought directly here to the carriage house, knowing better than to take a chance on its getting lost in transit.

It was no secret that Niall had resembled Monty Clift. In the early days of their courtship there'd been a moment when he held her face in his hands, ready to kiss her, and she asked him not to take what she was about to say the wrong way, but up close, she said, he looked even more like Monty Clift, and to be clear, she meant Monty before that awful car wreck altered his face and made him look like Monty's attractive brother close in age. Did Niall take her compliment the right way? He'd laughed inside her mouth, hearty and quick, with a *yes, yes* that landed on the back of her throat. *Thank you, love,* he'd murmured across her tongue, and his words became her words, his breath her breath, and that kiss made them feel like innocents, they both said it, so young and tender, so grand and brave, shivering like high schoolers afraid of getting caught under the bleachers.

Taking instant photographs with the Polaroid was number two. The chemical smell and *zip-zip* of the ejector was a full circle of satisfaction. Tracing a map with her finger was number four. The thick, nearly cottony paper beneath her sliding fingertip, the smell of dusty, yellowed maps, while searching for a place to go.

And number one? Speaking to her mother. Words strung together, flung together, in ways that didn't need to make sense. *Aperture, fractures, rifts,* on her lips in the dark, and then her mother's whispery replies in June's ears — *poppies, marigolds, fleece,* like cradle songs that gathered June safely toward sleep.

June told herself that if she could make it past sundown without taking a drink she would call the contractor and not hang up. She would follow through with asking, or at this point begging, him to restore the bungalow, as she was told his work was like no one else's, and she would sell the place by fall.

If this guy agreed to do the work, then June would swear to her-

self to get through the intrusion by drawing on her seven comforts, none of which were a drink, and she would allow these summer days and then the future beyond them to unfold with a new
neighbor living close by, and she would not try to control every
crease and corner of her life, would not try to be someone she
was not, and here she would vow that the season of summer, *her*
season of watermelons and berries and the blue and gold thrush's
return to the yard, could officially begin today, in this first week
of June, with Venus and the moon and a warm breeze deepening
with the last hint of decay from the by-the-wind sailors.

8

THE DAY HAD PASSED WITH NO third black mark. Sarah Anne hit the switch on her way out of the kitchen, throwing Jameson into darkness at her back. He glanced over his shoulder into the dim room, the blue kettle on the stove signaling morning, and he thought of the new day that would come for them tomorrow. They would drink their coffee with milk as slowly as they pleased, with no place to be, and there in his small chair, Ernest would have yogurt and Cheerios, making a show, at least once, of chewing with his front teeth and grinning, which would make them both laugh, and they would forget, yet again, all that happened today.

The hours might have folded away right then with Jameson turning toward the living room, Ernest to be scooped up and slipped into his bed. But the hushed, somnolent house was interrupted by the phone in the kitchen.

Jameson snatched the receiver off the cradle, held it to his ear, and faced the window with his fist on his hip. "What the hell do you want from us?" he said.

"I beg your pardon," a woman said.

"Oh," Jameson said.

"I didn't mean to intrude," she said with some kind of accent.

"I apologize," he said. "I thought you were someone else."

"Well, then. I'm pleased to say that I am just me."

Jameson smiled, perplexed.

She introduced herself, though he did not catch her name. Ernest was whimpering in the living room, and Sarah Anne was telling him that everything would be OK, while the woman spoke with a soft foreign lilt, her voice plush with a silky cadence that distracted from what she was actually saying. *"Jameson,* is it?" she said, with a strange bit of laughter that made him wonder if she'd been drinking.

"Yes?"

"You came highly recommended," she said, now sounding sober and clear. It was then he understood about the call, what it was she wanted, and his body flushed with relief. *"Oh,"* he said. "Well." He nearly laughed. And then he did laugh, quietly, at the ceiling. "Can I ask who recommended me? This number, it's not the one I give out . . ."

"What was his name . . . It will come to me. I phoned him weeks ago and he told me that you're just the man for this job . . . this particular house . . . my grandparents' . . ."

"Was it a guy from eastern Washington?"

"I'm not sure where he's from. He only said that he used to know you some years ago."

"Oh." The offer was so unexpected that Jameson moved toward the kitchen table, to the chair near the window, where it was all he could do to sit, grasp a knee, and remain still.

The small light popped on over the stove. Sarah Anne appeared with Ernest, a sight that often gave Jameson a jolt even on the best of days — a child on her hip — the fine wavy texture of his hair from behind, the familiar blond strands.

Jameson rubbed his eyes closed as if a headache were coming on. Perhaps one was. "Was he a customer or a contractor?" What did it matter? He opened his eyes to Sarah Anne's legs in cutoffs, and the sight filled him with a vague sense of guilt, as if he were doing something wrong, as if he were always doing something wrong, but especially here and now, alone in the dim light talking on the phone to a woman with a beautiful voice, a woman he didn't know, but who was, in fact, offering him some much-needed work.

"I apologize for the time. The day got away."

"Not a problem. I was just closing up shop around here."

"But your number, yes, I located it through information. The guy, whose name will come to me here, he used to be a contractor, hauling scrap now, as I understand, and the number he gave me no longer worked."

"Yes. Well. Here I am."

Sarah Anne tried to kiss Ernest on the temple and he leaned away. She bounced him gently and smiled into his eyes as if to say it didn't matter if he rejected her, because no way in the world would she ever be rejecting him.

"This fellow, I don't know him personally. Obviously." The woman caller laughed. "He said you'd be perfect for the house, and of course, I understand that you live on the other side of the state, and, I'm sorry, I don't want to put you out, but it's somewhat urgent. I'm afraid I've waited so long to get this project going, and anyway, I'm praying you might find the time on such short notice."

"How short is short?"

"The thing is, I've no idea what the work will involve. How long the entire project will take and all that, but I'm guessing several months, as I hear you like to work alone, for one thing, and I'd like to sell the house by fall, so . . . Something like this week. *Tomorrow?*"

Jameson couldn't contain himself.

"Oh. You're laughing. Is that a good thing or a bad thing?"

"Well," Jameson said, a little lost in the wonder of his luck. He was lost in so many things at once, like what else she might have been told about him. And what did *the other side of the state* mean? The coast? Portland? South along the California border?

"I'm glad you called," he said. "I appreciate it. Thank you for going through the trouble." Before he had a chance to ask where she was calling from, she said, "The house means a great deal to me, and he said you were better suited than anyone. I understand your work is a little unorthodox."

Jameson took a moment to let that sink in. He came close to asking if she cared to elaborate, even opened his mouth before clamping it shut. He didn't always know how to talk to people, and it seemed to have gotten worse in recent years.

"I guess," he said. "I don't know." But Jameson *did* know, and anyone who'd ever worked with him knew that stains and scratches spoke to him of smokers and drinkers and lovers and cooks, guiding him toward what needed to be done and where. Maybe she'd been told he began each job by strolling the rooms, resurrecting the lives of those who'd lived hundreds of years before, playing out the patterns and habits that marked their days. Every home filled with stories, and he followed along with the beginning, middle, and end. He would offer the place a new ending, but first he had to pay close attention to the ghostly silhouettes where chests and picture frames had come between sunlight and layers of wallpaper, until he knew where everyone had stood and sat and rocked and ate and thereby loved and despised and mourned and celebrated one another in every room. After that he would know what to do.

"Are you still there?" she asked.

"Sorry. This old wall phone goes in and out. Can you write down my cell in case we get cut off?"

She said she needed to grab a pen, but then she seemed to have not gone anywhere. "Right," she said. "I'm here."

He gave her the number, and then he asked how old the house was.

"It's a 1940 bungalow. A Sears kit my grandfather built."

"Oh," Jameson said. "Say that again?"

". . . I still have the instruction book."

"A Sears kit?"

"Yes."

"With the original manual?"

"That's right."

"Well, hell. Excuse my language. That's remarkable. You don't see them much anymore, especially not west of the Rockies." Jameson turned to Sarah Anne with a huge grin on his face, and she smiled with a raised eyebrow, a look of curiosity, pleased, he guessed, by what she was gathering was good news.

He shifted his shoulders toward the window and made a point not to let his hopes sail too high. Not yet. Work on a house of that sort could be extensive, complicated — not everyone knew how to build those kits properly, even with step-by-step instructions. The place might be a mismatched disaster, better torn down, and that would mean a waste of a workweek, driving out to wherever she was to tell her there was nothing he could do.

"And just so you know, my grandfather looked after the place quite well before he died a few years ago," she said, as if reading his mind. "It's fairly solid in spite of the winters out here."

"Where is —"

"I mean . . . oh, sorry, you go ahead," she said.

"No, no, please, you finish."

"Well . . . I was just saying that so far as I can tell, it was in decent shape up until he and my grandmother passed away. Three years now. I haven't been over there much since, to be honest."

"Has it been vacant?" Three years. He could practically smell the run of mice, squirrels, and raccoons. The attic, walls, and subfloors could turn out to be an ecosystem of nests, gnawed hardwoods, coated in fresh and petrified waste.

"I'm afraid so," she said.

Jameson caught himself midsigh.

"I was out of the country, and then I had my own circumstances — that is to say, my own house to deal with. I used another man. I mean, for my house. A different contractor."

He smiled. "Sure."

She let out what sounded like an enormous sigh. "My grandfather built my house, too, a carriage house next door. Another Sears. In 1937. He and my grandmother lived here first, before building the bungalow."

"You're kidding."

"No. What do you mean?"

"About it being another Sears."

"No, not kidding, not about *this* bit, anyway."

Jameson wasn't sure he understood her. He didn't know if he should laugh. "OK," he said. "So, that's where you live now, next door to the house that needs work?" He turned toward Sarah Anne with what had to have been a puzzled expression, and he saw that he'd caught her attention. She was staring right at him, her own puzzled look melting into another warm smile. She mouthed, *Work?* and he nodded, and she beamed and gave him a thumbs-up.

"Yes," the woman said, and Jameson wondered if she was what the British called daft.

He turned to the window. "That's just so unusual. Pretty rare to find these homes at all, let alone two of them together."

"Oh? I didn't know they were special to anyone other than my family."

"Well, *I* think they are. Not everyone would agree."

"You're just the man, then."

"I believe I may be. I take it this other contractor isn't someone you can or want to hire again?"

"He moved to Phoenix."

"Ah. Sunshine."

"Yes. I hear some people like that sort of thing."

"God help them."

She laughed, fully, out loud, just a laugh, that's all it was, and yet it sparked across the line with a clarity so pure it was as if she were suddenly with him in the room. He glanced at Sarah Anne's back and then the meadow outside, *his* meadow, she called it, and he realized the laughter reminded him of Sarah Anne from before, in years past, not the tone so much as the energy behind it, and it occurred to him to hang up the phone right then without an explanation to anyone.

He leaned forward. "Whereabouts did you say you live?"

"Right, yes, sorry, it's a little town on the northern coast," she said, and Jameson replied, "Oh," and Ernest said, "Ohhh," and Jameson knew without looking that Sarah Anne had handed him a vanilla wafer.

The woman continued talking, saying she would pay him more than his going rate if he could finish by September, when the rain made it harder to sell, but his mind wandered, lurched back, and wandered again to the Oregon coast. He thought of Sarah Anne carrying Ernest back into the house today, the red pads of his feet bouncing at her hips, his skinny back heaving from tears.

It was a matter of control, a practiced way he put a halt to the ping-pong pattern of memories, but not before the dead faces of his children in the morgue would appear behind his eyes, and the clutching of Sarah Anne's arm while rising from nightmares of identifying their bodies, screaming himself awake that they were only *seven years old!* And again, hobbling to retch in the grass near the children's tree swings while telling Sarah Anne to please get back in the house.

"Excuse me for just a second," he said. "I need a moment to see if I can switch some things around."

"Of course. I didn't mean to put you on the spot. Would you prefer I phone you tomorrow?"

"No, no. I just need a second."

He closed his eyes and smothered the mouthpiece with his palm. He could feel Sarah Anne watching from behind, or maybe he just wanted to believe she was. He concentrated on the lilt in the woman's voice, allowing it to drift through his mind without force or intention.

A carriage house.

He replayed her voice in his mind, paying close attention to the slant of her *o*'s, the slight roll of her *r*'s, and this single-minded focus opened a door he'd closed long ago on a life he'd known before this one. A life before anything had gone *terribly* right, in the old sense of the word, and *terribly* wrong in the new and fuller sense of the tragic.

He pressed the clunky landline against his ear and fell into what felt like the space just before sleep, his awareness not yet lost, his surrender not yet complete. It was then a series of windows flung open at the corners of his mind, and a distant row of vantage points came into view. He slipped his hand off the receiver, said, "Just one more second, if that's all right," and she said, "Of course. Take whatever you need."

Take whatever you need.

He tapped his fist to his forehead. They had no other income. No clue when another job might come along, and there was Ernest to think of.

Take whatever you need.

"Just checking one more thing," he said, and now he hoped Sarah Anne wasn't watching while he drifted into his twenty-year-old self, an impractical kid in college studying linguistics, that sheepish explanation he'd given his parents, and their inability to translate understanding the origin of words into a paycheck. "You don't even *talk* to people!" his father had said. "It's the wonder of the thing," Jameson had said, stopping short at mentioning the joy he found in puzzling out the ways populations arrived in a particular place and time, why some communities spoke to each other in a language vastly different from another found a mile away. He liked knowing how these lines had been drawn. "Like why Finnish is closer to Hungarian than any of the Scandinavian languages nearby," he'd said, clearing out what little air was left in the room. His father's eyes glazed over, his mother shook her head, no doubt counting the moment as a black mark on her life. "This is not happening," his father said, walking away. "Why not just take all the money we saved for college and eat it? Why not set it on fire instead?"

He cupped his mouth, the small grin, feeling younger than his thirty-five years for the first time in ages. In the seconds it took to consider all of this, his mind looped back to the kitchen, to the house, to his life, and he could not find a way to reconcile the jolt of pleasure he felt against the pain of the day.

It was Irish, her accent, in some pidgin form.

"So, three months to restore a 1940 Sears kit on the coast?" he managed to say. He turned in time to see Sarah Anne's mouth fall open.

"What do you think?" the woman asked. "Is it possible?"

"It is," he said to his reflection, and he could see Sarah Anne turning and opening the fridge. His mind wandered once more, no further than the last rain three weeks ago: a passing shower when they'd needed heavy rain, the meadow already a dry sea of purple and silver, like fossilized bone in the fading light.

It was going to be all right. They were going to be fine, though Jameson knew he should have told her he couldn't promise to finish a house in three months without seeing it. But it wouldn't be the first time he'd faced down rain, mold, and salt — a domino effect of untamable, weathering erosion. Not to mention creatures ready to protect their young against his hands inside the walls. There would be termites fluttering into his face and hair, their translucent wings sticking to his skin. But what the hell. This was his work. And anyway, this was not the third bad thing. Going back would save them. Going back was a second chance to make things right.

"What town did you say?"

"Nestucca Beach," she said, and a weighty knot shot through Jameson's calf where the bone had once pierced the skin. "I have . . ." he said, massaging his left leg. "I used to live there."

"Did you?" she said.

Jameson turned to Sarah Anne, as if the sight of her might convey what he needed to know, might afford him some comfort. She hadn't heard what he said, couldn't have, not the way she was bouncing Ernest on her hip. They were making faces at each other, their eyes opened wide as if practicing the expression of astonishment.

"Do I know you, then?" he asked. "I must know you."

Now Sarah Anne turned toward him with straight-faced concern. Ernest looked at Sarah Anne, then Jameson, in the same stark manner. They all turned away at once.

"I don't think so," the woman said. "Did you grow up here?"

"No. Just spent a few years out that way. I've been gone for a couple. But I thought I knew everyone, or they knew me."

Sarah Anne was frowning, biting her lower lip. She had heard him, he was sure of it, the way she didn't look at him or Ernest. She was busying herself at the open fridge, shifting the contents around with one hand.

"I suppose it's possible," she said. "Though I doubt it. Your name . . . I would have remembered your name."

"And your houses, I must know them. I can't picture where they are."

"I've been away, of course, so there's that. But the houses, yes, they're up the hill. Way up. I'll text you the address."

"But you? You didn't grow up there, right? I mean, your accent . . ."

"No, yes, well, I did — for the most part. It's quite complicated around here. Maybe I'll know you by face? I hadn't heard your name before he . . . Oh, it just came to me. Van. The guy who recommended you. Van Hicks."

"Oh," Jameson said. "*Van.* Yeah. I know Van."

Sarah Anne dropped a bottle of mustard on the floor and the crack startled Ernest.

The woman on the phone offered again to compensate Jameson for more than what he would normally be asking, for coming so far and for getting the house ready in time to sell.

"That's really not necessary," he said, feeling his irritation rise at the mention of Van. But what choice did he have other than to take this job?

"Well, then, I'll have to insist," she said, and for a moment he was caught inside a funnel of his fractured past, that stream of mourners at the door — "I'll get it, I'll get it," he'd told Sarah Anne with every knock — all those people pushing charity in the form of marionberry pies and casseroles when he had no appetite, their arms pulling him into an embrace even though he was on crutches with a broken leg and the last thing he wanted was to be touched. "The sand from my children's shoes is still on the tile," he'd told someone before shutting the door. "In the grout. It sticks to the soles of my feet."

It wasn't like him to refuse income. Especially not now. Maybe he'd flung himself around some benevolent corner, like his father, changing with age. Lately the need to make amends in every way seemed to cross his mind more often, and that was saying something.

Sarah Anne was coating a large soft pretzel with mustard, and Jameson suddenly yearned to be the one to offer it to the boy, to be the one who cared for him the most.

If Sarah Anne had any idea what Jameson had just said about the extra money not being necessary, she would have gladly filled him in on the necessary.

"Well, I have to say, it sounds like an interesting project," Jameson said, hoping his tone didn't give him away.

Something had come for him, an invitation, or command, to pay attention. This exact moment, the mustard jar in his wife's hand reflected in the window, his face and shoulders superimposed over hers, this woman on the line — he could feel it was the beginning of an end, a slip from the fractured life he'd managed to hold together for three years, and into another, unmoored.

Sarah Anne was wearing that sweater he loved, and as he was thinking of the honeycomb pattern, the cream-colored Irish wool stretched across her breasts, evoking the smell of her hair and skin, a persuasion had entered the room, an impulse, the first of many to come that would have him acting on the needs of . . .

"What did you say your name was?"

"June."

"Oh. Right. Well. June. It's just begun. It's your month." A dumb joke she'd probably heard all her life, and now he couldn't take it back, and didn't know her well enough to cover one joke with another.

"You still there, June?"

"Yes. Was that your phone?"

"No. Yes."

"Jameson?"

"I'm here," he said. "I was just saying that the answer to everything is yes."

PART TWO

9

JUNE OFTEN DREAMED OF COLORFUL, blooming dyes and rocky scapes — land or moon she couldn't say; they had the feel of porous tints and textures that she recalled come morning, a tactile sense of craggy coral beneath her bare feet. She climbed to get where she was going, and though she was never quite sure where she was headed, it seemed there existed a place she was expected to be. She ate lemons and wild strawberries and Grandmam's marionberry pie. The air smelled of animal and fermented earth, of salads and cocktails and sweets.

She'd wake after these dreams feeling a little queasy, and now that she was no longer drinking it seemed unusually cruel. The sun hurt her eyes the way it had when she was hung over, and it was all she could do to lie still and not think about the blue and red stains lingering behind her lids, not recall the tart flavors on her tongue. On those days she felt as if she'd already lost the plot before her feet hit the floor, and she would think how nice it would be to have a cup of cinnamon-ginger tea and a tangerine, how nice if there were someone to offer it up. But she didn't keep tea and tangerines in the house, the way she didn't keep wine, vodka, or beer.

Last night June dreamed of the hands of a man she'd yet to meet. Hands everywhere she looked, lifting and pulling and holding this piece or that of her grandparents' house up to the light, to give her an awareness of what was to come, a vision of the past resurrected. "You know I'm going to bring it all back," this man —Jameson?— said, and June woke in the dark, damp with sweat, and went to the window, her hands fumbling to close the blinds she'd already closed before bed. Was she a sleepwalker now? The world did not operate in a vacuum. Remove one thing, and another rushed in to take its place.

She'd returned to bed after that, hot and unsettled beneath the duvet, which she'd kicked off and laid on top of in her peach pajamas, made of a fabric so soft it was too soft, a silk that somehow left her feeling self-indulgent for wearing them while alone. So she sat up and undressed and lay back down, naked and wide awake for the next hour in the same Milky Way–blue light of her childhood, imagining the linens and shirtsleeves on the line wrestling in the wind. Imagining, too, Leigh and Cordelia in the claustrophobic kitchen where they'd been lingering, neglected, for over a month. She needed to get them out. She would get them out. The hour passed, and June gave up on sleep and went downstairs in her robe with the blue velvet hem to see if there was any chance *The Misfits* was playing on TV. She kneaded her velvet cuff and paced the braided rug with the remote in her hand, aiming it like a laser gun at the television set from different corners of the room. Infomercials flashed a different kind of blue light, and June wondered if her grandfather might have left a bottle of Jameson next door in one of the old shed cupboards where she'd yet to fully rummage all the way through.

10

EVER SINCE THE PHONE CALL, sleep had not come easy for either of them. "The crickets seem especially loud," Sarah Anne said, and Jameson thought the same. The chirrs had risen above the coyotes' howls, and Jameson was glad for it. Those haunting yelps often kept him awake, not the sound so much as his need to translate the messages, the chronic fearing and craving and the public admission of one animal submitting to another. The worst was the lone howl that went unanswered. It often caused Jameson to throw off the quilt and stand in the kitchen drinking a glass of water until it quit. Sometimes it didn't quit. *God bless the crickets and their love songs,* he now thought, those males pulsing with faith in all corners of the yard. Jameson's feet were too warm for the quilt and he lay on top of it in his boxers, shirtless, immersed in the rhythmic trills beneath the window. At last he began to fade.

"You're really OK with going back there?" Sarah Anne said. She'd startled him, but he didn't let on. It was his habit to protect her from every kind of slight. "I think I am," he said. "I am. We need the money."

"I know we do. I know. I'm just wondering. We could figure something else out. We always do."

His throat filled with emotion, his breastbone ached. He

wanted to tell her how badly he missed the children, but couldn't speak of it without keeping her up all night.

She rolled away, and Jameson reached for her, lightly, brushing a finger down part of her spine. Flickers of memory came to him the way they often did, like a battle of hurt, and he allowed for that, advancing steadily to the other side of so many memories to reach the one where he saw her for the very first time. Such a strange surprise to find a woman on a stool at a potter's wheel when he'd expected to find the room empty, the ceiling leaking from the damage he'd come to repair. But here, like some Flemish painting from a golden age, was a young woman dressed in a loose-fitting white dress, her feet bare, her back turned, blond wavy hair piled into a slack twist at her neck. He couldn't take his eyes off her fingers, her hands gliding so delicately, so lovingly, across the top and around the sides of the clay in same way they would one day glide over him. But even then, before he'd seen her face, he felt touched by her, aroused by her right foot pumping the kick, the wheelhead whirling with immense speed for such an ancient wooden tool. The place where it stood between her knees was nearly too much to take.

He didn't move, afraid his shadow might register somewhere in the room and startle her. Right from the start he made a point not to do anything that might frighten her. He watched her glistening hands, slick and orchestrating, the trail of caramel-colored water dribbling down her wrist.

He didn't need to see her face to know what she looked like. How was it that he already knew by the curve of her, by watching the loose threads of hair lifting and falling to the rhythm of the oscillating fan?

Recalling her this way gave him a sudden hard-on. He hadn't expected that, and didn't want it, not now anyway, not lately. But here it was, a charge, a pulse of life racing through his body. He locked his hands beneath his head, crossed his ankles, and drew in an extra-long breath. They had not made love for at least three months. Maybe longer.

In college he'd hired himself out as a repairman. At the start of his senior year he'd accepted a small project several miles from campus, near the Mackenzie River. A woman had a leak in a studio that her niece used on the property, and Jameson told her a leak would be no trouble at all, and that was how it all began, with a phone call from a stranger.

He'd arrived out there at dawn on a Saturday, and nearly missed finding it. The house was a long ranch, easy to spot, but the studio was a small outpost quite a distance in the back. He'd looped around the property twice on foot before coming across a path in the tall grass, which he followed to a small orchard of fruit trees — apple, plum, and pear — and there, across a rolling meadow full of foxglove and Scotch broom, stood the studio, its oversized windows reflecting the flowers and the knee-high grass. Red-tailed hawks and turkey vultures swung high against the rising sun. He'd fixed all of it to memory, including the shift in the air that day, the first crisp push taking them from one season into the next.

The deep and dusty path led to a red Dutch door, the top portion of which swung fully open, and beyond it in the middle of the room sat a young woman spinning clay. The morning sun lit the milky windows and plank walls and floor with an amber glow, and he took it all in as if he might never again see such a thing in his life.

He watched for what felt like several minutes before she snapped her head around, as if sensing him behind her. Her foot lifted from the kick, and a bowl flew sideways on the wheel. "Oh, hell!" she said, swiping at her hair as the fan came back around, leaving umber streaks across her forehead. "Are you the carpenter?" she asked, looking exactly as he knew she would, her eyes and mouth familiar in a way he didn't understand.

"I am," he said. "Are you the lady?"

This made them laugh and blush, at least he believed she'd blushed. He'd dropped his hot face downward so quickly he'd never known for sure. For certain she'd hurried out of his way, telling him her aunt had mentioned he'd be there early, but she thought other people's early wasn't the same as hers. He would have liked her immediately if only for that. She washed her hands in the sink and, without looking up, said she'd be just a second.

"Sorry I scared you," he said. "I'm in no rush."

She didn't answer one way or another, just gathered her things and darted past him, smiling at the floor.

It took three days to fix the leak, longer than expected, and when he was alone in the studio with the leak newly repaired, he traced a finger through the dry clay in the grain of the wooden wheel and felt the chalky powder between his finger and thumb as he hummed that old song about the carpenter and the lady and marriage and having her baby. He carried his tools through a warm rain across the meadow to his truck, and they seemed heavier than before. He drove down the country road until his cell phone gained service, then stopped to call the aunt for Sarah Anne's number, which the aunt rattled off without hesitation, and he wondered if Sarah Anne had said something about him. When she answered the phone, he asked if she would like to meet for pizza, and he waited in a mild state of dread as the wipers creaked and she told him to hold on, and she came back and asked him to hold some more. The third time she returned, she said, "Yes. If your offer is meant for today at noon." Noon was twenty minutes away, and so was she.

His shirt had dried to his skin as he drove toward her, and by the time he pulled into Marzano's parking lot, it felt shrink-wrapped, itchy against his ribs.

He sat across from her in a booth, and it was easy to do, suddenly the easiest thing he'd ever done. "I'm so glad you called," she said, as carefree a set of words as ever were spoken.

His hard-on was thriving now, lifting his boxers, his groin filling with heat, and he wondered how deeply Sarah Anne had
fallen asleep, and what she might think of this going on in the
bed next to her.

He knew that sometimes the mere sight of him could remind
her of things she'd rather not think about, just like the sight of her
with Ernest on her hip could do to him. But he was trying, and
Sarah Anne was trying, and every day was its own challenge, its
own big picture. He imagined a time when a road that led to letting go would reveal itself, or a valve in hand would turn toward a
release, some improved-upon system of life.

He rested his hand on Sarah Anne's hip, in the warm curve
where her waist dipped sharply. She patted his fingers twice, then
tucked her fists up near her throat. After a moment she placed
her hand over his where it stayed.

A year after they met, on another early morning like the first,
he'd walked down to the studio to bring her a second cup of coffee. By then they'd spent nearly every weekend at the house,
while Sarah Anne's aunt drove to Cottage Grove to help care for
an older, ailing cousin with whom she'd been close since childhood. For Sarah Anne and Jameson, the weekends became a
spoiled getaway, an escape from the strain of puny campus apart-
ments and crowded parties and into the quiet green and open air.
Sarah Anne woke at dawn for the studio, and Jameson woke with
her, each getting their first cup of coffee in before Sarah Anne followed the meadow path with sleep in her eyes. Jameson would
return to bed with a book, a novel if he was caught up on school,
and lose himself beneath the feather blanket they shared, even
as it became more difficult to leave for the jobs he'd have to begin by ten a.m. But on this particular day when he brought her a
second cup, Jameson had no work, and he found her in the studio
just as he'd found her at the start, facing away from him, pumping the kick. When he called out, so as not to startle her by walking in, she didn't answer. He called louder a second time, and as

he entered, she let go of the kick and squeezed the vase on the wheel to ruin.

He'd never seen her do this, leaning into the wheel, elbows on her knees, shaking her head no. He said her name, but she didn't move, and as he came toward her, she sat upright, swept her hair back with her arm, and turned. She had the most tender morning face he'd ever known, and here, even though she'd been awake for hours, was the look of having just crawled from bed, as if her body were still warm from the covers. The desire to hold her was intense. But he had the coffee in one hand, her own hands were caked in clay, and something was going on that required restraint.

"What?" he asked. "What's wrong?"

She placed her cheek on his chest, and when she looked up he could see that she'd been crying.

"Sarah Anne," he said.

She said, "If you want this life, it would be nice of you to tell me. And if you can't, you know, *say the words,* then tell me that. Either way I need to know, and I would like it to be today."

He was terrible at saying how he felt. There was no excuse for it. There'd been no childhood moment of shaming him against his own emotions, no kind of trauma to teach him to be afraid. And yet, for as long as he could remember, he'd kept things right next to the bone. It served no purpose, and most often it had worked against him, yet he did it anyway. Even here he was doing it, when something more was called for.

"This life?" he said, and already his words sounded forced, not to mention that gaze of hers, the deadly serious smile a clear message that Sarah Anne was surely wondering if Jameson was getting it. And then he *did* get it, loud and clear. What he didn't understand was why, why today, why did she need an answer right now?

Her smile began to fade, her sights shifting toward the coffee dribbling down his wrist. She was wearing his red flannel shirt, taken over as her own, and he saw past the buttons between her breasts and the curve of them too, and he gazed at her tanned arms beneath the sloppy sleeves rolled to her elbows, and he filled with worry over what to do next. Her shorts exposed much of her thighs, and the longer he took to answer her question, the deeper his desire for her grew. A strange yearning that seemed to be attached to something bigger than themselves, as if Sarah Anne had managed to gaze into the future through a magic viewer to the place where their lives were already set up and running, and she was bidding him to take a look in there, too.

And he knew, just as sure as he stood there, that a day would come when he'd tell their children — a boy and a girl with golden hair and olive skin just like Sarah Anne's — about this moment of proposal. *And her hands caked full of clay,* he'd say. *And dry cracks streaking her arms and cheeks, and she was getting a little annoyed with me for taking so long to say the words.* He'd describe the intensity of her beauty — always was and always would be, and how, at that wheel, her lovely soul hit hard.

She'd raised an eyebrow at the coffee meant for her, spilling and going cold.

"I do," he said, "want this life."

Now, beside him in bed, Sarah Anne's breathing was heavier, her hand having slipped off of his. That boy and girl, as yet unborn when he asked Sarah Anne to marry him, arrived seven months from that day.

He removed his hand from her hip and lay there thinking about when he'd stepped back into the house after learning the job in eastern Washington had been canceled, and that eerie silence settling over the rooms in the same way it had three years ago. He'd rushed to the living room and found Ernest asleep on the sofa and Sarah Anne sitting cross-legged on the floor, rubbing a circle on his back. The boy was sleeping, just sleeping, but Jameson had choked up and ducked into the kitchen, where he sat for a time before disturbing Sarah Anne with the news. After that, he'd made them breakfast for dinner.

Now Ernest began thumping his heel against the wall next to theirs. The pounding was one of the strategies he used to fight his way into sleep. Jameson often thought of him while hammering nails, the way the steady strike helped him fight through something, too.

"So you're going," Sarah Anne said suddenly, with a suck of air, returning to a conversation he'd thought was over.

A few seconds passed. "It's not like we have a choice," he said.

"No," she said. "Maybe we do. Maybe we should talk about it. I don't know. I hate to think of you going back there without me. I hate to think of you being there at all."

"I don't care for it much myself."

The thumping continued.

"That's an understatement," he added. "I'm going to miss you something awful. I don't know that I'll get much of a break, but maybe you could come . . ."

Ernest banged his heel especially hard, but didn't call out for either of them.

After a moment Sarah Anne said, "You need to get some rest, then. That's a long drive, and it sounds like a lot of work in a short amount of time."

"Wait," he said, pressing himself into her back. He was harder than before, nearly hard enough to burst, and this surprised her, he could tell, by the way she snapped her head around. It surprised him, too. He reached under her top for her breast, kissed her shoulder, the side of her neck, and she responded, slowly, her arms wrapping him in. And then she flipped forcefully onto her back, and they did not kiss; his mouth was on her breast, his hands, hers too, clutching fiercely onto the other with a clear-eyed greed. She reached down and around, shoving past clothes, and still his boxers clung to an ankle, her pajamas not fully off when he entered her with his fingers, and then himself.

Her nails dug into his shoulder blades and she told him to fuck her harder and he did just that, and no sooner had she spoken the words than she let go a cry, as guttural as any animal in the wild, and Jameson followed right behind, before dropping his head against her shoulder.

Within seconds he felt a well of emotion. He could not see her face in the dark, but he knew she was on the verge of tears, too.

She slid out from under him and cleared her throat while he rolled onto his back. They lay for a moment without a word.

Ernest kicked the wall.

Sarah Anne rose onto her elbow and kissed Jameson's forehead like she was kissing a child. She sat on the bed and fixed herself into her pajamas with her back to him. "Do you think this woman was the one calling and hanging up?"

"No . . . why?" he asked, though it had crossed his mind.

"No?"

"It doesn't make any sense."

"Yes. It doesn't."

Jameson followed the shape of Sarah Anne through the dark until she braced her way around the doorframe. He could hear her settling Ernest to sleep with the same soft lullabies the twins had always asked for. They'd been born within a minute of each other, and only Piper had cried, if one could call that little whimper, that tiny skirl, a cry. Nate had smacked his thin pink lips over his gums and gone to sleep. "They're so content, so happy to be here," the midwife said, hugging Jameson with an outstretched arm, resting her cheek atop Sarah Anne's sweaty head.

"Just one more," the children pleaded of Sarah Anne up to the week before they died. "Please. One more song and we promise we'll go to sleep."

11

JUNE SAT ON THE EDGE of her bed, the night clear, stars bursting through the black, the moon illuminating her tidy room, reflecting off the shiny worn surface of her brown rubber flip-flops near the bed. She couldn't sleep, didn't feel like lying down, didn't feel like getting up. The shadowy trees outside gave her something to look at, and she found herself humming *Too-ra-loo-ra-loo-ral*, the lullaby Grandmam used to sing to distract her from the howling winds of winter and the branches rasping the roof.

June had sensed a kind of safekeeping afoot. *Safekeeping* had been a Grandmam favorite. Never what she meant, exactly. Like storing the croquet mallets on the top shelf of the shed for *safekeeping*. It was really to keep them out of June's reach. Six years old, too small for swinging a mallet of that size, June wildly missing the large ball at her feet, and yet she seemed to have loved nothing more — the way Granddad turned his ear toward the *crack* when June finally did hit the ball, and he'd smile, and she understood, even then, that the two of them held a kinship for the strangest things. All the cracks and pops and snaps and jangles of the world. The zest of reds and blues and yellows, every color in between. *Have a look, June. Have a listen. Write it down.* But when their croquet game was meant to be over, June often refused to let go of the mallet. Why was that? Granddad would try coaxing it from her fists, the balls already put away, and June knew it was only a matter of time before Grandmam got fed up and shot across the yard toward her, and when she did, June ran, slicing the mallet through the air and laughing as she darted toward the trees. Sometimes, after she was caught, she'd manage to squirm free and swing the mallet against the white trees, and the mallet would bounce back with such force that it knocked her flat on her rear. This made her laugh even harder. She'd come to her feet like a tiny drunk, swinging at the ivy if she got that far, or back to the lawn chair on the patio if she'd managed a head start. Grandmam would win in the end, of course she would, a woman three times June's size, snatching her by the ankles, *cheeky, cheeky, cheeky,* she'd say, but June could see her stifled laughter as they wrangled to the ground.

Yet something about it wasn't funny at all. June remembered a kind of hostility in her hands, a fierce and frightening need to slug and pummel and thrash what now seemed a barely veiled painful existence into oblivion.

June's father often watched from the upstairs window. His *box seat,* Grandmam called it. Maybe his watching was the thing that inspired June to behave so strangely. Maybe she had wanted him to know she was down there having a life in spite of his absence, even if her child's mind couldn't call it that. Maybe she was having a normal childhood. Maybe she was having fun.

I'll just put them up here for safekeeping.

Niall had made her feel safe.

"May I join you?" he'd asked the first time she saw him, at a cocktail reception in Dublin in honor of a writer June had studied with in college, Eleanor Black. June was already three martinis in when he approached her, as she stood alone with her back to the rose-and-white floral wallpaper. It was a garden party, and June wore a violet sundress and leather sandals with a small wooden heel. She couldn't wait to go home.

She held up her glass and he chinked his to hers and said, "Thank you for coming. I'd like to talk to you about your work." He was serious, his round eyes a beautiful glassy green, cheeks the ruddy red of the Irish. He had locks of shiny brown hair, or would have had if he'd let them grow, but as it was, the waves were cropped rather short, and he wore light tortoiseshell glasses. Everything about him said smart, kind, and confident.

"My work?" she said.

"I hear you're a writer."

"I'm not going to sleep with you," she said, and it shocked her that she'd said it, but it didn't seem to shock Niall.

"Just to be clear, are you saying *tonight*? Or *ever*?"

"Tonight. I'm not going home with you tonight."

"When, then?"

"Let's give it about a week."

They laughed and chinked their glasses again.

He introduced her to other people in the room as "June Byrne, a colleague of Eleanor's from the States." He offered her cheese and crackers, and she offered him a glass of sparkling water when she got one for herself. When she sobered up enough to drive, he walked her to her car. Midway across the lot, he lifted her hand into his, and she was happy for it. When he kissed her at her car door, she regretted what she'd said about tonight.

"I want you to know I'm not in the habit of kissing my writers," he said.

"I'm not your writer."

"No, but I hope you'll consider me. I got a wee peek at your book from Eleanor."

June stepped back, feeling stricken. She didn't like for people to know more about her than she was aware. It unnerved her beyond reason.

"Oh, dear," Niall said. "Clearly I'm making a complete mess of this."

June turned, opened the car door, and sat without closing herself in.

Niall kneeled next to her. "I have no idea what I've said to upset you."

June got hold of herself, rubbing her arms as the evening chill slipped in. "It's nothing," she said. "I didn't know. You should have said something right away."

"I didn't want to scare you off."

"How would that scare me off?"

"You're right. That's not what I meant. I meant I didn't want you to think of me as a publisher first instead of a man wanting to have a conversation with you at a cocktail party."

"But you wanted to have a conversation with me because Eleanor gave you my book. Without my permission, I might add."

"She said you were shy. So shy, you weren't sending it out."

"Still."

"And anyway, it isn't true — that isn't why I wanted to talk to you. I saw you from across the room before I knew who you were, and I wanted to know you immediately."

June was published first in Ireland, and Niall had been the one to usher in her career. Their relationship had been a little lopsided from the start, though on some things they solidly agreed. Neither had wanted children. June could never picture herself having the patience for someone who might turn out to have a disposition similar to her own, some small version of the person she used to be. Children struck her as capricious creatures, grabbing things off grocery shelves, or being pushed around while strapped down like the mentally ill. They were hot little beings full of fits and tears, their tantrums ready and warbling just below the surface, full of violence too large for their bodies, a ferocity that erupted through moody and confusing demands. Perhaps June hadn't changed at all. Maybe she was still every bit of those things, only now it was worse, downright dangerous in the body and mind with the strength and power of an adult. Maybe this was the reason June was shy. Maybe this was the reason she drank.

What was certain was that, several years in, the life they'd made together left them with chronically tight, achy knots in their shoulders. Hectic. Everything was hectic. Deadlines and meetings and book tours. June started having blackouts, and Niall was taking more and more calls in his study.

Then one Friday morning he found June weeping in her coffee for reasons she would not talk about and saw no reason to explain, and Niall had suggested a picnic. A Sunday picnic. There were so few openings on their calendars. They needed sleep, that was the problem. That was what they said about everything that went wrong. Sleep! In the end it turned out to be true, in a way. But back then they hadn't yet hurled blankets in the night, or gripped their hair, gripped a windowsill, or smashed a fist through the glass. They were on their way, but back then they didn't yet know about weeping till dawn. They spoke of being tired as if they had a clue. *We're so tired all the time,* they repeated to each other while sighing up the stairs for bed. They didn't know anything any longer, it seemed.

June had awakened early that Sunday to prepare the basket, and to leave behind the annoying scraps of sleep that had come for her in the night. Back then, she often dreamed of falling off a rooftop, or being shuffled into unfamiliar rooms with a sea of others she did not know. But that night she'd been shoved onto a stage and was meant to dance for hundreds of people. She tripped and could not find her way up from her burning knees. Jeers lingered in her ears long after she'd opened her eyes to Niall sleeping wide-mouthed and facedown beside her. She lay without moving, thinking how life, her life, had become a series of missteps, of faltering and righting herself back into the rhythm of the person she'd once been, or had thought herself to be.

The light outside that Sunday morning was gray. She dismissed it as fog, and peeled the quilt from her body and let go her heavy thoughts. "A Sunday picnic," Niall had said two days before, and placed his arms across her shoulders and ducked his head in close for a kiss. She'd swallowed her own longing, stifled all signs of the pang from that achy, constant yearning for something other than what she had, as she closed her eyes. The feel of his lips on hers did nothing to close the gap between them.

A picnic. Yes. "It's only going to get worse," she'd said about their schedules.

They didn't know about worse when June placed plums and cloth napkins in the picnic basket. She was still grateful that Niall often kissed her and took hold of her hand, that he was still turned on by her after eight years together, though there didn't seem much time for sex, which made his arousal more theory than fact. They should force themselves to make time for it, tonight, perhaps, and by *forcing* June meant encouraging each other, which meant talking about it, and the idea was already losing its appeal.

A breeze had rippled the half-curtain above the sink, and when June turned to the yard a light rain was misting the lawn. It was not supposed to rain today. She continued with the cheese and bread and wine in the basket. She added dark chocolate, and the homemade applesauce she'd stayed up late making from their own apples.

By late morning, rain was lashing the glass door in the kitchen where June found herself standing — slapping at her face as if to mock all attempts to save her marriage. She stiffened when Niall appeared in the kitchen, and they turned toward the rain, and June shook her head and pursed her mouth to mean that they must not give up this day for anything. This was how people lost their minds, she thought. A rising desperation formed into tears ready to fall when Niall came to her and said, "Here love, here," and brought her into the living room, where he spread a wool blanket on the floor. He took her hand and kneeled with her and set the basket between them and said, "What does it matter if there are no trees?"

The living room picnic had infused them with something fresh for a day, a week perhaps, before they fell back into the same pattern, with Niall whispering and laughing on his phone behind the closed door of his study, and June pouring another drink in the kitchen, and Grandmam's alarming voicemails beginning to pile up.

The wake for her grandparents in Nestucca Beach followed Irish tradition, a celebration with music and drink — and there had been a child in attendance, a young girl no more than eight years old, with long red hair and a clear love of music. June didn't know to whom she belonged or with whom she'd come, but the girl was intently watching the fiddle player, a young man who nodded and smiled at her while playing Irish folk songs — "Danny Boy" and "Flowers of the Forest," the only ones June recognized. Everyone was drinking, and with a big open bar, people were starting to fall down. But not Niall. Niall was June's caretaker, the designated driver of her life.

He'd noticed the girl too, and while everyone was doing a jig, Niall asked her to dance. June watched them from a folding chair along the wall near the cake and whiskey. When the girl nodded and tucked her head shyly, Niall took her by the hand and showed her a couple of steps. The girl was hesitant, though smiling, and June rose from her chair. She set her drink on the table without taking her eyes away, her hands trembling. She knocked over the glass, spilling whiskey across the lopsided table and onto her dress and down her bare leg into her heeled black shoe. She remembered very little after that.

Later, at the carriage house, Niall had tried to calm her, at least that was how he'd explained it the next day. June could flash on scenes, but they didn't add up. She and Niall shed their clothes and crawled into bed, where they lay on their backs looking into the dark, listening to the cold hard rain, saying nothing. Then Niall asked June to follow him into the living room. He took her hand and pulled her from the sheets, not a light on in the house and not a stitch of clothing to cover them. This June remembered. And the outline of his chest and ribs in the dim light, his lean arms in the fused glow of the fire he'd made earlier and now stoked back to life. He tuned the radio to the "Cocktails and Crooners" station, and June shivered while Niall pushed the chairs out of the way with his knee and swiftly pulled her toward him, as if his moves were all part of the same dance.

The locals at the wake had been charmed by his warmth and Monty Clift good looks. June had watched the way people responded to his voice, his touch, his compassion. Others wanted to be near him the way she wanted to be near him; they stared long after he walked away. At their wedding Granddad had told June that Niall was the right man with the right woman. "You two remind me of us," he'd said. There had been no bigger compliment.

June remembered Roy Orbison playing on the radio while they'd swayed naked in each other's arms. She never cared for his voice, the desperation it gave off, and she never cared for that stillness he had while singing; his eyes, hidden behind dark sunglasses, giving nothing away, unnerved her.

It was during "Crying" that Niall held up a finger and went into the kitchen while June waited with her bare back to the fire. Her shadow filled the wall opposite, and she lifted her arms up and down like a swan or an eagle, for how long she didn't know, because suddenly Niall was there, laughing at her. He held a bowl of strawberries and a can of whipped cream, and June cupped the bowl with both hands while Niall squirted the cream over the top, and they swayed and ate the berries and cream with their fingers while the sounds of Tom Jones and Ray Charles filled the room.

And then? How many songs had played before Niall's mood shifted? His eyes narrowing as Leonard Cohen sang about having torn everyone who had reached out to him. Niall's smile had disappeared. What had June said? Where had she gone? He pulled her tightly against him and held her wrist as if she'd threatened to leave. "Goddamn it, June," he said, "do you know how much I love you?"

"Of course," she replied, but she was lost in a fog, and an old rage was making its way to the surface. She jerked free her wrist, her breath coming up short. Then she rested her head on his shoulder and he took her back into his arms. "What did I do?" she whispered. "What did I say to that poor girl?"

"You took her by the arm and told her to get out. You dragged her to the door and told her not to let that man look at her that way. Not to stand there and do nothing."

That was three years ago, and still June woke in the night and thought of that girl. She was probably out there, nearby, catching a bus to school come morning the way June once had. What if she'd seen June on the street since her return and recognized her? The moon shifted and the bedroom became darker, quieter it seemed, without the light.

It helped to think about other things.

The bungalow would be her priority above all else, with the exception of her sobriety. June would rid the house of any reason a buyer might have to tear it down, leave it as buttoned-up and move-in ready as possible. Too many of the original cottages in the village had been bulldozed in recent years, and cheap replicas made of fabricated materials built in their place. Granddad would rail against her from the grave if June were to let that happen to the bungalow.

"*Too-ra-loo-ra-loo-ral*," she whispered, and picked up the phone.

A nineteen-hour time difference between Oregon and Melbourne. She dialed Niall's number and he answered immediately. "June," he said. "Is everything OK?"

"No," she said. "Not really."

She heard rustling on the other end, and June imagined Niall leaving the room where a wary Angie stood with arms crossed and eyebrow raised, the same look June had given him when he would retreat to his study.

June pulled the blanket over her legs, suddenly chilled and filling with regret. "I'm sorry," she said. "This was a bad idea."

"Of course not. What is it? What's wrong?"

"I'm not drinking, if that's what you mean."

"I meant nothing of the sort. It's one o'clock in the morning there, right?"

"I suppose it is. I don't know why I called. I was just thinking about the time we danced naked in the living room. The next thing I knew I was dialing your number."

"Those strawberries," he said.

"You insisted above all that you loved me."

"I did, June."

"I know. I mean, I know it more now than I knew it then. Maybe that's why I called. To thank you."

"It was a terrible time. But you're better now. You sound so much better."

"Why did you call me last week?"

Niall hesitated. "I don't know. I've been thinking about it for so long. Always fighting it. But now things have changed. *Are* changing. There's been talk . . . We've been talking, Angie and I, about getting married."

June felt a tightening in her chest. She flattened her hand against it, and after a moment the feeling began to change shape.

"So you just, wait . . . Oh, bleedin' hell." June burst out laughing. "You're trying to be sure about marrying someone else by testing out any lingering feelings you might have for me?"

"Of course not."

"Making sure all your skeletons have been cleared from the closet?"

"June."

"You have my blessing, Niall."

"It's more complicated than that and you know it."

"You have my blessing," June said, and hung up.

Niall did not call back.

Their house in County Carlow seemed a million miles away, light-years, not even on this planet. June had rented it out to a couple and their three boys — ages nine, six, and four — trailed by an ancient collie named Umpire, and she wondered what they were doing at this hour, and if it felt to them like home. The family had glided along like a constellation on their initial visit to the house: parents in front with the stairstep boys fanned out behind them, Umpire at the rear. When the boys reached the backyard, they broke around their parents as if bursting into their own existence, the oldest child doing cartwheels, the younger two leaping back and forth over the rill. Their mother warned them not to fall in, saying they would wear their wet shoes home if they did. The youngest boy asked twice if this wasn't now their home, and June and the couple all smiled. She liked the idea of this family wrecking the place with crayons and purple juice and rocks and broken windows and overgrown weeds and holes in the garden beds, and the hollyhocks pissed to death by Umpire. But the boys had stood shyly behind their parents when they first arrived, politely turning down June's offer of apple juice, and even more politely accepting her biscuits from a tin, which was a moment June had planned for, the proximity of it, by drinking only vodka that morning so that the children in particular would not back away from the smell of alcohol when she bowed to their level. She had slipped up after hitting the boy on the bike.

She was sure to slip up again.

But not tonight.

Niall was getting married again. Things are changing. There has been *talk*.

June woke again at dawn, pulled her robe tightly across her chest, and made her way downstairs, where she stood at the kitchen window and stared at her grandparents' lopsided front porch. Broken lengths of copper gutter were scattered in the yellow weeds, catching the first rays of light when the tall grass swayed with the breeze.

The coffee was ready, but June remained at the window, imagining a stranger strolling the property, the shape of him becoming more familiar with every summer day. She would learn his habits and quirks, his limits on patience and care. She would know how many hours he slept and what he ate, and should he speak a little too loudly on his phone, the sentences would echo down to her, and she would know to whom he spoke most, and she hoped the sound of his voice would be a comfort to her.

After Granddad had fetched June home from Salem, he'd reintroduced her to kindness and grace, as if she were a dog learning to trust again after being used for vicious sport. That first summer without her father, when the days were long and the light barely dimmed at ten o'clock, the first bats appearing in the sky, Granddad would be out there whistling through the shadows. "Lord of his manor," Grandmam used to say with a wry smile. "Lord of the slugs and the birds and the leaves." The sound of him in the dark had calmed June and allowed her to fall asleep.

Yesterday's news claimed that today would be the hottest on record for the month, and when June looked again at the clock it was somehow eight a.m. Two cups of coffee were gone. Even so, she felt quiet beneath the weight of the coming heat, threw open all the windows in the kitchen, and was met with slow, warm air. She closed her eyes and wondered at the progress of roots and seeds and grubs churning beneath the hemlocks, the tender greens pushing up and open, to be burned by the sun.

"June! Get to work!" Granddad used to say with a giant grin, his arm sweeping in a wave above his head. What he meant was for her to get busy with *life,* with *living,* climbing trees, tending homework, reading stories about other places and other times. What he meant was for her to be absorbed in the act of making something of herself. To be engaged. What he meant, she understood now, was that she needed to keep her mind busy and bright so that it would not slip into the dangerous and dark.

The day her father died, a cool spring rain had misted the ridge by late morning, and the square windowpanes around the kitchen table were coated in steam. June had brought the fire to a roar in the living room, and the house was beginning to dry out when upstairs her father's bedroom door groaned open. Then came the soft sound of footsteps creaking in the hallway above her head, followed by the slow tap of each wooden step. June remained still in the middle of the living room as her father descended the stairs toward her.

He was not wearing his usual cardigan, white shirt, and jeans. He wore a chambray shirt with the sleeves rolled to the elbows and tan canvas pants, like a laborer going off to work. June smiled up at him. "You're here," she said, but her father walked right past her. He stood on a leather chair but did not say, "Here, there, and everywhere!" One by one, he snapped the drapes from the rods. "Oh," June said. "Are we washing today?"

He didn't answer.

The day before, June had gotten into terrible trouble at school, and that trouble had followed her back to the house, thick and palpable as the steam in the kitchen. Her father was making a pile of the cream-colored drapes on the floor, and the pile was part of that trouble, too. The windows were stripped clear, and even with the thick wall of gray rain beyond them, the room felt torn into the open, wide and vulnerable, the entire space reaching beyond the comfort of where it was meant to be.

"Just these," her father said, scooping up the heavy fabric into his arms and passing her on the way to the washing machine in the mudroom. June followed at first, then stepped back as he shoved the drapes aggressively into the drum. "It's raining, Papa," June said, because he seemed not to know. "We'll need to dry them at Grandmam's."

Her father shut the lid, turned on the machine, and spun to face her. "We'll do no such thing," he said, and produced a cigarette from his shirt pocket, lit it with matches from his pants pocket, and went to sit at the kitchen table.

June had never seen her father smoke. But he was smoking now, taking long, deep drags and releasing puffs of blue clouds that filled the kitchen, and June tried not to cough. He pointed his cigarette at her when he said, "You need to learn to behave."

Now June thought of how she had walked toward that golfer like a madwoman. She had shown herself like a half-naked ghost, and not without menace.

Somehow it was nine a.m.

She texted Jameson her address. As soon as she thought it reached him, she dialed his number. "Good morning," she said. "Is this a bad time? Can you talk?"

"June?" he said.

"Yes. It's me. June Byrne."

"Good morning, June Byrne."

"I just sent my address, but thought I'd mention a few details before you arrive. Before you hit the mountains and your service goes out."

"I've just stopped to gas up. Still here in the high desert. Got at least six hours to go, depending on the traffic through Portland."

June flashed on her father's map, the illustrated mountains a series of shaded triangles along the right side of the page.

"Well. Are you making it OK? So far, I mean?"

"All's well," he said.

"That ends well," she said.

"It's been said."

"You're good to come all this way."

"Your call came at a good time. It's no trouble, like I said."

For a moment neither spoke.

"Right, then," June continued. "You'll see the small shed between the houses that you can run all of your cords to."

"Sounds good."

Why did he sound so restrained? He seemed far friendlier when they first spoke. June cleared her throat, feeling defensive, protective of her home, her life. "Anyway, I'm telling you all this now because I probably won't see you when you get here."

"Oh?" he said. "All right."

Why had she said this? And how had he taken it — that she wouldn't see him at all? Or just when he arrived? Maybe she should clarify.

"You sure?" she said. "I mean, I'm not sure myself —"

"I'll know what to do," he said. He wasn't asking her to clarify.

"Of course."

"If you're not around."

"But I could be."

"Either way."

"I sort of hide from the world as it is."

"Oh. Well, that's . . . you . . . ?"

"Not *hide,* exactly. I do, I guess, but it's writing. I'm *supposed* to be writing. Usually I am."

Jameson didn't ask what kind of writer. Nearly every time she'd told someone she was a writer, the first thing they asked was what kind.

She could hear movement around the phone, and she imagined him drawing his hand over his mouth, sliding it down his chin, as if clearing a grin from his face. She could not picture his face, only his hands.

"Yes, well, the back door will be unlocked," she said. "It leads into the dining room. Just go on in and do what you need to do to get started. Let me know if I can help."

"I appreciate it," he said.

"But you'll need to go through the kissing gate first, the *gate*, I mean — my grandparents — it's what the Irish call it, but no matter, I wanted to say it's broken. Just shake the latch to get it loose."

"Got it," he said, with what sounded like a small chuckle. "I can always call if I have questions —"

"You can always call if you have questions."

"Right."

"Right," June said, certain now of stifled laughter on the other end.

She felt her body go stiff, her mind switching strictly to the issues of broken sashes and the sagging bathroom floor. She mentioned the storm that took out the tree and the gutters. It sounded as if Jameson were wrestling all over, perhaps changing clothes. She heard small grunts and moans and imagined him bending over and pulling on socks.

"What's going on there?" she asked.

"What do you mean?"

"The grunting."

"Oh. I'm cleaning my windshield. Was I grunting?"

"Groaning. Grunting. One could say so, yes."

"My father used to do that. I'm turning into my father."

Crisp shadows fell all around the yard, the chickadees and juncos taking turns at the feeder, and June considered telling Jameson not to come after all. She wasn't sure she could manage the invasion of her privacy, the work she was struggling to get to, not to mention the strains of her new and solemn sobriety. No, no. It was just that she had barely slept.

"Before I forget," she said. "I put you up at the San Dune Motel." It wasn't true. She'd planned on it and forgot to follow through.

But saying it had a way of keeping him at a distance, placing him anywhere but here.

"That's not necessary," he said.

"But of course it is. I can't expect you to pay —"

"No, I mean I'll just sleep in the house."

"In the house? What do you mean? The house is a mess. It's un-inhabitable. You're coming to repair it. The electricity is off, the panel needs updating..."

"You just said I could run my cords to the shed."

"Jameson," she said, and his name in her mouth gave her a jolt. "There won't be any heat."

"Not exactly an issue."

"I guess not."

"How's the plumbing?"

"The plumbing. Well, the water runs and the toilets flush, if that's what you mean. But I'm not hopeful about the state of things underground. I just had everything over here replaced."

"It doesn't matter. There's a campground with showers in the state park if need be."

"Listen," she said, "there aren't any beds in the house. No fur-niture at all."

"I've got my sleeping bag and mat. I'll make a pallet on the floor. It's what I do."

"It's what you *do?*"

"Well. Yes. I thought you knew. You said ... What was it you said about me ... *unorthodox?*"

"I meant your work."

"That's what I'm saying."

"I didn't know this."

"What *do* you know?"

She hesitated. "I'm not sure."

"OK," he said.

"If you prefer," she said. "Whatever you prefer. I suppose that's all."

"Thank you."

"Certainly not."

"June," he said, and now *her* name in *his* mouth gave her the same kind of jolt. "I promise it's fine. I've done it this way for many years."

Several beats passed. It wasn't his turn to talk.

"Van told me you're a stickler for period detail, which is great, but you should know that my grandmother changed a few things." What was wrong with her? Her grandmother had done no such thing.

A clear sigh traveled across the line. "Are you saying you don't want me to change those things back to the original?"

"I hope you won't be disappointed, but maybe we should keep it all as is."

"Well," he said.

"It's not too late to say no, I mean about the whole project. You're uncertain, I can tell."

"No," he said. "I can work with you on this. It's not a problem. I hear how important it is for you to have it the way you want it."

"Well, thank you. My grandfather would appreciate you saying that. He came over from Ireland with just enough money to mail-order a house." She could hear her own accent thickening at the mention of her grandparents. "He cleared the land and built everything with his own hands, and he loved it all."

"I'm guessing I would have liked your grandfather."

June brought her fingers to her lips. She dropped her hand. "Then I'm guessing you would have, too."

After a moment he said, "So . . . I'll see you or I won't."

June smiled. "Yes. That is exactly right. Goodbye, Jameson."

"Goodbye, June."

"Wait," she said. "Just one more thing."

"What's that?"

"Your name."

"Like the whiskey," he said.

"Yes. I'm aware. It's just . . . *Jameson*. I'm a dry drunk. And your name . . . it's funny. Don't you think it's kind of funny?"

"If you're laughing, then I'm laughing," he said.

"The house where Jameson was needed," she said, and for a moment no one spoke.

"Listen," Jameson said, "it keeps slipping my mind, but have you replaced the roof?"

"Not yet. The guys will be here in a couple of weeks."

"Ah. That's not what I wanted to hear."

"Why is that?"

"It's the order of things. I can't really be inside while that's going on. It'll jar my teeth loose."

"Oh."

"Did they say how many days it would take?"

"Two," she said.

"That means four," he said.

"Does it?"

"You need to double whatever they say at the very least, to make allowances for trouble and slackers."

"And what does that mean for you?"

"It's one of the reasons I prefer to work alone. I can get things done when I say I can without relying on unreliable people."

"So, then . . . what will you do when they come?"

"I'll be having a few days off."

"I see. All right. I'll still pay you, of course. I'm so sorry."

"You're paying me by the project, not the hour. It's my fault. I should have asked, and planned to come after they were done, but no matter. I'll accomplish what I can before they get there."

"I appreciate you working with me on this."

"I've had that impression."

"Well. It's true."

"All right, then," he said.

"All right."

"Cheers," he said.

"Cheers to you," she said. "Here's to seeing you or not seeing you."

"Sláinte," he said, and June quietly hung up the phone.

12

JAMESON HATED STOPPING FOR GAS. Mini-markets attached to the stations in particular left him with a sickening unease. Oregon drivers weren't allowed to pump their own gas, and he was grateful to remain behind the wheel and distract himself from the smells of corn dogs and burnt coffee, which he imagined to have been among the last perceptions on earth that his children would have taken in before the terror of what was happening overtook them.

It was worse for Sarah Anne. The first time they pulled into a station after the twins were killed, she got out of the truck and vomited into the garbage can next to the pump. Jameson was still fumbling out of his seat belt when a woman rushed over to help with a handful of paper towels. Jameson got out and held Sarah Anne's hair as she continued to vomit what little breakfast she had eaten. The woman asked her if she was suffering from morning sickness. It was eight a.m., and Sarah Anne collapsed to her knees.

When June called, Jameson was sitting at a station ninety miles from home, drinking the last dregs of coffee from his thermos while the attendant filled his tank. He was watching a young couple in rumpled clothes hold the hands of two young girls dressed in matching blue sweats of different sizes. They rounded the corner to the bathroom at the side of the store, but not before Jameson saw the younger girl stand in place and cry, as if the parents had woken her hours before she was ready. The mother, he guessed it was, lifted the girl to her shoulder, and Jameson was seized by a gasp, a sob he tried to restrain.

And then a text, and then the ringing, and there was June.

It took some effort to concentrate on what she was saying. He watched a silver-haired couple in a blue Mercedes coupe next to him, reading and typing on their phones, the blue light of the screens reflecting in their glasses, faces devoid of emotion. He turned toward a tall man in leather pants, shoes, and jacket, just off his motorcycle, removing his gloves and helmet. The man rubbed his hand around his face and hair, and the burning knot in Jameson's leg fired up.

Everyone at the station seemed to have the same weary expression of early-morning fatigue, having strayed away, gone adrift, far from anywhere, certainly far from home. Jameson replaced the lid on his thermos and looked in the direction of the highway. His windshield was filthy.

June's voice was as magnetic as it had been the first time they spoke. He'd leaned back into the headrest, wanting only for her to keep talking. But the entire conversation couldn't have lasted more than five minutes.

The attendant had startled Jameson at his window, handing him the receipt. Jameson reached for it while June spoke of the gutters and a storm that had ripped them loose. "Eighty-two-mile-an-hour winds, according to my grandparents. Two years ago, I think."

Jameson eased his truck to the side of the station and shut the engine. He and Sarah Anne would have left the coast by then, and they had shut the world out, the nightly news especially, for the better part of the following year.

June mentioned all the things important for him to know, but he could not squeeze past the melodic sound of her voice and on to the meaning of her words. Her accent slipped on and off her tongue, and he found himself trying to predict which words carried more brogue than others, and whether or not it was random. It wouldn't be random.

I can work with you on this. It's not a problem. I hear how important it is for you to have it the way you want it.

He'd never said anything like that to anyone he worked for in his life. He had a compass of conviction, and the side effect was the confidence it instilled in homeowners. They felt their property was in good hands, and because he believed in what he did and the way he did it, they believed it, too. And yet he'd said what he said several hours ago to June.

And all the rest? What was *that?* There was something she wasn't saying, even as she'd openly shared her problem with drinking. Jameson hadn't found a way to ask her if there was something else she needed him to know. Maybe he was reading her all wrong. Maybe talking at the gas station had spun him off in the wrong direction. But he'd sensed some kind of trouble. Of what nature, he couldn't say. He'd gone silent on the phone when he'd meant to speak up, and he was sure it had made her uneasy.

When he'd hugged Sarah Anne goodbye this morning his heart had moved nearer to hers, his face buried in her hair, her arms gently rubbing his back in the bright cold dawn. He'd felt her presence when he was on the phone with June at the gas station, her spirit swirling past whatever was happening. And what was happening? Nothing he could put his finger on.

Sarah Anne had woken early to have breakfast with him, heating up the leftover omelets and biscuits from two days before. He'd thanked her, but she didn't have much to say, just shuffled around the kitchen in her underwear, an old, boxy white shirt of Jameson's, and white cotton socks. Her silence was only a symptom of not enough sleep. That's what he told himself. She didn't bother to run her fingers through the back of her hair; she walked around with a teased clump sticking out in all directions.

Now hours had passed since he'd spoken to June, the high desert giving way to evergreen forests and the summit dotted in clumps of old snow. The Willamette Valley sprouted tulips and stretches of grass and gangly strings of hops. The coastal range was choppy with clear-cuts, brutal scenes of stumps and sky where ancient trees were supposed to be. Those views were hideous, hillsides stripped and taken against their will. A rape, he thought. The ravaged landscape. Ever since his children were killed, his thoughts, without warning, could twist repulsively in dark directions, bracketing innocent phrases with a perverseness he could not control. He looked out onto the land and thought, *Slaughtered, gruesome, monstrous, obscene.*

He turned the radio higher than was comfortable and passed the time by guessing snippets of songs between the static. He dialed in a Mexican station with a crisp clarity, and the cab of the truck filled with bright and tinny mariachis and a stream of trumpets that mocked his sober mood. The world felt as if it were falling even further out of context, becoming dreamlike, without a hold.

"*Viva America!*" a man sang, and Jameson rolled down his window as he veered onto Highway 101. The scent of the Pacific Coast reached him before he could see it, so thick he could taste the moisture and salt, and the pine, too, coming for him like an invitation from someone he loved but could not trust, someone waiting on the other side of a door with bad news, even as they called out sweetly for him to come inside, asking with equal kindness what had taken him so long.

13

A PALLET ON THE FLOOR? How odd he was. How odd that she'd laughed like that, making jokes at her own expense. He had lived here while she was abroad, but having lived here wasn't enough to make him feel so familiar. Not enough to put her so at ease. *I'm a dry drunk,* she'd said. Heaven help her.

Was it the one a.m. phone call, the strange dreams that had her acting this way?

Niall was moving on.

After a third cup of coffee her hands were trembly and damp. She missed her mug and she missed her pillow, and she missed Niall with a goddamn fury that pressed so hard it seemed as if the bones in her chest might crack if she didn't shorten up her breath. She sat at the table and kneaded the velvet hem of her robe.

A flash of Leigh and Cordelia flittered at the corners of her mind. June stood, looked around as if spooked. She lowered herself back into the chair, stood again, unsure what to do, as if doing the wrong thing might jinx her.

They could keep their beer, she thought. No rewrites on that. Hadn't they been through enough? Weren't they about to go through much worse before things took a turn for the better? June could appease those young women; it was the least she could do. They could have their drinks, and she would get them off the kitchen floor, get them standing, at least one of them, for starters, could hand the other a beer. June's problems were not their problems. Mostly they were not. One of them ought to enjoy a cigarette, too — nothing like a kitchen filling with clouds of thin blue smoke on a hot summer day.

June poured the rest of her coffee down the sink, not quite ready, though certainly on the verge of taking up the pen, as it were. It was at this table all those years ago where she'd sat across from her father while he smoked, and here where she'd tried so hard not to cough, and tried harder still to gather her thoughts for what to do. Excuse herself and run next door? Or do nothing at all, and her father might tire and get up and return to his room. Trouble had gotten on everything. "The music so loud in there you couldn't hear your own voice," he'd said. "You couldn't hear your own thoughts." He laughed and shook his head, and June asked what he was talking about. And then the washing machine clunked to a stop, like a signal for him to stub his cigarette in a coffee mug. He rose without a word, piled the wet drapes into the laundry basket, and carried them, barefoot, out into the rain. When he began hanging them on the line, June started to cry. "Where are the pins?" her father asked. June remained paralyzed at the back door, shivering as the warm air from inside pulled the smell and heat of the fire past her legs in exchange for the cold. She searched across the yard for Grandmam — and here she came, suddenly at her father's side, and Granddad too, exchanging glances behind her father's back. "Get inside, love," Granddad called out to June, and then, as if at the sound of his own father's voice, her father collapsed in a heap.

June had stepped back out of the rain. "One, two . . ." she whispered, counting her footfalls to make sure she'd done it correctly, as if everything needed to follow some code to keep the whole of it from breaking.

Her grandparents held her father on each side, and the three of them stumbled into the kitchen. Everyone was crying now, her father worst of all, sobbing like nothing June had ever heard, a wild misery that, to this day, caused her eyes to well up at the thought. Every bit of what was happening was happening because of the trouble with June.

Grandmam remained upstairs with June's father while June helped Granddad warm up yesterday's soup and potato bread, or rather watched him from a distance. His energy seemed to have been dialed down to the end of the gauge. He was upset with her. Everyone was upset with her, and how could they not be? June had overheard Granddad on the phone with the principal the day before, agreeing to pay for Heather's medical expenses. But Mr. Oliver, a man her father's age, was asking for something more. "But you're telling me the cut was superficial," Granddad had said. "The girl didn't need any stitches. OK, several. All right. Yes, Heather. I *do* know her name. Of course it matters, son, but to not allow June to return to school . . ."

By the time Grandmam came downstairs an hour had passed, and June and Granddad were reading quietly in the living room in front of the fire. "I could use a little something to eat," Grandmam said, and she sighed loudly, and Granddad sighed too, and together they met in the kitchen and spoke Irish, and June had never felt so alone in the world, and that was before she knew the full extent of what it was to be cast aside and forsaken.

Nearly nine months later, Granddad burst through those dreaded double doors in Salem and found June coloring at a table with two other girls in a room so quiet June could hear the breath of each girl next to her, smell the oil on their skin and hair. Every girl had her own coloring book with pages of empty houses and trees, even the teenagers. Every girl had a set of five crayons. Granddad called out for her, and June startled and stood as if she were about to be disciplined. But it was Granddad, not the director, taking June by the wrist. They scuttled out with several of the staff following in protest. Granddad didn't look at them, not once. His brogue was thick and loud when he said, "Do not go near this child. And you best not come anywhere near me."

He brought June home to the carriage house, to her old room, her father no longer upstairs, no longer anywhere. Grandmam was in the kitchen — a version of her was, stiff and hollow, a stranger, really, compared to the person June had known and loved all her life. Here was a much older woman greeting June with a cursory hug, looking around at everything other than her grandchild. When her eyes finally did meet June's, it was June who turned away. To be seen by Grandmam made her chest ache. She, above everyone, seemed suspicious of the secret corners of June's mind and heart, Grandmam's eyes like spotlights aimed at every bad deed, and there were plenty. More than before she'd gone away.

That first night back home, she had asked in a trained tone of politeness if she could sleep in her own bed, if she could go on living there, because to let it go, though she did not say so, was to let her father disappear completely. Her mother, too. Her grandparents spoke to each other in Irish before they agreed. For years after, until June was sixteen, they slept in the carriage house with her — Grandmam in June's father's old bed, Granddad on a cot next to his wife. The nights were no longer filled with the sound of a clicking typewriter or the scent of grilled cheese and tea and tangerines. No more *Buttercup Byrne* or *What's the news?* No maps, no plans, and all the laundry was done next door, as were the hours of homeschooling with Grandmam and a tutor named Mrs. Crowley, who came twice a month to see that June was keeping up with the state requirements.

June had spent entire afternoons cradling her knees to her chest on the lounger in the carriage house yard, her eyes closed to the sun, when there was sun. She must have appeared lonely, bereaved, and disturbed, or at least bored and dulled by a lack of social interaction and friends. June was some of those things but not all of them, and not all at once. She was grateful to be home, if grateful was the word. It wasn't, but she could think of no other. She was where she wanted to be, and yet everything ached. She hurt when she climbed the hazel tree, hurt when she looked up at the window and her father was not watching for her, not sitting sideways in the stuffed green chair that matched the set at her grandparents' house. She hurt not seeing his eyes seeing hers, his small smile matching her own.

Happiness had confused her ever since. It pulled like an adhesion across her chest, had no give, and burned. It made her anxious and fazed, and only afterward, when some distance was afforded her, could she feel pleasure in the form of relief. Joy was no better, coming for her with a deep roiling in the gut. The idea that she was not entitled to anything good had taken hold.

Heather Atkinson's mother told Grandmam that Heather was afraid to go to school, that she couldn't trust the other children not to hurt her, and Mrs. Atkinson herself was having nightmares, which she expressed to Grandmam in a high-pitched stream of emotion at the front door a few days before June was sent away. And how was it possible for things to get worse from there? June never even tried to save the girl who slept closest to her when Mr. Thornton came around in the night. *Did he touch you?* Granddad later asked. *Did he lay a hand on you?* Claire Young was the girl's name. She was two years older than June but smaller and quieter, and June had not made a sound when Mr. Thornton sneaked her away. Mr. Thornton liked to hit the girls. He'd chosen only the sweetest girls, the ones who shared their crayons and cookies and socks and who cried when they saw others cry. He took them into the storage room down the hall and smacked them with his bare hand while their pants were down, and he forbade them from making a noise or he would take them into the cellar, where they could scream all they wanted and no one would ever hear. The other girls, those who, like June, had not been touched by Mr.

Thornton, girls who had been at the school for years, told her the full story on the first night she arrived. These were the mean girls who fought and stole and kicked the staff, and more than once it occurred to June that if anyone deserved to be hit, it was them, but they were not the ones Mr. Thornton chose, and he did not choose June, and she understood this to mean it was because she was as bad as the others, and of course this was true, given the way she pretended sleep when Mr. Thornton came for Claire.

Here's to seeing you or not seeing you.

June stood and wrapped her hair into a knot.

14

THE ELECTRIC-BLUE HORIZON TURNED Jameson's breath into small wisps of air. The view was the same as it had always been — layers upon layers of churning color — ultramarine and jade and snowy whitecaps crashing against the outcroppings, and craggy spruce clinging to the iron-stained rocks above. Junipers shaped by the winds pulled like beasts reaching for land, and the evergreen shoreline sliced through with the light gray bark of alders, and all of this at once was a sight above every other on earth, if you asked Jameson.

He shut the radio off and grabbed his cell to let Sarah Anne know he'd arrived, but his phone was still out of range. She'd be checking the time, waiting to hear. He wanted to say that the staggering beauty still broke his heart the way it always had, even from before, in that other life, the one they used to share. *It's magnanimous,* he wanted to tell her, *still,* he'd clarify, *even now.* He was overcome with mercy. This thing here was something they could count on, its grandeur as heavenly as it ever was, and he would tell her how he wished she were with him now, and that he'd hated to leave her alone.

I'm not alone, she would say. *Of course,* he'd reply. *Of course you're not alone. How is the boy?*

Seven hours and hundreds of miles had accumulated in Jameson's lower back and hips, and by the time he pulled into the driveway and stepped from the truck, he felt drowsy and stiff, shaking his legs to get the blood moving again. He slipped off his cap before it was lost to the wind, and the familiar tang of briny air this close to the sea slapped him awake. He pressed his cap to his chest like a man pledging his devotion, though in truth he was standing in the gravel drive facing the house June had hired him to restore, and he was second-guessing everything.

No Trespassing on the front door and fence made him wonder if anyone had ever tried getting in. *No Trespassing* always struck him as rude, an affront to the kind people who'd once lived there, and to the people without any ill intent who might walk by.

He glanced next door, and again at the house in front of him. He looked up and down the street, and there didn't seem to be another house for hundreds of feet in either direction. He didn't know these Sears houses were here. He'd never been this far up the road.

He dialed Sarah Anne again. This time the call went through, though it rang until her voicemail picked up. "I'm here," he said, his tone flatter than he'd intended. "I made it just fine," he added, nodding at the ground. "Call me when Ernest goes down. Hug him for me. I love you, Sarah Anne. Oh, and the house is way up the hill. A place I don't know. I'm relieved. You know. I don't know these people and they don't know me. They don't know *us*. So. OK. I'm here."

Unlike Jameson, Sarah Anne possessed a reserve that kept her steely and straight, even as she came across as soft and clear-eyed, which was as genuine as the rest. As far as he could tell, Sarah Anne became more of what she'd always been after the children died, while the best of what Jameson might have been had thinned out, diluted by anger, guilt, and grief. He did not know how to live in a world where such things could happen. And maybe it was also a fact that he did not carry the same appreciation or kindness for the world that Sarah Anne had to begin with.

This place was a downtrodden mess. June's grandfather may have kept it in good condition when he was alive, but it had definitely fallen into full disrepair. Most people were shocked to see how quickly an empty house could go to rot. But homes like these were made from living things, ashes to ashes, no different from human beings, and just like human beings they needed to be cared for in order to keep going, to keep giving something back.

An overgrown footpath led to the south-sloping porch, held up by a truncated beam meant to brace the pitched roof. The roofline was a complicated collection of A-framed dormers. The shingles were warped with moss, and some were missing altogether, which meant leaks on the inside and deep-seated rot he'd have to root out and fix.

He wiped his forehead of sweat.

The absent gutter had taken a fair bit of trim with it when it fell, and the cedar siding was thin, the color of driftwood, a faded gleam of silver-white in the late-afternoon sun.

"Can we leave our siding like that?" Sarah Anne had asked years ago when they bought their first home, two miles from where he now stood. She'd loved the well-worn look, called it homey and cozy. But he'd been forced to replace most everything. She hadn't understood the hidden rot underneath. By the time they sold it, the shingle siding was solid and a rich chestnut brown, the entire house eerily perfect. He wondered if the family who'd bought it still lived there. If they'd taken care of it, and felt at ease in all of its rooms.

Oh heavenly hell, his father used to say. Jameson had made a commitment to work here, and that was a fact, and he would get to it like his father had gotten to it, like his father's father had gotten to it before him.

It was apparent right away that June's house stood in clear view of her grandparents', and he guessed he'd be seeing quite a bit of her if she wasn't hiding. The front porch had a panoramic view of the ocean, as well as a view of what Jameson deduced would be June's kitchen and living room on the first floor, and the north-facing bedroom upstairs. He wondered what she thought of selling a house that came with this kind of built-in observation of her life.

By contrast to the abandoned bungalow, every inch of her place appeared plumb and stout. Aside from the ungainly hazel tree separating the houses near the road, her property was tidily buttoned up. There was the shed near the fence with the electricity June told him he could run his utility cords from; its cedar siding matched that of her house, a velvety chocolate brown that made the white trim appear brighter, newer than perhaps it was. A walkway made of river rock led to her front porch, lined with swaying, silvery blue oat grass. A small patch of manicured front lawn spread out like a blanket beneath a set of red Adirondack chairs facing the ocean, the whole scene a picture of perfection, or should have been. Jameson couldn't get past the feeling that the place was slightly off, as if everything had been staged.

Hydrangea, lavender, and euphorbia encircled the immediate area of the house, and out to the sides of each property spread a thick cluster of trees, acres of conifers casting long shadows from the sun. The familiar, acidic scent of pine reached him in waves, the way it used to every morning when he opened the patio doors and stepped out with a cup of coffee to watch the juncos and towhees vie for the feeder in the yard.

He slammed the truck door and gripped his hips and looked around while a light wind cooled the sweat along his hairline. He had not imagined the closest homes would be so far away. There were stretches of knotted spruce with bulbous burls, salal underbrush breaching upward of six feet with pale berries still raw this time of year. Deer fern filled in the rest, everything in its own shade of green. He put his cap back on, tore it off, and mussed his damp hair into place as if trying to present himself, as if someone might see.

The ocean crashed at his back a hundred feet below the road, and he closed his eyes and couldn't help recalling the way he used to begin every day for years — with sun, salt, gusty winds or soft rain pattering spongy moss beds beneath the windows. The feel of Sarah Anne's body next to him, her legs, her feet, traces of sand in the sheets. He did not have the luxury, the immunity, to recall those days without recalling the children, too, the backs of their blond bedheads, their soft pale pajamas, the sound of them whispering down the hall so as not to rouse their parents, who were already wide awake, facing each other, smiling at their children's clumsy, thoughtful efforts.

What did it take to be here now? Bravery, as Sarah Anne was suggesting with her questions last night?

His ghost children lingered in this wind, these trees, that ocean pulling out and swirling back. They lingered in the Nehalem River where their infant toes had been dipped, the very waters their toddler bodies had unwittingly run toward repeatedly, and every time — just in time — scooped up by their parents. Here was the shore their perfect hands dug into all summer, their clever minds and fingers creating sand castles, bridges, and moats, their legs sprinting over the dunes while tangled kites trailed them the way their parents once had.

Jameson wanted these memories more than anything on this earth. He wanted them in his sleep and in the water he drank, in the mirror when he shaved, and in his hands when he looked down to see how they'd aged. He wanted them crushed, too, into absolute oblivion. He wanted to set them on fire until the flames turned to smoke, and the smoke disappeared in the rain, and the rain into the great blue beyond, where nothing could have ever existed to begin with.

What did he think would happen if he came here?

He remembered Sarah Anne holding Nate next to him, so close he could feel his son's breath against his arm. Piper was folded against Jameson's chest, and strands of her hair blew upward, tickling Jameson's neck and chin. Let this be. Let these twins dangle once more in their parents' arms. Let them laugh as their parents laughed, and their small hands reaching, she for him and he for her, an instinct they carried from the womb, their secret language of gestures and cues still alive in this world.

He wondered now, as he had not done since the day they died, if they'd reached for each other in that final second. He hoped they did. He believed they knew what was coming in the store that day, that they would have seen the gun pointed at them. Their double dose of mind and spirit like a two-headed creature not meant for this world, a single entity able to see in all directions at once.

Who was it had said to Jameson afterward that at least one of them had not been left behind without the other? Who was it he had slammed to the ground and kicked? It brought Jameson no comfort beating this man, nor the coroner's explaining that the children had left this world within the same fraction of a second. Was it Van Hicks who had said that? It seemed that maybe it was.

15

THE BOUTS OF MONOMANIA BEGAN after Granddad brought June home, her thoughts snaring and clamping for days or weeks at a time on a singular thing that needed to be taken care of. It lessened a bit as she grew older, and then served her well when she became a writer. The generative nature of such thinking carried one scene into the next, bringing June closer and more clearly to a bigger picture in the end. It had not, however, served her well in relationships. *But you said, you said, you said. For you I will not drink, I will not drink, I will not drink. Who are you to tell me not to drink? Who are you? Who. The. Hell. Are. You?* June would collapse under the weight of looping arguments, her narrow focus never translating into solutions, impossible when the variable was another person who could not be controlled or predicted or imagined into being. The elusive how and why of what happened would not leap up to her like plot points from her box of obsessions, but remained trapped and feral, viciously rattling the cage.

Niall had been patient with her at first. As kind as he was baffled. But she had not wanted kindness and patience. Who does not want that? What she wanted, what she needed, was for him to make her stop. To take her by the wrists and demand she curb such nonsense, that he tell her she was wrong and unkind and she needed to put an end to the behavior that was destroying them both.

What can I do to make you understand, June? What can I do to help?

She used to get so angry at him that she couldn't speak or sleep, and she did not even understand who or what she was angry with, so she would take long walks in the Carlow countryside and search for the Seven Nobles to calm her down. Oak and ash and holly were the easiest to find on the trail. The yew was her favorite, with its fleshy red aril surrounding the seeds, ornamental as Christmas lights, even from a distance, and she would think of Granddad, who was still alive and well on another continent, keeping track of that other world without June in it, collecting every last detail as if one day someone might ask to see.

The Nehalem River breached its banks and entered the little town at high tide on this 24th of January, and there was no sign of birds, not even gulls, when I took the johnboat down and ferried the three sisters, Ruth, Henny, and Sonja, to safety at Jack and Mona Henderson's place. This seems a yearly occurrence now, once or twice in the least. The fierce winds shut down everyone's light and most everyone's heat, and here a lone squirrel took advantage of the vacated grass and trees by the time Maeve and I got around to reading the morning paper at dusk, with the aid of candlelight and the hearth.

She wanted to collapse into the world that had belonged to her grandparents. Like falling backward into a feather bed tucked with fine pillows and soft cottons and everything smelling line-dried in the sun.

After June finished speaking to Jameson she began to write. It wasn't much, a few pages, but it was something, and more than she'd written in a month.

But then her thoughts turned to the kissing gate, to the idea that Jameson would travel all this way only to wrestle with the latch in the midst of getting his heavy things in and out of the backyard. It was a thought too irritating to bear, and June dressed and headed to Granddad's shed, where she found a chisel and hammer, tools she'd never used in her life, but she used them now to chip away the frame on the gate. Like some clumsy sculptor, she shaved and splintered the lopsided wood that had prevented the latch from hitching. Her touch was mild at first, amounting to little more than nicks on the grain's surface. Then she slammed with a force that removed a large chunk of the frame. When she pulled the latch toward herself, it would not attach to the opposing hook, did not even come into contact with it anymore. The gate swung on its crooked hinge in either direction, and June's anger returned.

Those safety scissors were dangerous. She didn't know. When she'd snatched them up and held them open, one blade had turned into a knife. She didn't know. She was seven years old and maybe she should have known, but she didn't. She didn't even know what was in her hand, what it was she'd actually raked down Heather's back, until after, long after, because at first everyone was so quiet. When Miss Cassandra finally spoke, she said, "Dear girl. My dear, dear girl." She was speaking to June in that whispery tone, not to Heather. The tenderness was the shocking thing, the look of mercy in her eyes even more so, and it caused June to stagger. Miss Cassandra sat Heather down and checked her back, then asked Jennifer Catton to stay right there with Heather, hold a painter's smock against her wound while she whisked June to the principal's office and sent back the nurse. In the hallway, her touch was light around June's shoulders, the scissors still in June's hand until Miss Cassandra stopped halfway to the office and asked if she could have them.

All right, then. Jameson could swing the damn thing open with his hip, swing it like a saloon door and push on through. He could remove it, too, of course. He *should* remove it. She should have just told him to remove it. June breathed the way Niall had taught her to breathe in all of his patience, and for the first time in a long time June wondered if she was, after all these years, going to lose her mind.

Her hands still trembled as she replaced the tools in the shed, and now she was searching in the cupboards and drawers for a drink. That's what this was. Of course it was. The silt at the bottom of the river was the thing she was after. She'd resisted raiding the shed in the middle of the night, though she had gone as far as finding a flashlight and putting on her shoes. And now here she was, riffling faster, spilling screws and metal wire onto the floor, telling herself that if she found something it would be *good,* because if she found something she could *get rid of it,* and then she could go forward with the certainty that nothing would be waiting within her reach, no temptations this close to home to lead her astray. Her fingernails were rimmed black by the time she closed the shed door and walked away empty-handed.

After that she focused on slipping a check inside a large manila envelope containing the blueprint and manual for next door. She added several photographs of the house from during its prime and made handwritten comments on sticky notes, which she attached to the back of each. She pulled off more than half the notes and rewrote them, believing each draft was more accurate than the last, though none seemed accurate enough by the time she walked across both yards in the same line of grass her father last walked, and she placed the envelope on her grandparents' counter. Then, just like her father, she went through the house and out the front door to the porch, though she did not cross the road and throw herself into the sunset.

She went home to the carriage house.

Now she was fresh from the shower, and she heard what sounded like the slam of a car door. It was too early for Jameson to have arrived, wasn't it? Had she taken so long writing and fixing the gate and rummaging through the shed? Maybe it wasn't him. Maybe he'd sent someone ahead to drop off supplies, maybe Van Hicks to help haul something up the hill.

She stood in the kitchen in her underwear and bra, wet hair dripping a steady stream down the curve of her spine. She shivered and searched the drawer for the binoculars she was sure she'd returned the day she saw the elk on the golf course, certain she had put them back right here, where they could always be found, and where suddenly they were not.

If it was Jameson, then he'd driven too fast, well above the speed limit.

Where were the binoculars?

She searched the cabinet behind her, shelves stacked with a food processor, hand mixer, Grandmam's holiday bowls, candle holders, and a gravy boat. She searched the drawer below the first and found pencils and pens, two kinds of tape, a ruler. She looked in the third and it was full of her father's maps, which she'd temporarily forgotten, and slammed the drawer shut. She returned to the first drawer, and there, as pretty as you please, lay the binoculars, atop a pile of rubber bands.

She peered through the half-closed blinds until she caught the lean shape of a man in faded jeans and a dusty black T-shirt. He had a mess of dark hair, jaw prickled with whiskers, a smattering of freckles across his cheeks and nose. His eyes were dark — *Spanish eyes,* Grandmam would say — serious and focused and intense. He was tanned — the desert, she assumed — and the corners of his eyes were creased and weathered, though the whole of him was quite *the bee's knees* — Grandmam again. His truck was the same model as her father's, in her driveway, but much newer, at least a decade and a half newer, and baby blue.

She grabbed her cell phone and sent a text to Jameson, asking what time he thought he might arrive. She watched as the man outside reached into his pocket. *I'm here,* came the reply.

And so he was. A stranger come to spend the summer next

door, three months practically living with June. This morning he'd woken in the high desert, with scorpions and avalanche lilies and dormant volcanoes, and now he was here, a world away, in the lush, moist green of the Pacific coast. June wondered what he was thinking as she gazed at him through the binoculars, and those thin rings beneath his eyes, were they caused by not sleeping last night in anticipation of today? Maybe this was how they always appeared, maybe he had a history of insomnia that reached well beyond the days leading up to this one.

He was facing her house now, facing her, looking to see if she was home, no doubt, and expecting her to open the door and greet him, the way any decent person would greet someone who'd traveled a long way at her request. June could see close enough to sense a history in his eyes, crammed and impassable, and she took a step back into the shadow of her kitchen and adjusted the binoculars. Her face was warm while the rest of her filled with gooseflesh.

He appeared to be . . . what? Looking into the cab of his truck. Now up at her grandparents' house and . . . No. What? Crying? Was he *crying?* She couldn't see actual tears, but he held his bottom lip between his teeth, and June wondered if his tears had dried earlier, before she'd found the binoculars. Maybe he'd already wiped them away. Wait, he was wiping his eyes this very moment. A gold band on his finger caught the sun.

June lowered the binoculars.

I've never met anyone more selfish in my life, Niall had told her when she'd first asked him to leave. Every bit of his patience used up. Her entire body softened with relief.

She zeroed in on Jameson again, the thin scars on his hands and arms, and she was struck with the feeling that she might know him, or had known him, at some point in her life. Was that possible? Surely she would have remembered his name. But she didn't, and couldn't recall where she would have seen his face.

And yet she couldn't ignore the familiar shape, and the recognition, or whatever it was, tugged at her with the feel of an actual memory on the rise.

I'm guessing I would have liked your grandfather.

Then I'm guessing you would have, too.

June watched as his lips fell slightly open, a little puckered as if he were drawing deeply on the air to regain his breath. She could see his chest rising and falling, the expression he wore like a man aroused, encountering something sensual, or something dire. There was no way to tell on which side he was falling. But falling he was.

Maybe she had written a character like him, a man who lived in her imagination, as alive as the real world for all the time it took June to know these people, years of intense study before she could understand and sympathize and forgive them all their sins, years before she could predict what it was they were likely to do, in a way she had never been able to with people in her own life story.

His mouth went slack, his eyes lightly closed, and after a moment June's own breath began to mimic his. She stared and stared, and he didn't move, and it felt like she was inches from his face, close enough to smell the scent of his clothes and hair. The way he stood, the way he breathed, so close to something and someone she knew.

June returned the binoculars to the drawer.

With the windows open and the crosswind drifting from the front porch to the kitchen, she could easily hear the sound of the truck door opening and closing, and June sensed that this would be a summer of sound and movement and a stranger's presence, even when he went unseen. She closed her eyes to the faint echo of boots on gravel, the clap of wood being tossed into the yard, listening like writing — coming to her, at her, for her, on streams she had never understood and never questioned. What was true and what imagined? Were they not one in the same?

She opened her eyes to a knowledge of something she did not yet understand.

Long after the sky lowered its gray blanket onto her skull and the rain fell without end and the air turned to thin, stringy wool in her lungs, long after her body became heavy upon rising and her mind slipped into dark, familiar places, she would recall his fluid shape in the sun on the hill exactly as it was in this moment, and the memory would take over like branches rupturing her heart, sprouting stems of white heat, and she would welcome the pain, all she had left of him, even as her ribs seemed to crack with every breath, she would smile while drinking her morning coffee, and she would smile at the unrelenting rain.

16

AN OLDER MODEL OF JAMESON'S TRUCK was parked next door in June's driveway. It had lost its luster, but Jameson knew it had once been a beauty: two-tone orange and cream. It seemed the kind of truck that suited an old man. June had said she might not be here to greet him, but she never said one way or the other if someone else might be around instead.

He studied the sunlight hitting June's shingles, the ravens cawing in the trees above her roof. The blinds in the windows were tilted at nearly identical angles, just enough to block out the world, and raised several inches from the bottom to allow for a breeze through the screens. He couldn't see any movement, but he knew houses better than he knew people, and as staged as it all might appear, her house did not feel empty.

When the terrible storm she'd spoken of had battered the hillside, a giant spruce — the stump still there — had heaved from the saturated soil, taking a wide and pointed swing at the house as it crashed into the yard. Jameson could picture it clearly, how it'd wrenched the gutter free of the entire south side, and the immense weight continued to snap it loose until it came undone like the seam of a dress, the rusty nails splitting one after the other, weak and fragile as thread. It was a wonder the roof had not caved along with it.

The roof shingles were swollen, misshapen, waterlogged from rain and moss, especially along the front pitch of roof where a wet and relentless wind had slammed into it for years. He knew what to expect before he entered the dank cave of that house, wondering, sight unseen, if it would have been better to raze the place, send it into oblivion, which was saying something coming from him.

He dragged the larger toolbox and his duffel bag to the edge of the truck bed and considered what a pain it was going to be to haul the table saw and workbench up the side of that hill. It was four p.m., a few good hours left in the day, so he shucked off any trace of whining and trekked on up with the bulky toolbox in tow.

He stopped to catch his breath and ease his shoulders. The extra sunlight of long summer days would be no small grace. From the looks of things, he'd need to make use of every waking minute through September.

He was nearly out of breath when he reached the kissing gate. He set the tools down and placed a hand on top of the gate, and it gave easily beneath his shove, swinging open and shut several times on a crooked hinge before he held it to the side with his knee. He checked the latch and found freshly hewn pieces missing from the wood.

It wasn't until he looked up again that he realized he had a clear view of the backyard, and a complete view of June's backyard, too, but it was this yard he was in, the one where his feet were firmly planted, that caused him to step forward in a kind of daze, the gate creaking behind him. He might have sucked in a breath. Surely he would have needed to after trudging up the path. But he was saying "Heavenly hell" right out loud, and gripping the corner of the house, and the wind threatened again to take his hat. He yanked it off and shoved the rolled bill into the front pocket of his jeans. His heart felt as if it were trying to escape his ribcage, banging, banging, banging.

The sight before him blossomed out of the ground like a fairy tale, an enchanted drawing from a picture book he'd read to the children. Columns of paper-white birch, some of them shooting three, four, or five trunks from a single clump, bordered the backyard, and their heart-shaped leaves formed a shimmering curtain that dangled halfway down the trunks. Just beyond this narrow white forest was a blanket of emerald — a golf course, *the* golf course, the Nestucca Bay Club, stretching into the stark blue horizon.

Tell me about what happened on the motorcycle, Sarah Anne had asked more than once. She had a right to know. But Jameson never cared to speak of it. Never cared to revisit the horror and shame of that day. There had been witnesses. A police report she could read, and did read, but still she asked him to tell her, and so he said he didn't remember exactly what had gone on in the moments leading up to it, even as it burned vividly behind his eyes on any given day while he worked, and any given night while he slept. It played out in nightmares, and in daydreams while cooking omelets and hash browns at the stove.

He always recalled what had happened with a bird's-eye view, as if floating in slow motion over Highway 101, while below him a white Pontiac bore down on a motorcycle going twenty over the limit in the wake of a heavy downpour, and that man on the motorcycle was Jameson. He had lost control in the same instant the Pontiac was hydroplaning sideways across the stretch of highway toward him, gliding on wet, glassy asphalt, its silvery chrome and the road each a blinding reflection of the sun. To the west, a golf course, and a hefty man who'd just taken a swing, his arms and club held upward, frozen in the air. Then the full collision with the ground, the snap of bone shearing Jameson's Levi's, *clean as a bowie knife* was what he'd thought, *heavenly hell,* he'd thought, sliding and sliding as if he'd never stop. His skin was shredding and his leg had snapped in half, but he did not feel any pain, and he did not see his life flash before him, and in not seeing it, he assumed he would live. Seconds before he passed out, he did see his father's hands, palms patting Jameson's boy cheeks, patting them even after Jameson would become a young man, his father unafraid to show his son affection, his father saying his name, and then Jameson looked up in time to glimpse the elderly driver behind the wheel of the Pontiac, that moment of reckoning playing out across the man's face when Jameson collided with his fender.

Back then his existence was still a tightly woven object, a solid piece of something he'd known how to care for and protect. And yet he'd been reckless with the people he loved most, giving in to small-minded grievances with Sarah Anne, speeding away from her, knowing she wouldn't like it, knowing she would worry, and worse, speeding away from the children. They had heard the fight. They were standing at the window when he tore out of there.

"Their last thoughts of me as a father, Sarah Anne."

"Don't."

"It's the truth."

"It was an accident. And it had nothing to do with anything else that happened that day."

"I made a terrible mistake."

"Yes. But not the one that killed our children."

What he wanted was that anxious hum beneath his skin to go away.

When he'd gained consciousness in the hospital, it was as if he'd spent years in a coma, though he had been knocked out for only a few hours, and then several more for the surgery on his leg. He woke in the middle of the night with a profound understanding of things that once baffled him, and though he didn't think he had the language to explain, he'd wanted to try it out on anyone who might listen, especially Sarah Anne. For the first time in his life he'd been completely lost to the physical world, and every part of him had felt sheltered and at peace. But there was no one standing vigil when he'd opened his eyes and said hello. By morning he was relieved to see the staff, though everyone approached him with odd, furtive looks that he did not know how to read. He asked after his wife all morning and was told they'd put in a call to her, but he did not believe anything anyone said.

Sarah Anne had finally arrived near noon, wearing the same clothes she'd had on the day before, trembling and pale, her eyes darkened and more deeply set than he'd ever seen, and he believed it was because of what he'd done, his idiotic lapse in judgment, and he smiled at her while apologizing, and he called her baby, and he said, "No, no, I'm OK, Sarah Anne, I'm so sorry I made you worry." He went on and on like that while she stared out the hospital window at a tulip tree, and it took a while before the new and unimaginable began to creep in. It wasn't him at all that was troubling her. Something else had gone wrong. He wasn't even on Sarah Anne's mind right now. It was the children. It had everything to do with the children.

The way Sarah Anne spoke when she was able to form the words made it clear that she'd been given some kind of sedative. That's when Jameson knew, before she'd said those awful things. The unthinkable had happened, it was already done, and it could not be revoked. Sarah Anne mumbled and wept to get the words to come, words that should never be spoken and were not to be believed but she was saying them nonetheless. A gunman had killed their children in the market at the gas station.

Jameson passed out in the hospital bed and seconds later came to. He saw Sarah Anne holding his arm and yelling, and just before he lost consciousness again he realized that she was shouting at him, and others were taking her by the arm, but he heard her say how she'd left Piper and Nate with Chloe, their sitter, so she could race to the hospital to be with him, and while she was sitting right here, watching him sleep and heal, Chloe decided to distract the children from worrying about their father by driving them to the lighthouse to spot whales through the bin-

oculars they'd received for their birthday. Chloe had needed to
stop for gas.

When Jameson woke sometime later, he had to be restrained.
He'd jumped up and tumbled off the bed, his leg in the cast not
enough to stop him, and he managed to tear free his IV before the
staff tackled him back onto the bed.

Sarah Anne denied she'd ever said such things. Later, she
agreed that it was possible. Later still, she said she'd been heav-
ily drugged and he couldn't reasonably expect to get an answer.

Two weeks later, Jameson had phoned Chloe. He needed to
understand how it was that she had survived and not his children. "The clerk lost his keys," she said flatly. He guessed she was
still in a state of shock, and though it crossed his mind that he
had no business calling up this eighteen-year-old girl and forcing
her to revisit that day, he could not stop himself from digging in.
"'Where did I put my keys?' the clerk said, and he was looking all
around the counter, and that's when the guy with the gun walked
in, and I heard the noise of it, the gun, I think I did, some prepara-
tion of it, I don't know, and people just started screaming and the
front glass blew out with a huge bang, and then, I don't know how
long it lasted, but it seemed like a long time before it stopped."

"Where were the kids?" he asked.

"At the candy. At the front."

Jameson swallowed. "Where were you?"

Chloe hesitated. He could hear the guilt rising in her voice, and
he did not try to make it easier. "Where?" he asked.

"At other the end of the aisle. I was crouched down, getting
ChapStick off the bottom shelf."

For a while neither spoke.

"I'm sorry," Chloe said, emotion choking her voice.

"You've got nothing to be sorry for," he said, but he understood
her anyway. Sarah Anne had been telling him the same thing:
nothing to be sorry for. Yet his children were dead, and they would

still be alive if he hadn't sped off instead of talking it out with Sarah Anne.

"People keep saying I'm lucky," Chloe said. "What a horrible thing to say."

When Jameson hung up, he saw more clearly the scene that day. The two teenage attendants, boys the gunman had gone to school with, both dead near the pumps. The clerk in front of the counter, inches from Nate and Piper, inches from the gunman, who shot himself immediately after. Jameson grabbed his crutches, hobbled into the backyard as far as he could go, and threw a crutch into the trees. He gripped the rope from the tire swing to be sick in the grass, and when Sarah Anne came running out, he told her to get back in the house.

Jameson felt his stomach lurch at the memory. If June was inside her house, he was glad she chose not to come out. He did not want to see another face, not for days if he could help it.

He lugged his tools toward the dining room doors at the back.

A warbler lit on the lowest branch of the nearest birch and watched as Jameson stomped through wiry bunches of lavender tangled in milkweed and ivy and four inches of hemlock cones. The lavender crushed under his feet released its scented oil into the air and onto Jameson's boots, and everything smelled of Sarah Anne's bubble bath, of her neck when they'd made love last night, and again when he'd kissed her goodbye at the door, where he'd turned away too quickly from her welling eyes, trying not to read too much into them.

By this time of day they would be taking cover from the heat, dodging scorpions and bees, slathered in sunscreen, Ernest especially, reeking of its chemical scent. Jameson had hugged them both goodbye, Ernest straddling Sarah Anne's hip, sleepy-eyed and distressed by another in a series of too many farewells in his short life. The two of them were a package Jameson tightly embraced. When he'd leaned back Sarah Anne was looking through him, all the way to the single thought he was sure they both shared: if there was mercy to be found in this world, let it find them now by not taking Ernest away from Sarah Anne, not ever, but certainly not before Jameson got home.

He sat on the rickety back stairs of a stranger's abandoned house and missed his wife with an ache he had not felt for her in years.

17

"THE PRIMROSES ARE READY," Granddad had told June, hours after having to take her out of school for what she'd done to Heather Atkinson. He could barely conceal his disappointment in what she had done, his shock, too, filling his eyes and mouth, which he repeatedly cupped with his hand while drawing a large breath. June thanked him for telling her about the primroses, her voice laced with exaggerated gratitude, a tone of hyperappreciation. She plucked a handful from the yard and placed them in a jam jar on the table. By then Granddad was already walking toward the bungalow, leaving her there, not bothering to see the arrangement she'd made. His announcement of the flowers being ready had just been something to say, words to fill the quiet trouble weighing down both houses.

After placing the flowers on the table, June stood back with an animal's instinct that her father was no longer resting upstairs the way Grandmam had left him, that he had instead come out of his room and left the house without her seeing. When June reached his room she found the door slightly open, and she knocked and it gave. He never left the door like this, whether he was in the room or not. June slipped inside for the first and only time she could remember. The air smelled of the musky-sweet pomade her father used to control the waves in his hair. Clothes hung over the sides of open drawers as if washed up on rocks, the furniture draped in shirts and pants and jackets June had never before seen. The piles were jettisoned across the floor and bed, and everywhere in between her father's maps and atlases were folded or crumpled or torn, along with wadded balls of typewriter paper. The room was heaped and bundled in layers of brown, ash, and green.

June searched the rest of the house, but she wouldn't find him. She knew this, but felt it necessary to plod step by step for the sake of order, because with order she might be able to reclaim the day, and their lives would fall back into the place where they had always been and belonged. She would make amends with a posy of bluebells and daffodils and sprigs of thyme for Mrs. Atkinson. She would apologize to them all, and they would forgive her because *when a person stepped up and took responsibility,* Granddad said, *others could not help but show mercy.*

When June reached the back door, she saw that the clothesline had been cut away, lopped off at the center, pieces of line dangling from each post. The scissors from the kitchen drawer lay in the grass.

She'd remained in the doorway for what must have been only minutes, because how long could a child stand in one place like that, though it felt in memory like hours before her grandparents told her to get inside and shut the door. Grandmam said, "He's gone to see that woman, Mrs. Atkinson, to apologize for something he's done." And Granddad said, "What *he's* done?" and Grandmam gave him a look, and switched to Irish.

18

WHEN JAMESON ENTERED THE BUNGALOW that first day, he was hit by the familiar musk of animal odor and traces of mouse turds in the corners of the rooms. Squirrels had taken up residence in the attic and walls, as he'd figured, their frantic claws scattering at the sound of his boots creaking the floors. The air was warm and stale, with the scent of dust and droppings and mold and several kinds of decay, thick and palpable as steam. The bare fact of the work facing him here, work that required him to rally his body fourteen hours a day, seven days a week, shoved his thoughts into overdrive, with a focus on putting this place right, and filled him with a kind of answered prayer.

But as he walked the rooms to get a take of things, sadness followed him, grief that was not his own but a sorrow that belonged to the house. This was often the case with old homes. He once found a small grave on a piece of rural property in southern Oregon, marked on a hill by a rudimentary stone in direct view of the kitchen window. Whiskey rings and tobacco ash deeply embedded a corner of the porch, where the headstone could also be seen from the place where two grooves of a rocking chair wore away the pine planks. One summer evening a flare of lightning lit that side of the house, and Jameson saw the trailing marks of urine stains deep in the clapboard siding, and he understood how a man could be reduced to pissing on his own home.

He gutted rot like he was scraping away cancer, like he was exorcising sorrow and the deepest mourning. And if, for some reason, Jameson was unable to bring a home back to life, he guessed this was how a surgeon might feel when losing a patient. It was personal and grievous. Of course, a house was not a human life — he knew too well what it was to lose the lives of those he loved, and he didn't mean to compare the two — but there had been times when he'd reached down and drawn back ancient wood grain that crumbled into pulp in his hands, and the loss of it moved him to tears.

He ran his hand over the board-and-batten walls and the planks of the dining room floor, and could see that they needed only a good buffing, red and golden as they were, and he imagined saying to June that he could stare all day at a patina like that — and saying, too, that his work sometimes made him feel the way he'd felt in church as a kid, as if something was happening that meant a whole lot even though he couldn't put it into words. *The color, the weight of it, as strange and wondrous as a fading sun.* He didn't talk like that, but he stood there imagining how he might talk like that to her.

And then he thought of things beyond this house and grounds, like fractured bones and a sack full of strawberries and turkey sandwiches under the shady eave out back, and he could feel the way summer's end would bring a well-groomed close to this house, and the exhaustion of the days taking shape toward that end, and it already struck him as coming too soon.

The house was making him think this way.

He crouched near the French doors of the dining room, swung them right and left until the sunlight caught and revealed the wave of antique glass in the panes. It seemed a miracle that they were still intact, and that the doors themselves were plumb all around. He stood, feeling a small victory, knowing what it would look like when rain blew in and rippled down the wavy glass, and by the time that was happening, he'd be gone.

He gently pried open all the windows upstairs and down, careful not to damage the frames and sashes. Soon every corner of the house was swept by a north wind, and the odors stirred into an acrid stew before releasing in some small measure to the outdoors.

A manila envelope lay on the kitchen counter, and he jiggled free a check and blueprints and below that the large instruction booklet for the house. A smaller envelope contained ten photographs, half of which were black and white, fine and parched as dry leaves. The other half, instant Polaroids.

The delicate condition of the older prints didn't seem to be a concern. June had fastened sticky notes to the back of each. "Just like this," read the delicate cursive, tacked to a portrait of a young woman — June's grandmother, he assumed, taken in what must have been the mid-1940s. She stood in the very spot Jameson stood now, her back to the countertop, hands gripping its edges at her hips. He gauged his own hips against the counter and figured that she would have been nearly six feet tall, a couple of inches shorter than he. She had a wry grin. *Go on,* it seemed to say, *I dare you.* He wondered if she looked like June.

"Everything needs to be the same," read another, this one attached to a photo of the living room fireplace. Her grandmother was there, too, her right hand clutching one of the large round sandstones of the mantel. Jameson sifted through the rest and found it odd that no matter the room, every photograph included June's grandmother. And now Jameson was starting to feel a little odd, a little weak with the familiar. Some of the images were a bit too gray and grainy to make out all the facets of the room, and he held them to the sunlight and wondered what June had meant for him to see.

The woman. Jameson couldn't help but stare at her classic,

old-world face — wide cheekbones and large almond eyes. The
feeling that he somehow knew this face crept through his chest
and throat. His ears went hot. He blinked and swallowed, but
he could not think of who she might be, and he wondered if it
was only that she might be reminding him of someone else. Most
likely hers had been a face he'd seen around town when his children were still alive.

He was meant to be studying the rooms, not the woman, to
get a feel for the vision June had for the place. He didn't need the
photographs, but having them prodded his curiosity. He glanced
around and knew what to do. He set the photographs down
and patrolled the kitchen and dining room and living room. He
dragged the half-open pocket doors out from their dusty slots in
the walls and found the wood on both sides with barely a scratch.
Her grandparents had indeed taken good care.

Offhand, he didn't see anything that could be considered an
add-on, as June had said, something not part of the Sears kit
that she claimed her grandmother changed. Nothing struck him
as unconventional or slapdash; everywhere he looked appeared
true to form. The clear-oak floors were original and dull but in
fairly good shape. The softer fir in the bedrooms might not have
held up so well, but he expected that.

He went back and lined up the photographs on the counter
in the order he thought would match his timeline. After that,
he imagined what it would have been like to live here. "The best
room in the house," the sticky note read on the photo of a young
girl eating an apple at the dining room table. The child looked to
be around five years old and was most likely June, ankles crossed
and dangling above the floor, barefoot in a white, cottony dress.
June's skin, eyes, and hair were darker than her grandmother's.
Her gaze was one of pure joy, turned up in affection while her
grandmother's hands cupped toward her. The two of them appeared to have been caught in the moment right before her
grandmother must have held June's cheeks and kissed the top of

her head. The child was grinning behind the apple in her mouth. Jameson could barely see the room fading out around them. What had June wanted him to see? Joy? Innocence?

Instinct is a strong negotiator, his father used to say, and his mother used to say, *Did you run all the way home from school to tell me you love me? All this way,* she would say, and he understood, even then, that she held for him a strange and almost unpleasant kind of love, but that didn't mean she didn't love him.

Jameson could back out of this job before it began. He could tell June he'd come down with something or had a family emergency. He could leave the check and walk away. But he would not leave. He could do no such thing.

He gazed once more at June's grandmother, in the Polaroid taken on the front porch while she snapped green beans into a bowl. He guessed it to be the most recent picture, and Jameson could practically hear the clink of beans against the white metal bowl in her lap. He carried the photo into the living room and looked out the front windows at the view she would have seen from the porch. The world looked to him now as it would have looked to her — the downhill slope of road, dunes in the distance, the ocean churning, the lighthouse, the soon-to-be-setting sun over the ridge into the sea.

When he glanced to the left he felt a deep stillness over June's house, and he did not fight the feeling coming over him that he had seen her grandmother before. He had known her in some context, and he was certain that something had gone wrong in this place. He hoped he would know all the right things to do, so that this particular part of the past was not here to stay.

He began by removing the orange signs that warned others to keep out.

19

WITHIN DAYS OF JUNE'S DISCOVERING the pink piece of paper with the phone number from Heather Atkinson's mother on her father's desk, she woke in the night to what sounded like a woman's laughter. Then weeping. June scrambled from beneath her quilt and stood in her doorway, looking down the hall. Dim light from her father's bedside lamp shone on the glossy planks beneath his bedroom door.

Then other sounds, like misery, a man's misery. Her father's groans and a sob-like cry.

June put on a pair of wool socks and padded across the wooden floor to her father's room. The keyhole was large enough to make out the nightstand and lamp alongside the bed. The gap beneath the door allowed her to see the floor at the foot of the bed and shadows shifting in the lamplight. There was someone in there with her father. This had never happened before. June felt hot, her mouth grew moist, and she swallowed so loudly she feared he might hear. Through the keyhole she saw a woman lying sideways on the bed, her blond hair draped over the side in front of the nightstand. June's father crawled on top of her, was kissing her lips and cheeks, her throat and forehead, and June reared back and lowered herself to her knees. She placed her head on the floor and looked under the door again, and her heart could not be contained. White sneakers with green half-moons on the back of the heel. June had seen them on the wet asphalt at the bus stop. The pink slip of paper passing into her father's hand.

When June told Niall what she'd seen that night, and what she'd done the next day to Heather Atkinson, he held her and told her, in the same way she'd been told by more than one therapist in her life, that whatever she had done back then she did as a seven-year-old girl, and she shouldn't be so hard on herself. *True, true,* June said to them. But the crimes did not end there, and besides, it wasn't as if she didn't know the facts. The problem was that the facts didn't *feel* true, and that other people insisted they were true wasn't helpful. That kind of talk only served to make June feel worse, defenseless against a different kind of truth that was shrewder than anyone seemed to know what to do with. "Your mother hates you," June had said to Heather. "She came to my house and told me she hates being your mother."

"Your mother is *dead,*" Heather said. "And you're a liar."

June's mind had disappeared, her small body lost inside a clenched rage, thoughts snapped off and disjointed, though she would understand this only much later. In memory she had looked around the room and saw the chalkboard smeared in layers of arithmetic, the four rows of desks with five desks each, the coat rack in the corner with thick metal hangers and her own red sweater dangling on the end, the top yellow button closed to keep it in place, the long wall of paned windows facing the hemlocks and Neahkahnie Mountain, a bald eagle with a small catch in its talons flying above it all — June had seen everything exactly this way. And she had seen Miss Cassandra. That puzzled look, her mouth falling open, eyes gazing at the two girls in the second row, then on just the one, just June, standing three desks from the back.

Apparently June had reached for the closest thing at hand, and she would be asked again and again why she had done it, and there was no answer, none ever given. In memory it happened slowly, but it must have gone off at great speed, with Heather shoving herself away from her desk in front of June's and turning to run, while June's arm, like a trap coming down, sent the scissors slicing through the air, shearing the back of Heather's lilac blouse. Blood ran in a straight line, then bloomed like algae into odd shapes of purple, spreading here and there in the fabric. June cut from neck to tailbone, and Heather did not scream. No one screamed, not even Miss Cassandra, and thinking back, this was why it appeared at first as if nothing too serious had happened. Even after June was sent home, she wasn't thinking about Heather or the blood or anything of the sort; she had shut it all out and was thinking instead about finishing her two library books that were due in three days. After putting the primroses in the jam jar, she had sat in her room, and no one disturbed her for hours while she read. And when she emerged it was to ask Grandmam if they could have BLTs again, and it was only with Grandmam's quiet shake of her head that flashes of the day would return to June, yet she still couldn't think of why the principal had stuck her in his office alone and closed the door until Granddad arrived to take her home.

It wasn't until months later, when June was living at the Infirmary of Innocents, that she would learn how suffering could bring about such deadening silence. It could turn one's voice to dust, crush thought and reason, cause memories to go dormant until the body carrying them around would no longer recognize from where an incessant humming continued to spring.

Who was June fooling? She knew exactly why she drank.

"I hope you live long enough to regret this," her father had said to her, and then he'd walked out the back door, across both yards, and into his parents' house, where he'd been born and raised, as if traveling his life in reverse. He stepped out the front door and

across the road and straight into nowhere, which was somewhere
— that is, the rocks below — while back up on the ridge, sitting
safe at the table, was June with her glass of chocolate milk, the
swirl of sugared cocoa and raw milk on her tongue, and across
the way a view of misty rosemary and sun on the wet leaves,
dangling.

PART THREE

20

A WEEK PASSED BEFORE HE FINALLY saw June. The only visitor
had been the warbler, and on that first day Jameson had bent and
crimped a scrap of copper gutter into a bowl-shaped birdbath,
wedged it into the ground so that it would not tip, and filled it
with water. The warbler jumped right in, and Jameson wandered
beneath the shade, entertained by the bird's spastic bath, a small
act offering them both an oversized pleasure, that day and every
day since.

Now here it was midafternoon, and Jameson felt the day's heat
at the workbench, even in the shade, his vinyl safety earmuffs
damp and dripping perspiration down the sides of his neck. The
table saw ran through a strip of yellow pine trim when some kind
of movement caught his eye. The warbler had returned to his
bath, and directly beyond him, into June's backyard, lay June.

Jameson lost his grip, slipped forward, and came within inches
of severing his hand at the wrist.

June was dressed in jean shorts and a white tank top, braless
— from twenty yards away he could see through her sheer white
shirt, see that she was tall with long, tanned legs, her knees bent,
feet flat on the ground. Sunglasses covered her eyes, her hair a
dark round mass beneath her head, and she reached back and

scooped it off her neck and to the side so that it lay halfway off her blanket on the grass. Then she crossed her thighs and swung her dangling foot like she was waiting for something, or losing patience in the waiting.

Jameson closed his eyes and swiped his hairline. When he looked again, June had dropped both legs flat, crossed her ankles, and spread her arms out to the sides like wings.

Evenings, he'd noticed the lights on in her kitchen and upstairs bedroom, and the shadows behind the blinds appeared to belong to only one person. He understood the need for privacy, but how hard could it have been for her to step out of her house for five minutes and say hello? Now here she was in the wide open, and there was no way for her to think he couldn't see.

They had shared one phone call since he arrived, when she rang to ask if there was anything he needed, anything she could provide, and made no mention of her absence. He said he couldn't think of what was lacking, though in truth he'd thought of a mini-fridge filled with a few cold beers. He didn't dare say it, even as a joke, and in thinking about it he wondered if maybe she had fallen off the wagon and this was the reason she hadn't left the house. Then he guessed such thinking was the go-to when something went wrong, or right, with a person getting sober, everything stemming from a singular cause. People had thought such things about Jameson and Sarah Anne: no matter their moods or actions, their lives became defined by a single event. The looks, the sighs, the *I admire you two after all you've been through,* as if Jameson and Sarah Anne could never be motivated by anything else, never *be* anyone else, other than the couple whose children had been gunned down in a gas station convenience store.

As she lay there, he thought a person with a hangover wouldn't want to be out like that in this heat.

"Are you sure I can't put you up at the San Dune while you're here?" she had asked again during the phone call. "I'd be relieved —"

"I've already made my pallet in the dining room. I'm comfortable as can be."

"The dining room?"

"Is that all right?"

"Of course. But it's so warm with all that direct light. I'm sure the whole house is warm. And you don't have a fan. Oh, I should have gotten you a fan!"

"It's not bad at all. The air cools things off by ten o'clock." In fact, sometimes that didn't happen until one o'clock in the morning. He had slept on top of his sleeping bag in nothing but his boxers, and did wish he'd had a fan. "I don't need anything," he told her, unable to accept, once again, her offer of kindness. "I'm right as rain."

He could ignore her now, he *would* ignore her, by returning to other work inside the house. But it was hotter inside than out, and after trying to nail down trim with salty sweat in his eyes, he returned to the yard and looked again for the sole purpose of seeing her, and she was there as before, lying on her back, arms spread wide as if waiting for something or someone to drop out of the sky.

He had told her on the phone that he was doing just fine, and it was true. A week in, and not nearly as bad as he'd feared it might be. He began each day with the sun devouring that old-growth grain of the walls and floors, surrounding him with a radiating, cadmium orange, a glaze of color like a cast-iron pot that his mother once owned. His sleeping bag lay along the far wall, and mornings arrived like an alchemy of senses, a yellow dawn behind white trees, chattering songbirds, a steady crash of waves. His arms and legs filled with the kind of low grade satisfaction he'd had no name for in his youth, a way of moving through the world untroubled. It was gratifying to boil water on the propane burner for pour-over coffee to drink with his morning banana bread from Helen's Bakery. Gratifying to be right there and nowhere else.

June had gone quiet on the phone when he didn't accept her offers. Jameson worried he'd offended her. "I prefer it this way," he said. "You understand that, right?"

"I cannot say I do. But if you insist, I can certainly go along."

"I insist," he said. "And thank you."

"Certainly not, don't thank me," she said. "But I do like hearing what you've said about the dining room."

"The colors —"

"Oh. Well. Yes. And the view of the trees. As a child I would sit in there and . . . just, well, sit, I don't know. I would sit and think and *feel*, I suppose, if that is what children do."

"I'd say they do just that," he said, and closed his eyes and prayed she would not ask if he had children.

"Anyway . . ." she said.

"So was this before or after you moved away?" he asked.

"What do you mean, moved away?"

"Your accent. It didn't come from Nestucca Beach."

"Oh. *Oh.* Yes. I've one foot in and one foot out my entire life, I suppose. The Irish think I sound American. Everyone here believes I'm foreign. A citizen of nowhere and everywhere."

"Sure," he said, and though he wanted her to go on, he didn't know what else to say. "Well," he said after a time. "I guess I should get back to work. I'm not getting paid to make conversation." It was a stupid thing to say.

"I shouldn't like to dock you," she said.

"I shouldn't like that either," he said, sounding a bit like June.

"Are you mocking me?" she asked, in a tone that meant she was mocking him.

Jameson gave a small laugh, and then, perhaps it was the way her voice fell on the last word, he felt a sudden seriousness. "Goodbye, June," he said.

"Goodbye, Jameson," she'd said.

That was days ago. Now he was looking right at her, with the heat nearly tropical and his perspiration streaming as if he'd been dunked into a vat of hot steam. And then she lifted her phone, plucked a finger around, and brought it to her ear.

His phone vibrated on the workbench. He glanced at her, then the phone.

"Jameson here," he answered, and she said, "Hello, Jameson," with a tone of such familiarity that he wondered again if she might be drunk. "How's it going up there?" she asked, a little more American than usual.

"*June.* It's going. About what I expected. No surprises. Not yet, anyway." He took several steps back, stuck his free hand in his front pocket, pulled it out, and scratched behind his ear.

"Well," she said. "Good. *Good.*" Her knees were back up, one leg was thrown over the other, and her foot was swinging and swinging. She lifted her head slightly and ran her hand through her hair, then she loosened the whole of it again so that it sprawled from her head like a dark and twisted tail. "I'd like to pop over if that's all right."

Jameson turned in a half-circle, looking up at the house and down into the yard, which was full of junk piles, the mess rising before him as if it had just appeared out of nowhere. "Of course."

"I know you don't like to be disturbed."

"I know you don't either."

Then silence.

"It's your house," he finally said. "Please. Come whenever you like."

June was saying something, but his phone began to beep with another call. He held it out and saw that it was Sarah Anne.

"Well. If you really don't mind," June said as the phone reached his ear, "there are a few things I want to talk about."

"Not at all. Listen, I've got something coming through on the other line. Do you mind if I call you back?'

"No need. Sit tight. I'll see you in a bit."

He nodded and switched over the call, feeling the full discomfort of sweat weighing on his clothes. He backed up and sat in the shade against a white trunk.

"Hi, baby," Sarah Anne said, an endearment neither of them had used since the children had died.

"Sarah Anne. How are you? How's the boy today?"

"We're both well, really well. I've got news. I don't want to get your hopes up, but Melinda called Jessie to ask about the adoption."

Jessie. It took a moment to realize Jessie was the caseworker's name. "Oh, you mean . . . she's asking how to do it? She's asking how to let him go?" He was glad to be sitting down.

"Yes. That is what I mean. And you sound tired."

"It's hot," he said. "I'm sure it's even worse for you."

"Of course it is, but Jameson? Did you hear what I said?"

This heavy wave of fatigue . . . Had he not been getting enough sleep? His dreams had come to him like fleeting, hovering moods, forgotten as soon as he woke.

"Yes, yes, I did, of course, you didn't call to talk about the weather. You caught me off guard with my hands full."

"Aren't you happy? Is everything all right?"

"I'm good, no, this is great, just . . . a little exhausted and all that, but listen, I don't want you to get your hopes up. Melinda says a lot of things . . ."

"I think she means it. I really do. Jessie had a serious, very honest conversation with her after our last visit. I think . . . well, do you want it, if it's true?"

"Do I *want* it? Oh, Sarah Anne. Of course I *want* it. Of course I want *him*." Jameson stood and fanned his shirt. He closed his eyes, opened them, and looked down to see that June was no longer on the lawn. "I've got my hands full, like I said. In the middle of a thousand things."

"I'm sorry. I figured as much. It's OK. Call me later. Will you call me later?"

"I will. In a little while. I'll call you by this evening at the latest."

He hung up and stood, trying to collect himself as sweat ran through the grime and sawdust on his face. He lifted off his T-shirt and crossed the yard, using the fabric to dab his face, and then he thought that June might be watching, and figured the only thing to do was keep walking and dabbing his neck in a way that seemed mannerly and considerate of her seeing him, though it made no sense, and still he steadied his pace so as not to give anything away.

He rinsed his face and neck at the kitchen sink, dried himself off with his dirty shirt, and pulled a clean, wrinkled T-shirt from his duffel. He didn't know that he could parent that boy. He didn't know that Sarah Anne could not. He drank two full glasses of water and shook his damp hair like a dog.

21

JUNE BEGAN TO PANIC DAYS AGO. She had lived long enough to regret plenty of the things she'd done in her life, and she'd spent the past week terrified and certain that if she left the house at all, even to lie out in the yard, she would walk away from the property and down to the store and return home with several bottles of wine. She closed herself off like her father, and understood him in a way she had not before.

But every day that passed she had been sneaking looks at Jameson through the blinds, memorizing his gait, the way he favored his left leg now and again. He often set down whatever he was holding, gripped his hips, and tipped his face to the sun, as if remembering suddenly that it was there. He kept his eyes closed for ten seconds or so before he dropped his head back down and gave it a little shake, as if freeing his mind of the thoughts he'd allowed in. Watching him put her in a trance, and June didn't trust a trance. A trance was too close to a stupor. Jameson must think her incredibly rude.

But today arrived with a new distraction. It was June's birthday, which she preferred to forget. Every year Grandmam tried forcing a celebration with cake and presents, as if no one could hear June's father weeping and pacing upstairs in his room. She needed to get out in the sun.

When she opened the back door, she paused for a long breath and then stepped into the yard and stretched her arms in the air. One year older, more than one month sober, and the air smelled of freshly seared wood, lavender, and the clattering sounds of work next door, and everything tightened June's chest with relief. Life was about to get better. Surely it was. It was already better. A few bad scenes were not the end of the story.

She got the camp blanket and lay down on it, thinking how she needed to call Jameson. She must go next door finally and introduce herself. She took out her phone.

"Please," he told her. "Come whenever you like."

Now she was in her bedroom, about to change clothes and go meet him. She happened to look through the window and see him taking off his shirt in the yard. She lowered herself to the edge of the bed and stared as he dabbed his face and throat with his wadded-up T-shirt. He blotted his cheeks and forehead and swiped the back of his neck, and June did not turn away, though it struck her that his movements, so private and tender, were not meant for her to see.

As he walked shirtless across the yard and into the house, June sat motionless on the bed. Moments later, he returned wearing a different shirt, and June felt her breath shorten at the thought that he had changed his shirt for her. The blinds were angled upward, and she guessed that if he looked over he would see her, too, and she removed her tank top without taking her eyes off him, and, mimicking him, she wiped away the sweat at the nape of her neck and between her breasts, and by the time she'd changed into something new, she was fairly certain that he had not looked up, and was not aware of her at all.

22

FIFTEEN MINUTES HAD PASSED and Jameson was starting to wonder. The wave of fatigue he'd felt earlier had been replaced by adrenaline, and as he paced the yard and rooms on the first floor, an awareness evolved, a wider disarray coming into view than the one he'd noticed thirty minutes before. He shuffled and scrambled and shoved tools and clothes and takeout boxes from the counter.

And then he waited, leaning into his workbench from the side opposite where he normally stood, gaining leverage while yanking nails from a piece of trim, a little busywork to bide his time. Standing on this side of the bench offered a clear view of the debris along the edge of the yard, and he was thinking about the call he'd have to put in to Van Hicks. Someone needed to haul away all this busted wood and rusted wiring and the gutter pieces and crumbled drywall that Jameson had raked into four separate mounds. It was getting out of hand.

When he woke this morning his right hip and shoulder had ached tender as a bruise, and it was only after three cups of coffee and a slice of banana bread that the soreness had finally disappeared, and he was sure now that he *had* slept well, because when he'd first walked outside, his right cheek reflected in the windowpanes of the double doors, he saw the lines carved in his face where he must have lain for hours without moving his head from the pillow, lines deep and varied as a map of deltas.

The air suddenly shifted at his back. Jameson turned to find June several yards away, holding a Polaroid camera in one hand and a coffee cup in the other. She took a sip and then lowered the cup, leisurely, to her chest, her face slowly coming into view. Her eyes were large and dark and unblinking. Her cheeks were bright from the sun, and the whole of her seemed as strangely natured and beautiful as he now realized he'd feared. She was a perfect match for the lilting, airy voice on the phone.

Jameson rushed to the other side of his bench like a fool running a store, a man caught slacking on the job.

June stepped forward and lifted her hand with the cup as if to touch his arm, though she was too far away to reach him. She was dressed in a thin blue tunic that billowed in the faint breeze, out and around and in between her ankle-length jeans. She seemed to be holding back laughter. "I didn't mean to startle you."

The blood pounded in his ears and his pulse was so loud he feared he wouldn't hear whatever it was she'd come to say.

"I hope you don't mind the intrusion," she said.

He shook his head. "Of course not."

"It's my birthday." She glanced toward her yard and back. "Sorry, that must sound strange."

"No," he said, though it did.

She lifted the camera to her eye, aimed at Jameson, and clicked the red button without a word. The photo spit out the front with a zipping sound he had not heard since he was a child. June plucked it from the camera with the fingers she'd looped through the handle of the coffee cup, and the coffee sloshed over the side.

Jameson stood dumbfounded.

"Well," she said, fanning the air with the photograph. "Anyway..." She turned toward the piles of junk, then peered in the direction of the open double doors into the dining room, where his rolled-up sleeping bag and duffel were stacked against the far wall. She nodded with a sense of propriety, as if to say she approved of everything, and then the cup was at her lips, and Jameson saw how much she resembled her grandmother.

He ought to come around and shake her hand. But the distance between him and any kind of protocol was like a widening river, and besides, she did not have a free hand to shake.

"Oh, I'm June," she said, "as you may have guessed."

"Nice to finally meet you." The piece of trim was still in his hands, and he tore at the nails without looking down. "I suppose it's pretty clear who I am."

Did that sound sarcastic? Clarity was a slow train coming, and willing it faster did nothing to help. He looked down at his hands; they might as well have belonged to another man for all the sense they made. He looked up and blinked, then found he couldn't stop blinking. "Sawdust," he said, wiping his lids with the back of his hand.

"I meant to say, I'm Jameson." He yanked a little harder at the nails, and when he looked down, he saw he'd busted several off at the base. When he looked up, the sun had lit the outline of June's shape through the fabric, the contour of her hips and the sides of her breasts now well defined. Her skin was deeply tanned, and her long hair, a coppery brown, was swept into a twist at the back of her head. Loose strands fell from her temples and others curled at the back of her neck. She was barefoot, but he did not tell her to be mindful of splinters and nails. She had watchful eyes of her own.

"The piles are filling up," she said.

"Yeah . . ."

"You seem to be making a lot of progress in a short amount of time."

"It's not as bad as it might have been. You were right. Your grandfather knew how to look after the place."

June nodded at the ground. "I'll give your friend Van Hicks a call."

"He's not my friend."

"Oh?"

"I mean, we worked together in the past, that's it."

"All right."

"I'll call him." Jameson's face burned with heat.

"Are you interested in doing any of the landscape work?" she asked. "I keep forgetting to ask."

"Depends on what you need."

"Not much. The hazel tree could use pruning. But I'd like it to remain a bit rascally, as Granddad used to say."

Jameson let go a small laugh.

"And once the house is done, I'd like a row of cypress planted between the properties for privacy."

"I can do both of those things if you like."

His thoughts shifted to Sarah Anne and Ernest, the extra days being tacked on at the end.

"I'll pay you fairly."

"I believe you will. Thank you for the check. You didn't need to pay so much up front."

"For your trouble," she said, and he did not contradict her. "I also wanted to mention something about the chimney."

He let go of the trim and the hammer, wiped his hands down his thighs, and made every attempt to focus on what she was saying.

"The stonework around the mantel is vulnerable in places not visible to the eye. My grandfather made a note of it before he died."

"I gathered, after poking around."

"Well." She took another sip. "It's just that we really need to take good care."

"Of course we will. I will."

"I was thinking we might need to call for backup."

"How so?"

"I mean, *if* we end up needing help. Probably not best to wait

until the last minute to find someone. I know you like to work
alone, and I got so lucky with you on short notice, but I don't expect that to happen again. How do you feel about working with
Van Hicks again?"

Jameson's jaw tightened. "He'll do if I need someone, but I
don't think I'll be needing anyone." He felt a tightness in his neck.
He didn't know what to make of her request.

"There's something I need to show you," he said, as if someone
else had stepped up and come to the rescue. "Do you have a minute?"

June swallowed her coffee. "I do."

She followed him through the dining room, and he turned in
time to see her looking down at his belongings.

"You didn't bring very many things with you," she said.

He didn't turn when he spoke. "I don't need a whole lot."

"Hmm," she said, and followed him up the stairs and down the
hall.

When they reached the master bedroom, Jameson walked to
the far wall and opened the west-facing window all the way, and
then he did the same to the one facing east, though barely a crosswind stirred. June stood just inside the doorway. The room was
about eleven by fifteen feet and echoey.

June kept the camera at her side, her cup to her chest, and
Jameson could see that the coffee was nearly gone. She went over
to the window facing the ocean, her movements a kind of grace-
ful, injured elegance. She looked out and drank the last of her coffee, and he could see the shape of the photo she had taken in the
front square pocket of her tunic.

"I don't remember it ever being this warm," she said. The depth
of her sigh was audible.

"That's because it's never been." Jameson slipped on his work
gloves and picked up the pry bar in the corner of the room. The
gloves were hot on his hands, and his clean shirt was already
sweat-spotted. He crouched near a row of planks at the center

of the room. "This," he said, not looking up, but in that moment he was studying the imprints her bare feet made across the dusty floor, and then her toes.

He glanced up. She had the camera raised to her eye. "You don't mind, do you?"

"No," he said, but he was feeling strange, pulled into something he didn't quite understand.

He shifted his weight into the pry bar and yanked hard, popping the rotten wood loose. "This is what I wanted you to see." He told her the flooring would have to be replaced, and he talked about the leaky roof and the termites, and how he'd expected much worse after seeing the outside.

June clicked the camera and the film zipped free.

Jameson wedged the pry bar deeper and yanked again. This time the dry wood snapped with a violent crack that caught him off balance.

He stood, favoring his left leg in a way he did only in winter. He let the pry bar slip to the floor as if he were alone, and it made a clattering crash that startled them both.

"I'm sorry," he said.

"Not to worry," she said, lowering the camera and fanning the photograph dry.

When he walked over to set the pry bar upright in the corner, he realized he was walking with a limp.

"Everything all right?"

"Yes," he said, and removed his gloves and covered his mouth. Then he dropped his hand and shook his head at the floor before meeting her eyes. "But the chimney," he said, "I don't want you to worry about that. It's a simple fix."

She started to speak, then stopped.

"Don't worry about any of this." He spoke with a kindness he hadn't expected or even intended, he didn't think he did, but that was how he said it, and he saw in her face that she'd received it that way, too. The corners of her mouth and eyes lit with a spark of understanding, and Jameson wondered what it would be like if things were turned around. When was the last time, if ever there had been a time, when he'd been told not to worry about *any of this*? When had he not felt responsible for every last thing in his life and for every last thing in the lives of those closest to him?

A moment of quiet, then June nodded and lowered the mug and thanked him. "There's that tile around the hearth," she said. "Are you able to find a match for the broken piece?"

"I've got a guy in Portland. I ordered a few extras in case another one cracks."

"Thank you."

"Sure."

"I have to get going," she said. "Is it all right if I come back tomorrow?" She stepped into the doorway.

"You can come anytime."

She began to turn away, hesitated, and gripped the doorframe. "Don't take this the wrong way," she said. "But I'm curious." Her eyes narrowed. "If you don't mind . . . I'm wondering how you live with the isolation."

Jameson shifted his hip, leaned into his bad leg, and shifted back. He balled his fists into his front pockets like a boy, wondering what Van had told her about him. She knew. She *had* to know about his family. She could have been part of the blur of people who'd pitied him and Sarah Anne, that onslaught of sympathy coming at them in the form of hugs and marionberry pies and easy-to-reheat side dishes. Before their hunger had vanished, another stew arrived at the door.

"Are you sure we've never met?" he asked.

June drew a long breath. "It's hot in here."

"We can go downstairs."

"No," June said. "I mean about meeting. I'm not sure. We could have. My history. You know. It's a little spotty."

"Oh. Well. Actually, the thing is . . . so is mine. That's why I'm not sure either."

June appeared puzzled by his reply.

Jameson held up a hand. "Oh, I'm not a drinker. I mean, I *drink*, but it's not a problem."

June nodded slowly, and it was all he could do to wonder if this was what all drunks said, and he guessed it was. He had no idea how to make plain that he didn't actually have a problem without sounding like he was protesting a little too much, so he let it go, and thought again of all those meals coming at them, until they'd run out of room in the fridge and freezer and began dumping everything in the trash, turning everyone's good intentions into garbage.

"So . . ." he said.

"What I mean is," June said, "what stops you from going mad inside all these rundown homes, year after year, with no one to keep you company?"

Jameson crossed his arms, realized it made him look defensive, and placed his hands on his hips, though he knew that was just a different look of defense. "I've worked this way ever since my wife and I were in college." The mention of Sarah Anne felt pointed — no accidental slip. Some part of him felt the need to set something straight. He was not so isolated. He did not need her pity.

June nodded at the floor.

"The thing is . . ." he said.

"Oh, listen. Sometimes I just say things. I don't know why I asked you that . . . I apologize. I've gotten so personal. And I've kept you long enough."

Her accent thickened with what appeared to be nervousness.

"No. I'm happy to answer your question," he said in a voice that seemed to come from elsewhere, from that bright blue desert sky back home for all he knew, because *happy* was most certainly not what he meant, and she seemed to know that, and it held her in place. "I piece together the lives of other people," he said. "I guess that's what saves me." *Saves me?* It had already slipped from his mouth, and he didn't want to come across like a man lacking confidence by stumbling to take it back. The truth was, no one had ever asked him such a thing before, and the answer he offered sounded eccentric to the world outside his ears.

June smiled, and faint lines appeared on both sides of her mouth, which he thought handsome. There was no other way to say it.

Jameson glanced at the floor, at her bare feet at the top of his vision. She crossed one foot over the other at the toes.

"That's pretty much what Van told me," she said.

He looked through the window at the ocean. "Is that right."

"Do you ever wonder what they'd think of your work, the people who lived so many decades ago? Do you worry whether or not you're doing justice to a place? I guess that's what I mean, not in any awful way . . . not in the way it probably sounds."

How was it that he felt a terrible, pleasurable pang for a woman he surely did not know? He wondered if he'd gone a little pale, the way her eyebrows drew together as she waited for an answer.

"Yes," he said. "I *do* worry. All the time. In fact, I think it's safe to say the dead inform my every move."

June smiled openly, and it caught his breath. "I'll see you tomorrow, then," she said. "My birthday and all. Not that I'm going to celebrate or anything. It changes as we get older, doesn't it? Forgetting, like that. Becoming just another day. Anyway, it's back to work for us both."

"Happy birthday," he said, watching her go, listening as she took the stairs one by one, and then the soft creak of the dining room floor, which stalled for a moment, and he guessed she was standing not far from his things. And then the creak of the back porch planks, but not the final steps. She'd hesitated again.

He waited.

June called back through the house: "I've got a pail you can have!"

Jameson came to the top of the stairs, puzzled, smiling. "Do I need a pail?"

"For the bird. It won't tip when he bathes in it."

"Oh," Jameson said, wondering why he had not thought of it himself. Then the click and zip of the camera, the groan of the steps, and she was gone.

23

June woke at six-thirty a.m. to the buzz of her cell phone.

Victory International Shipping was apologizing for the early call, apologizing for having taken so long to get back to her, apologizing for the short notice: the truck with her belongings would be arriving early this afternoon.

"Today?" she sat up.

"We're pleased to confirm you'll be home to receive the truck, and we want to thank you for your patience."

June cleared her throat. "There has been no *patience* here." She glanced at the Polaroids on her nightstand. Here was Jameson caught off guard at his workbench, and there crouched over the rotted floor with the pry bar in his hands. In the latter he appeared to be looking into the near distance where June was standing. He seemed to be looking at her feet. What was wrong with her, taking her camera over there like that? He must think her insane.

"We appreciate your business."

"You people are quite something." June hung up and realized that she'd mostly forgotten about the boxes, and now their arrival felt like an intrusion. The day was already taking off like a train without her. The hammering had begun next door.

Sixteen parcels from her other life were about to arrive, and she would need to make room, and there was no room to be made. She would have to shove the boxes into her father's bedroom, and the stacks would fill all the free space in the room. She could barely recall what she had packed. And after everything was dumped out, what then? Where was it all supposed to go? She had lived for months without any of these things.

She pulled open the blinds. The ocean was calmer than she had seen it in months, the horizon a tight, steady blue line. Today was set to be as hot as all the others, and June, to her surprise, was beginning to tire of the heat.

As far as she could tell, Jameson worked nearly every daylight hour of every day, and she wondered if he was drinking enough water. Niall used to ask June that very question, and it had gotten under her skin. She took it to mean that she'd had too many martinis the night before, and it sounded like an accusation, as if he were simply calling her a drunk, calling her a child, too, in need of a minder. June thought she was probably wrong about all of that. Niall was often driven by kindness; he had only ever been kind, for the most part he had. June grabbed her robe and cinched it tightly around the guilt rising in her gut.

Last night she'd lain awake replaying her conversation with Jameson, running through the beginning, middle, and end, recalling all the details, the sticky give of her soles on the dusty floor, the crash of the pry bar, the way he had said they would take good care.

We really need to take good care, she had told him. *The stonework around the mantel is vulnerable in places not visible to the eye.* What could have prompted her to say such a thing to a man who knew better than anyone what was called for? She'd felt the blood rush to her face as he looked away, and again minutes later when he nodded at the bedroom floor where he'd ripped out the wood that could not be saved, and she blushed again with the memory. A good portion of the wood could not be saved. This was what he'd told her in the bedroom, and he'd removed his glove and covered his mouth and sighed as if thinking of a way to tell her that it *could* be saved, a way to change the truth staring up at him. The gold ring on his finger was dull and scratched, a little loose in fit, and she couldn't help but think he had brought it to his face so that she might see it and consider what it stood for. *But the chimney,* he'd said, and when he lifted his eyes to her, he seemed to be thinking of something other than a chimney, something other than a floor that could not be saved.

I've worked this way ever since my wife and I were in college.

Her mug. Her pillow. What else had she packed?

Last night she'd listened to Jameson working up until the final ray of light, around ten o'clock, the same as he'd done since he arrived. But when she saw the shadows from his lantern, she imagined being inside the house with him, sitting knee-to-knee on the dining room floor. She imagined leaning close to his ear to say all the awful details she'd never said to anyone, not even Niall. The way the blood had run down Heather's back from the scissors in June's hand, and the sight of scrawny little Claire being led through the dark while June lay safely beneath her blanket. There was more than that. Much more, and June could feel the words forming in her mouth, feel the air of freedom as if she were being let out of a cage.

"My God, the theater of your mind, child," Grandmam once said, and looking back, June guessed she had meant that there was now something wrong with her. Something ruined and beyond repair. Grandmam's side glances when June spoke or ate, as if looking for the weary signs of instability like that of her own son. Before June was sent away, Grandmam had laughed with her whole body. She would hold June close and kiss the top of her head. When June returned from Salem, it was different. "She does not have the constitution to overcome all that has happened in her short life," she told Granddad when June was supposed to be out of earshot. "She's a lionheart, Maeve," he'd said. "More her mother than her father."

Victory International Shipping had said early afternoon, but the roar of the moving van was echoing up the ridge before June had a chance to finish her coffee.

24

WHEN JAMESON RETURNED SARAH ANNE'S CALL, her excitement had carried across the line with a charge he had not heard or felt from her in years. It got into him and all over him, until the enthusiasm he offered her in return was genuine, straight from the heart.

And yet, he'd thought about the rumpled warbler while Sarah Anne was talking, the joy of witnessing this little bird in a bath, the smallest pleasures he'd lost track of these past three years, but he didn't speak of it to Sarah Anne. What he did say was "I'm going to be taking a few days off when the roofers get here. What if you and Ernest come out and we rent a place down the coast?" Sarah Anne got her calendar and said how good it would be to get away, the three of them together, and Jameson said, "Yes, yes," and he could feel the way their words were igniting the system of life, the way so much of what was said was leaving out so much of what was not. But that night he lay awake imagining Sarah Anne driving across the state with Ernest in the back seat, having to stop for gas and pretend there was nothing wrong with her, that she had gotten a grain of sand or speck of dust in her eye, while Ernest stared at her in the rearview mirror, absorbing her lie.

Now here it was early the following morning, and from the back of the bungalow's yard he heard the distant roar of an engine in low gear approaching. The ground shook, and Jameson stepped out to the front porch to see a large moving van lurching up the hill. It came to a stop in front of June's house. It was seven a.m.

June was on her porch, dressed in the same shorts and tank top she'd worn while lying in the sun, but this time she was wearing a bra. Her hair hung loose down her back, well past her shoulders. She was barefoot.

Three men climbed out of the truck, came toward her, and shook her hand. Then she caught sight of Jameson and, looking up into the eastern sun, made a visor with her hand. "My things from Ireland!" she yelled, sounding not very pleased.

"Can I help?" he asked.

She shook her head and thanked him and said something about there not being much, while the three men began hustling around her, bringing boxes into the house.

He expected her to say she would see him later, but she disappeared inside. After a number of trips two of the men returned to the front yard, removed their hats, wiped their heads, and waited in the Adirondack chairs. They didn't appear to say a word, just sat looking out at the ocean and drinking from paper coffee cups they'd retrieved from the truck. Jameson recognized the cups from Helen's, where he'd been grabbing sandwiches and banana bread since he arrived, and it gave him an idea.

He washed his hands and drove down and bought a cupcake for June.

When he returned, the moving truck was pulling away. There was no sign of June, and he did not see her for the rest of the day. She didn't call, and he got the impression she didn't want him to call her, either. He didn't know, but the air had shifted, and come evening her kitchen was dark, and around nine p.m. Jameson ate the cinnamon-spice cupcake with buttercream icing, and twice caught himself moaning at how good it was.

June didn't show up the next day, or the one after that. Jameson didn't see her for another week.

And that was fine. He had plenty to do before the roofers came, and before Sarah Anne and Ernest got there, and he was glad to see the flooring he'd ordered arrive on time. He worked twice as hard as he believed he was capable, carefully pounding in the subfloor and every tongue-and-groove plank into place. But he couldn't help wondering if he'd said or done something he shouldn't have, and if he had, whether it was the thing that was keeping June away.

His desire to talk to her grew. He wanted to ask her things: Did she listen to the coyotes at night, and did she think those signals were a call to come closer or to stay away? Did she leave her windows open the way he did? Or close them tightly so as to not hear a thing? And how about the flickers drumming the cedars in the early afternoons? Had she heard their amplified clatter from across the golf course? The first time the sounds caught his attention, he thought someone was using a jackhammer.

Morning after morning came for him as if by prayer or meditation, a rising sun like a rising benediction for a man who was never quite sure he deserved all the good he'd been given, and in turn everything else seemed a punishment he'd rightfully earned. Back home Sarah Anne and Ernest would be battling a heat much harsher than the one Jameson was battling here, and without much comfort of a breeze, and they'd have to wait out the day for the night desert to cool things off. By then Ernest would be asleep, and Sarah Anne would be alone in the house without him, and he wondered why she didn't call him a whole lot more than she did.

When June left the other day, Jameson had gone on standing in the bedroom, staring at the empty doorway, recalling the time he'd discovered, in another house, a strange impression on a bedroom doorframe. He'd placed his palm into the groove about even with his head, and his hand fit just right in the indentation, and he imagined that a man had stood bracing himself in that doorway, looking into the room, again and again, for what must have amounted to years. What would hold a man's attention this way? Had more than one person come to stand there? If so, they would have been of similar height. It didn't seem likely. Jameson wanted to believe a sick child had been watched over from this place at the door. Or a parent, a grandparent, someone in need of care. He would never know, but even if he had known, the truth didn't always turn out the way he'd like for it to be. Over the years he'd seen all kinds of things, like evidence that a dog had spent a lifetime clawing to get out of a room. He'd found wainscoting ruptured by bullets, and the spread of black stains in subfloors, proof that at least one person had made his mark. Slivers of green glass burrowed deep inside floorboards might have been the result of carelessness, but there were times when Jameson felt certain that a jar had been thrown in a moment of anger or despair.

So he'd stood there the other day thinking about all that when June had called up to him about the pail, and he'd forgotten what it was he was doing.

When Sarah Anne was speaking in rapid-fire excitement about adopting Ernest, Jameson's heart had pulled toward her. "I know you don't want me to get my hopes up," she said, "but Melinda actually requested the paperwork, Jay. She called Jess and initiated the entire thing."

"I didn't mean it like that. Not really. The last thing in the world I would ever wish for is for you not to have hope."

He'd listened and thought about holding the boy, the feel of his tiny arms up against him, but then he couldn't help recalling Piper and Nate, the weight and smell of them, the sound of their voices, their laughter, their tears, and a hollowness filled his insides the way it always did when Jameson reached out to this boy.

Sarah Anne was caught inside a fever of her own happiness, if that was what it was, and Jameson believed it was, some form of happiness, and he hadn't said a whole lot during their conversation, and that was fine, he was glad not to have to speak, and by the end of the call he wondered if he could have been anyone on the other end of the line, so long as Sarah Anne had a person with whom she could share the good news.

It had been June's birthday that day, and he guessed she hadn't celebrated, hadn't even remembered until later in the day, and so far as he could tell she had spent the rest of the day alone, and he didn't know what to make of that. He assumed by now that she lived by herself, and of course he'd noticed that she didn't wear a ring. To each his own, he thought, but it didn't seem right spending a birthday by oneself, and he wondered if she thought so little of who she was that she could forget the day she was born, no matter her age. But that didn't seem possible, to look at her.

He was thinking that he might prepare a little something for the next time she called up and said she was coming over. Like lunch. Not lunch, not really, but what to call it? She could bring that blanket she'd been lying on in her backyard, and he could pick up a few things from Helen's Bakery after he consolidated the piles out back and made room for them to sit in the shade. Or maybe they could sit on the front porch and watch the ocean while they ate. But how on earth to ask? And what if she agreed to join him for something that looked an awful lot like a picnic?

For starters, he would need a topic of conversation, something he could rely on once they settled down and unwrapped the sandwiches. He would ask about her own work. How could he not have asked her about it already? He imagined her swallowing politely while he talked, waiting for the point he was trying to make, but even in his own imagination he wasn't saying a whole lot that made good sense and he wasn't putting either of them at ease. He chewed too quickly and for too long, wiped his mouth more than was needed, and nodded his head without purpose. And what *was* the point? He didn't know, not the full spectrum of it, though he was pretty sure he was no kind of man to be offering a picnic to a woman who was not his wife.

This wasn't like him. He didn't think this way. He'd never been involved in anything that could have been interpreted the wrong way.

But there *were* points to be made about the house. Practical details about ceilings and floors, and whether to replace the cabinets in the kitchen and bathroom, or not.

I bought some sandwiches and berries.

It didn't sound right, even in his own mind.

Would you care to have lunch with me?

No, that was all wrong.

I picked up enough for the both of us.

Just, no.

People have to eat.

Maybe this was all just the heat going to his head. Maybe the salty sea air and all that lavender poking purple through the weeds and that swirl of bees had gone to his head. Maybe her accent muddled his clarity of mind. Maybe the coyotes yipping in the night weren't helping matters. He'd listened in complete darkness to their sounds of yearning, and he knew without knowing that she was listening, too.

But now here it was, a week since he'd seen her, and in two days Sarah Anne and Ernest would be here, and the roofers would take over the place. Jameson thought about all of that at once while washing his hands at the sink.

Then June appeared.

She rapped a knuckle on the open dining room door.

He startled so badly he cursed.

And then he laughed at the sight of her holding up a brown paper bag he recognized from the bakery. Beneath her other arm was the rolled-up blanket, and in that hand, dangling at her side, was a white pail.

"I haven't heard you stop to eat yet today. I thought you might appreciate a sandwich."

"Come on in." He dried his hands on a paper towel.

So she was listening for the way he did things over here, was watchful of his habits throughout the day. This house held the strange and prescient. She was here, and she was holding the very things that had been in his mind, and he wondered what else. "Well," he said. "All right. Thank you."

June set the pail down on the porch, stepped inside, and glanced around. Her eyes grew larger. "It's beautiful. You've already replaced the trim . . . and the batten walls, the floor . . . Everything looks the way it's supposed to." Her arms fell to her sides and her mouth hung slightly open. "Aw, Jameson."

He looked away at the sound of his name.

She took a step back and seemed to shake off whatever thoughts she was having. "Right, then. How about we sit on the front porch?"

And just like that, the blanket was rolled out and the food was uncovered. They talked about the corner column he had replaced, and how the slope of the porch was plumb for the roofers, and she was saying how she'd been busy writing, and how it pleased her that there had been a bit of a draft. She apologized for not returning before today, explaining that sometimes, if she was lucky, the work swept in and took over, and when that happened, she had to run with it or lose it, and there'd be no guarantee of its return, and no real idea what she may have lost to begin with — those hours were particular to that moment in time and could never come for her again in the same way.

Jameson had to stop himself from staring at her mouth. He didn't know how to add to what she was saying, but it didn't seem to matter. He sat with the wonder of it, and as far as he could tell she didn't mind him listening to her that way.

Then the sandwiches were gone, and they were having what was left of the berries, and Jameson was poking his plastic fork into a blueberry just as June asked what the weirdest part about his work was.

"Weirdest?"

June shrugged. "Unexpected, I guess. The kind of thing people don't realize or guess about."

Jameson had never been asked that question, but he already knew the answer. "The stuff I find hidden in the walls."

June leaned back and raised an eyebrow. "Oh my."

"It's more common than you think. Things show up beneath floorboards and the corners of attics. Wallpaper and crown molding are perfect for slipping letters and documents behind, the kind written on that old thin paper."

June faced him crossed-legged. "And what's one of the more interesting things you've found?"

Jameson didn't have to think about that, either. "A keepsake tin full of photographs of women in varying stages of undress."

He could hardly believe he'd said it.

June's eyebrows shot up, but she was laughing, and now he was laughing too.

He didn't tell her how the women's legs were open and their knees raised, and he didn't mention the crude drawings of male and female genitalia that accompanied them, but he was seeing it all behind his eyes, and could feel the heat in his face.

"What about love letters?" June asked, and his heart kicked an extra beat.

"Yes," he said. "I've found a few."

"Oh?"

He looked down at the berries, stuffed a few in his mouth, and felt certain he was veering into territory in which he ought not go.

"Can you tell me about them?"

"Well." He swallowed his last bite. "They mostly end up in shoe boxes in attics, a lot of them written on tiny folded stationery that's hard to decipher."

"And others?" June smiled boldly, and God help him, he nearly reached out and touched her beautiful face.

He curled his hands and closed his fists on his knees and told her that most had to do with lust, though it seemed that people chickened out before mailing off that kind of stuff. "Most weren't postmarked, but maybe they were handed over in person."

June leaned away and placed her hands on the porch, behind her hips. "Lust," she repeated.

He didn't want her to see him blush. He ought to change the subject, but something had gotten hold of him and he kept on. "And other things, of a different deal." He'd said too much. She was going to ask what he meant, and he was going to tell her.

"Such as?"

"Cravings," he said, speaking to her as if he had a right to speak that way, free and familiar. "Strange kinds of desires."

June's mouth opened slightly. She leaned toward him and looked directly into his eyes.

"I mean, I've read all kinds. Where one person wants to hurt another for pleasure. Or a woman longing for another woman. A man crying his heart out for another man while having to make love to his wife."

June lowered her chin and raised her eyebrows, and she did not take her eyes from his. Her hands were clasped in her lap.

Jameson was first to look away.

"There's more," she said. "Tell me."

"No, it's just that those letters were as desperate as anything I've ever come across. Hard to shake all that misery and longing. And I feel pretty awful about it. None of it was meant for me to see."

June's breath had quickened. She was looking at the ocean, and he was looking at the way her chest and shoulders lifted and fell when she breathed.

"But not every hidden thing was so dark, right?" she finally asked.

"No. That's true. People leave behind whimsical, peculiar things. Everyday objects made mysterious by the act of hiding them. Like a red plate or a canning jar full of green cat's-eye marbles." The word "marbles" shifted the conversation, ushered in a reprieve, and June leaned away again. "One time I found a slide rule twisted with twine onto a compass. No idea what that was ever meant to be or why someone needed to stow it. I found an awful painting of a mermaid. I imagined a child had done it after reading Hans Christian Andersen, but why hide it?"

"What do you do with all that stuff?"

"I give it to the owners."

"Of course."

"Some places leave behind a whole mess of things. Others not a trace." He guessed she wanted to know, too, if he had found something in her grandmother's house, something that rightfully belonged to her.

"One time I found a gold bracelet tucked inside a potato sack behind a wall, and next to that a newspaper article on a railroad that was never built. The article was wrapped inside a handkerchief monogramed HG. No one knew who that could be. Not the owners who had searched the archives of the local papers, not the elderly neighbors. Not everything makes sense. In fact, most of it doesn't seem to."

His voice had taken on an excitement, an energy not so different from Sarah Anne's on the phone. But whatever he was saying did not appear to be taken in the way he had meant it. June's face had a look of concern, and then a small judgment, it seemed, as if she were hearing something beyond the words he was saying.

"You ever get a little lost in their lives?" she asked.

Jameson cocked his head. "I guess I do. Kind of a perk, I suppose."

"I do, too. Get lost in the lives of others."

They turned toward the ocean. In the quiet Jameson felt the temperature slowly begin to cool.

"So that's it, then," June said. "All the weird stuff you've found?"

"Well. No. Let's see."

He watched as she drank from a bottle of water, her head tilted, exposing her throat.

"I've come across a couple of suicide notes," he said.

June set the bottle down, wiped her mouth with the back of her hand, and leveled her eyes at him.

"One inside a wallpaper seam where no one would ever read it. A draft, I guess. Practice on a work in progress."

June stared, eyes stark and piercing, the corner of her bottom lip suddenly held between her teeth.

"I'm sorry," he said. "I didn't mean to sound so crude."

June shook her head. "Of course not."

Jameson offered an apologetic smile.

"What did the note say?" she asked.

"Oh, you know. Like you'd imagine: Please forgive me for what I'm about to do . . ."

June nodded once.

"I'm sorry. This doesn't seem like the best topic."

"Have you found anything like that here?"

"What, like a suicide note?"

June nodded.

Jameson felt like an idiot. He drew a deep breath. The sorrow in this place. The source of grief. Whoever it was and whatever the circumstances, it was being resurrected inside of June, forming across her face this very moment. "No. But I'm not done here. Who knows? There's still plenty to deal with." That could not have been close to the right thing to say, yet June seemed pleased.

She smirked, looking at the porch.

"Is there something I should be on the lookout for?" he asked.

"Not necessarily."

"I see."

"Do you think the person who hid that note behind the wallpaper took his or her own life in the end?"

Jameson hesitated. "There's no way to know . . ."

"I mean," she said, "if the note was hard to find, it doesn't make sense. Don't you think if this person had done it, the note wouldn't have been hidden away?"

"Logic would have it, but logic doesn't always enter into the equation."

"True."

"The other one I found was tacked to a stud in the attic where a person would have needed to go looking to find it, and in that same house in another room I came across bits of frayed rope on the top edge of an exposed ceiling beam. There was a groove worn in the wood. A man would have had to hang a long while to make a groove like that, so yes, at least *that* man seemed to have done it in the end, I suppose."

June appeared shocked for the first time.

"Oh God. I'm sorry. That was crass. I don't know why I'm telling you all of this stuff." He started to get up, but June stopped him.

"Because I asked you to," she said.

"Yes, but. I'm getting a little liberal in the tongue."

"I appreciate your honesty."

"All right. Well. I think it was . . ."

"Maybe he was just heavy," she said. "The man."

Their laughter was stifled at first, and then nearly wicked the way they let loose.

25

JUNE'S PHONE BUZZED ON THE DESK. It was Jameson. She looked at the manuscript, the phone, the manuscript, and then she picked up the phone.

"Sorry for the intrusion," he said. "I forgot to ask . . . I wanted to double-check one last time about the roofers. It's on my calendar for tomorrow. And I'll be taking the next few days off. I mean, I've made a plan to do that, so . . ."

"Oh shit," June said. "Yes. They'll be here tomorrow."

"All right. Sorry to disturb you."

June let out an audible sigh. "Not a problem." She was suddenly irritated by the whole thing. Not his phone call, but the fact that he'd be leaving and replaced by roofers, who'd make an awful racket. So many of them, tromping across the yard and over the roof, their nail guns and hammers banging away for days.

"I just needed to know. Like I said, I made plans."

"No, listen, I meant to call and come by. I'm swamped over here. Haven't even *touched* those parcels yet. Are you headed somewhere on the coast? Sticking around? Going home?"

"A little south of here for a few days. A cabin on the river."

Though June had lived abroad and traveled widely, the idea of getting away had not occurred to her in some time. She'd not left the property since she arrived from Ireland. Two months, and she'd hardly gone to the beach. She stood and looked outside. The day had gotten away from her. It was later than she realized, nearly dusk.

"I think I'm finished here for the day," Jameson said. "There's no sense in me starting the next thing until I get back."

"Would you like to go for a walk?" she asked.

"A walk?"

"Yes. I haven't been down to the shore in ages. I could do for a break myself."

"Yes," he said. "All right."

June waited for him in the Adirondack chair, watching the bright blue dragonflies float around the yard like props on strings. And then, as if on cue, a doe and her fawn peered from behind the spruce at the edge of the yard, flicking their tails, their eyes wide and watchful. Sometimes it felt as if this small holding on the hill had been written into existence, as if it were not of the real world at all but a conjuring of the imagination.

June squeezed her knees, turned toward the bungalow.

Now this man, coming across the lawn toward her, seemed conjured, too. He wore a sage-colored T-shirt and dark jeans with the hems rolled, and carried a long-sleeved flannel shirt in his hand. He appeared scrubbed clean, changed in a way she couldn't quite place. He wore flip-flops, as did June.

"You couldn't have chosen a better night," he said, and June stood and faced west, toward the water, the direction of endings.

She led the way down the long footpath to the beach. Campfires already lit the shore, and groups of shadowy figures moved in the distance. The wind lifted voices toward them — ungoverned teenagers, children singing with their parents, couples laughing, an entire world clamoring with life, and June didn't know if what she was feeling was envy, because she didn't know if, in truth, she wanted a family the way other people seemed to want one.

She and Jameson walked along the tide line barefoot, carrying their flip-flops. The sun had dipped below the horizon. Venus glowed brighter than the sliver being offered by the moon and clusters of stars.

Jameson said, "I used to come down here with my children."

June stopped.

He looked toward the water when he spoke. "They loved being barefoot in the sand."

The way he spoke the words, his throat constricted, conveyed something dire. June felt confused. "You're talking about them as if—"

"They were shot to death when they were seven years old."

She clutched his arm, paralyzed by shock. She searched his face for an answer, for a clue to what she should say or do next. Then slowly it dawned on her. Everything began to unfold at once. Who he was. What had happened to his children. Another wave of shock hit her and she stepped back to keep from stumbling.

"I'm sorry," he said. "I didn't mean to say that."

"I think we need to sit. Do you mind? Oh God." June turned for the dunes. She lowered herself in the sand. Jameson sat beside her.

"I know who you are," she said.

"I figured—"

"No. I mean, I just now realized who you are, and I'm *so* sorry for what happened. I know . . . what happened."

"I suspected you knew all along."

June stared as if seeing him for the first time. "I can't believe it."

"What?"

"You rode a motorcycle."

"I did."

"And that's what happened to your leg."

"You can tell?"

"A bit of a limp." June's eyes began to fill. "My grandfather was the man who hit you."

Jameson jerked his head up.

"Did you not know?" she asked.

"What?"

"No?"

"I didn't have a clue."

June shook her head at the ocean. "Is this a coincidence?"

Jameson's jaw tightened. "I don't know."

"Well, it's rather astounding, wouldn't you say?"

Jameson shrugged slightly and narrowed his eyes. He didn't appear as dumbstruck as she.

"My grandmother kept calling me in Ireland, leaving all these messages," she said. "She kept saying something about children. Children that weren't in the accident but who died that day. Of course I heard the whole story later. And even now, the town still talks about it..."

Jameson nodded at the waves.

"Your grandparents weren't actually hurt, right?" he asked. "We were told they were OK."

"They were fine. Just shaken. A little bruised."

"The road was wet. I was speeding."

"My grandfather shouldn't have been driving."

"What do you mean?"

"He felt responsible for the accident. And also... your children. What happened to them later that day. If he hadn't lost control of the car. His vision and reflexes were not what they used to be. I'd told him, Niall had told him."

"Niall?"

"My husband."

"You're married?"

"Was. Not anymore."

"I have a wife."

"Of course you do." June recalled her voice on the phone. *What is it you want?*

"She's coming here tomorrow."

June glanced at the sand, gave a nod. "Has she been back here since...?"

"We moved away within a year. No, she hasn't been back. This is the first I've been here myself."

"I see. A cabin. Well. That will be nice."

"I can't work with the roofers here."

"No, no, I probably can't either. They're going to be ten times louder than you've been, which is to say you haven't been an intrusion in the least, just so you know, but I'm sure the nail guns will be echoing off my house and through the trees. They'll be yelling for each other from all sides of the house." What she was saying wasn't at all what she meant.

"So I'll just take these few days," Jameson said.

June raised her head. "My grandmother left so many messages. She kept saying it was all their fault, because the story was, well, I learned later what the story was."

"I lost control before your grandfather did. How ridiculous for them to believe it was their fault."

"It was *no one's* fault."

Jameson looked at her sharply.

"I'm not overstepping my bounds here," she said.

"That's not what I was thinking."

"What were you thinking?"

"Never mind."

"I see." After a moment June added, "My grandmother brought you a pie."

Jameson looked at her, his eyes dark and serious, especially as the sun dipped deeply out of sight. "When?" he asked.

"I don't know. It was a message she'd left. I don't remember much from that time, but I remember that. She took you a pie and you told her something awful about the sand from your children's feet still on the floor."

He stiffened, lips pursed, and he turned away, clearly not wanting her to see him, though he nodded as if to say yes, I remember, yes, that was me. And then he pulled his knees up and held them to his chest. He lowered his forehead onto his arms atop his knees, and June could no longer see his face. The waves and the voices down the beach were not enough to muffle his sobs.

June placed her hand in the middle of his back and caressed him in a small circle, feeling the ripple of muscle and bone.

After a moment he raised his head and laid his cheek on his arms and looked at her, smiling sadly, and she offered the same smile in return. And then she lifted her hand from his back.

"I haven't cried like that in years," he said, clearing his throat.

"I can't begin to imagine your pain."

"Well." Jameson leaned back and dropped his knees and swiped at his eyes. "I'm not sure I believe you," he said.

June could feel the glare in her eyes. She did nothing to soften it away.

"I think you've lost somebody too," he said.

"I have. But it isn't quite the same."

"How so?" he asked. "How do you measure such a thing?"

The ocean rolled in and out, stars littered the black sky, the fires along the beach burned brighter in the dark, and June watched as a child's marshmallow caught flame on the end of his stick. His mother jumped up and blew it out.

"So you've got these days free, then," June said. "For you, and your wife."

"We have a foster child now."

June studied his face. He seemed to be waiting for her to say something more. Something he didn't want to talk about. She stood and brushed the sand from her jeans. "It's getting late," she said.

Jameson came to his feet. "What else did Van Hicks say about me?"

"What do you mean?"

"I don't think it was a coincidence that he had you call me."

"I'm not following you."

"That guy, who shot my children?"

"Yes?"

"He was Van's son."

June stepped back. Held her hand to her chest. "Why would he . . . I don't understand. Why would Van tell me to call you, of all people?"

"I'd like to think it's because I do good work. But I'm not sure. I don't trust him. I took this job because I needed it. I *had* to take it. That's just the fact."

June felt a little sick. All this time she'd been putting Jameson through something of which she had no idea. All this time she'd been a part of something that may have been underhanded.

"He said you were perfect for the house. That you would know exactly what to do, and the quality of your work was —"

"I believe you when you tell me that he said all that." He narrowed his eyes up into the sky.

"Well."

"I've spent the last three years beating myself up over that day," Jameson said. "That fucking motorcycle, excuse my language. I was riding too fast. Your grandfather had nothing to do with it, OK? If I hadn't taken off like that, my children would still be alive."

"And if it hadn't rained and Granddad had given up his license and that young man with the gun had not been lost inside a world of insanity . . . Where is a person supposed to draw the line?"

"That's easy for you to say."

June stiffened, fury in her bones. She turned for home. "You know nothing about me."

Jameson walked after her. "I'm sorry. I shouldn't have said that."

June spun around. "Easy for me to say? I've lived my whole life retracing my steps, checking off all the false moves that did me in. All the moves that did in the lives of other people around me."

Jameson started to speak, but June cut him off. "My own mother is dead because I was born," she said. "You think I give a shit about my birthday? That's the least of my problems."

Jameson took her hand. He held it tightly at her side.

June began to cry. "Oh good Christ."

"I had no business saying such a thing," Jameson said.

The breeze lifted the campfire smoke and now the singing and laughing was louder, mocking them, standing as they were, facing each other's grief.

Jameson squeezed her hand. "I am cracked and broken in more ways than I know how to fix," he said.

"I understand," she said, and then Jameson wrapped his flannel shirt over her shoulders to help stop her shivering, and he told her it was time to go home.

26

MORNING, AND JAMESON WOULD NOT work today, did not even feel like working, and that was new. He'd rolled up his bedding and placed it and his duffel in the hallway closet, and he filled the pail from June with water and wedged it in the ground beneath the birch that the warbler favored most. He would ask the roofers to leave it be.

He swept the finished rooms clear of sawdust, wiped down the walls with a damp rag. He mopped the newly laid wooden floors, then rolled out brown builder's paper from wall to wall, to protect the flawless planks, and taped the paper in place around the perimeter. The window guy would arrive in a few weeks to fix the broken sashes, and by the end of July the electrician would have finished updating the circuit panel and wiring, and Jameson would replace the walls. By the end of August he would paint the interior, and a house painter would scrape off the exterior trim and give it a fresh coat and stain the shingle siding, and the new gutters would go up. The house would stand solidly against the rain and wind to come. Jameson was saving the kitchen for last, and by the start of September he would have finished replacing the fixtures and sanding and staining the wooden countertop and cabinets, the latter to be painted a fresh white at June's request. His final act would be screwing in the green glass cabinet knobs and wiping every trace of himself away.

And then the market would do its thing.

That was how it worked.

Jameson had done this time and again, and yet he stood looking out at the backyard, the white trees, the glimpses beyond the fairway, and had a hard time picturing where to go from here. He was like a house himself, refurbished and retrofitted with metal bars, a homestead of a man whose leg leaned a little, and sometimes ached more than a little with winter rain, a man still rising from beds and chairs and floors, heading to and from places he needed to go, and was forced to go, but it had been so long since he was headed to a place he wanted to be.

Those piles in the yard needed to be dealt with. It was past time to call Van Hicks. It could be taken care of while Jameson was away, but first he'd have to make the call.

He glanced up at the mountain, turkey vultures trailing each other in slow, deliberate circles in the distance. A heron swooped toward the bay on its giant, prehistoric wings, and here in the yard, in spite of the mess, a fleet of golden-crowned kinglets darted into the pines like hummingbirds — stationary one second, zipping in a flash the next on their tiny, rapid wings. Strange feeling to not want to work. Stranger still to think about what he'd said to June.

He was raised near a clear blue lake in the center of Oregon, and now he thought how nice it would be to sit on a grassy bank along a river with a fishing pole and a beer. He was raised on the virtues of work, and it did not easily shake loose from his mind. He no longer knew how to relax the way he used to when he and Sarah Anne first got together. To lie in a bed and read a book had become as foreign to him as a language he'd never learned to speak.

He arched his back and shoulders and drew in a breath of

briny air, and he felt calmer than he'd felt in years. He dialed the old number from years ago.

When the line picked up, Jameson heard wheezing, coughing, a man trying to get a word out.

"Is that you, Hicks?" Jameson asked.

"With whom am I speaking?" Hicks could be a smartass. *Whom* was not a word he normally used, just a kind of inside joke he played with himself when he thought he was speaking to a stranger.

"Jameson Winters. I'm calling *on behalf of* Ms. June Byrne." Two could play the fake-eloquence game.

Hicks wheezed like a man who shouldn't be on a phone but on oxygen instead. When he finished he said, "So you came. You're here."

"Not for long. I'll be begging out for a few days starting today, and I would appreciate you coming by to haul off this load of scrap while the roofers have the house."

Hicks sounded as if he were swallowing something. The cough and wheeze subsided.

"Are you up for working?" Jameson asked. "Doesn't sound like it. If there's anyone else in town, I'd be glad to call him."

"I'm up. I'll do it. Go ahead and beg out."

"Good deal," Jameson said, and hung up.

His hands were shaking. He looked at the one that had held June's last night, turned it palm-up as if expecting to find something there. He opened and closed his fist several times and it calmed him.

From where he stood behind the house, he couldn't be certain if the tide had gone out or if the widened shoreline was glossy and mirroring the sky, with white gulls and black cormorants and the immense wingspan of a bald eagle, but Jameson knew without seeing that it was exactly as he pictured. His ears were as attuned now to the rhythm of the waves as the days when he'd lived on this coast, and if he were to walk down the footpath of the ridge, he would see that he was right about the tide and the sand reflecting everything above. His children would be ten years old now, taller and changed in ways he could only imagine, other ways he could not. Might their hearts have already been broken by crushes? What books would they have fallen in love with? What quarrels might they have had with each other? Would they have continued to look so much alike? He could not picture how they might have changed. The color and texture of their hair, the clothes they would have wanted to wear, Halloween costumes they might have chosen. Would there ever be a year when children came to the door that Jameson didn't wonder if one or the other of his own children might have worn that same costume? And yet he couldn't help but imagine the ways his children would have been devastated had they lived long lives, the kinds of people in this world who could have hurt them, including those who claimed to love them. What indelible sorrows were they protected from now? Of course it made no sense. The worst thing that could have happened to them had happened.

He recalled their translucent cheeks and lips in the morgue, their matching cold blue hands, and he gripped the nearest birch and dropped his head and prepared to be sick. When nothing came he understood that he'd driven back his rage and despair like so many times before, and he would drive it all back again the next and the next. He understood, too, that he had done this, stuffed it all away from the start, for the sake of Sarah Anne. The only place where he lost control was in his dreams.

He checked his watch. Sarah Anne wouldn't arrive for a couple more hours. The roofers were already late. There was no sign of movement next door, and he wondered if June had even gotten out of bed, or what she might dream if she dreamed at all, or if she'd lain awake in the night, replaying their conversation the way he had. What he wanted was to knock on her door and ask if she wouldn't mind having something cold to drink, a lemonade, out front in the Adirondack chairs, the way the movers had done.

They wouldn't have to talk, either, just like the men, but sit side by side, looking west into the blue.

Thirty minutes later, Jameson was still shaken from the sound of Hicks's voice. He yanked hard on the drawer in the work shed where he planned to stow his cords; the rabbet joints came loose, separated, and a false drawer collapsed into his hand. Two small notebooks tumbled free. "Ah, hell," he said, setting the pieces of busted drawer on the workbench. This was a complication he guessed June did not need. It was none of his business. He slipped the notebooks into the back pocket of his jeans and left the shed.

After that, he set off on foot down the road, conscious of his leg, the way his foot turned in and his hip gave a little when he came down on that side. She had noticed.

The bakery was the first thing a person came to from this direction, and Jameson had not gone much past it since he arrived. He wasn't sure how many people in town knew he was here, but Helen had a way of chatting, so he guessed everyone knew, including people who'd never heard of him. *And him up there working on their house. Life sure is strange.*

Jameson walked down the main street, past the toy shop with the whirling kites on the roof, the taffy shop, the Little Grocer, all the way to the end, where he entered the bookstore beneath an archway of twisted wisteria. He asked the curly-haired clerk, who gave him a second look, if she might have what he was looking for, and she said of course she did, right over there in the local-author section, and she smiled like she knew more than she was willing to say.

27

IT WAS LATE MORNING, and aside from the crash of waves it was dead quiet, and June could not think, could not sit, could not seem to breathe as deeply as a body needed to keep from passing out. She'd hardly slept, her neck in a knot, her shoulders, too, and she wondered if Jameson had lain awake as she had. Every time she'd drifted off, she dreamed of being barefoot on craggy rocks, and she woke clutching her feet, searching for open wounds.

She'd been watching him sweep the front porch, carry handfuls of his things to his truck, coil up electrical cords and store them in the shed. He made a brief phone call from the backyard, but his voice was low and curt and she couldn't make out what he said, but he didn't seem happy, whatever it was.

She went through the motions of showering and getting dressed, to temper the anxious hum beneath her skin. It did nothing to calm her. She wandered into the living room dressed like a person who had someplace to be. She fought that off by going stiff in the middle of the rug, as if in protest against the drink she imagined having, the dark pub booth she imagined settling into. She was a stock-still statue erected as a symbol of silent battle, while at once counting all the reasons she could step forward and have just one, just today, to move her beyond the feelings taking over, feelings that had nothing to do with needing a drink.

She gathered two of Grandmam's teacups and matching saucers, the sugar bowl and creamer, set them on a tray, and took them out back, where she arranged the settings across from each other on the patio table. *One for Mum, one for me,* as she used to say.

How long had it been since she had drawn on her number one comfort? She had forgotten so many things while drinking. Faces, names, entire days and weeks unrecognizably smeared.

She returned to the kitchen for her Polaroid camera. The silver trim on the cups and saucers would glow on the instant film. The chemicals and filtered light would give the illusion of an image that was decades old.

And then, the strangest thing. She startled in the patio doorway.

Raccoons, a mother and three kits, were climbing onto the table, grabbing hold of the tea set. They leapt around like a band of mischievous, costumed children. The smallest snatched a teacup with his tiny paws and looked at June and then the cup he was holding, as if he were waiting to be served.

June rushed forward and the raccoons dropped the cups and saucers onto the table. When they scampered away they sent the tea things flying, crashing to the ground.

She roared with a fury she didn't know she possessed. She whipped what remained of a saucer in their direction, but they were already free of her, the smallest one trailing, looking back at June, as if he did not understand her or anything that was happening here, and then he, like the others, disappeared in the thicket of trees.

The dishes could not be replaced. June would be plucking shards from the grass for weeks. She would need to wear shoes out here.

Then laughter coming from her grandparents' yard. For a fractured second she didn't understand how that could be, how anyone could be over there, and the sound haunted her, frightened and confused her.

Then she turned to see Jameson, braced forward with his hands on his knees, laughing.

"You saw that?" she called.

Jameson straightened up and nodded.

"Bloodin' hell," June said.

Jameson came toward her, smiling. "Bold little bastards."

June shook her head. She lifted her hair off her neck and wiped the sweat away, her hand there suddenly recalling the way his shirt collar had wrapped around her last night.

Jameson was looking in the direction the raccoons had gone. "Weird," he said.

"Curiouser and curiouser," she said.

Broken cups and saucers lay across the table and on the ground.

"I didn't mean to intrude. Looks like you were expecting company."

June felt the heat in her face. A child planning a tea party with an imaginary mum. "Excuse me," she said. "I'll just be needing the broom."

She grabbed her flip-flops and the broom and dustpan, and she twisted her hair atop her head for the heat. When she returned, Jameson was right where she'd left him, watching her now as she swept the slivers from the patio. "I was going to get some shots with my camera. I wasn't expecting company. Certainly not raccoons."

"How long have you had that camera?"

"My father gave it to me when I was seven."

Jameson looked at her closely.

"Would you like some lemonade?" she asked, and stood upright with the dustpan full of shards in one hand, the broom like a staff in the other.

Jameson shrugged. "Thank you. The roofers are late." He glanced behind him at the bungalow. "I want to have a word with them before I head out."

"What time do you leave?"

"She should — Sarah Anne — should be here anytime."

"Well, then. I'll bring extra glasses for her and the boy — what's his name?"

"Ernest."

"Ernest." June smiled to one side, gave a soft nod.

"Can I help you with anything?" Jameson asked as June stepped toward the house. Her mind flashed on all they had said to each other, their hands clutching, and after lightly touching as they walked together to her front door, where Jameson stepped back as if embarrassed by his behavior, and abruptly said good night. He was smiling now, different, as if he'd awakened in a fine mood. His wife was on her way. Maybe that was it. He hadn't seen her in weeks.

"No need," June said. "I'll just be a moment."

Inside, she gathered what she needed from the kitchen and returned with glasses full of ice and a pitcher of lemonade on a tray, and they sat facing each other at the table.

"I made that drive once," June said. "That she's — Sarah Anne — is making today. To the high desert. With my father. Though technically I *returned* with my grandfather. A long tale for another time."

Jameson glanced at an imaginary watch on his wrist. "I've got time."

June poured them each a drink and relaxed back in her chair. "My father wasn't well," she said, with such seriousness that it surprised her. "We took a road trip, as I mentioned. The first and last time we ever went anywhere. He was talking to me about my mother, which he rarely ever did. And he closed his eyes while driving. He did that. Closed his eyes often when he spoke, as if it were a terrible struggle. I don't know, I was a child, but when the truck veered off, I have to say I wasn't terrified at all."

"Were you hurt?"

"My front teeth were knocked out."

Jameson cupped his mouth.

"To be fair, they were already loose. Baby teeth."

Jameson smiled faintly, and June wondered what he was thinking behind the faraway look on his face. She guessed his own children. "What were you, if you weren't scared?" he asked.

June swallowed the tart lemonade. "I was a bit thrilled, to be honest. My first thought was that I was going to see my mother."

"Oh."

"Now look who's being crude."

Jameson shook his head.

A dreamy kind of quiet exhaustion settled in. They glanced toward the golf course, then the chickadees zipping for the feeder, the juncos hopping on the ground beneath it where June had sprinkled seeds just for them. Then June looked directly at Jameson and he at her. They were free to say what they liked to each other, she thought. He would soon be gone, and they would never see each other again, so what did it matter?

Jameson said, "That little kit up on the table with the cup. It was like he'd come for tea."

June smiled.

Then he spoke of his children, haltingly, spoke of their love for each other and how it seemed to be not of this world. The words caught in his throat, but he said them anyway, said some part of him believed that they must be better off, having left a world where such a thing, the thing that happened to them, could be allowed to happen.

What she saw in his face, and in his shoulders and back, was relief.

"I was sent away to an awful place when I was their age," June said.

She told him about the young girl who had needed her, had needed someone, anyone, to help her, while June did nothing, never even spoke of what had gone on in that place until she was grown.

Jameson started to speak, and June cut him off.

"Please, if you don't mind, I'd rather not hear how I was just a child and didn't know any better. I've heard it all before."

"I was going to say that every saint has a past and every sinner has a future."

"Oh. Oscar Wilde."

"Yes," he said. "And that your guilt must feel overwhelming, even now."

June's eyes welled up. "Yes," she said. "It does."

"I don't think I can be a father to that boy," Jameson said. "Sarah Anne needs him as much as she's needed anything in her life, and the cruelest thing I could ever do is deny her the child, and the next cruelest thing is to go along with the adoption when it isn't what I want."

June nodded. "I understand how a person can get into a predicament like that."

"How so?"

"When I was young, Granddad used to chop and stack the fire logs near the side door under the eave over there. By the time I was seven I was in charge of keeping the house warm, and my father sometimes surprised me by coming out of his bedroom to stand in front of the fireplace with the camp blanket wrapped around his shoulders like a shawl. He'd thank me even though he didn't look at me. His eyes were closed as if it were the only way to absorb the heat, and I would stare at his lids and lashes, his cheeks prickled in whiskers, his reddish hair made lighter by the orange glow. My love for him caused a terrible ache." June paused, caught her breath, feeling the very ache. "The space between me and my father was never going to be the center that held up the world. He didn't want to be left with me. He didn't want me from the start."

"My God, June. What an awful burden to bear."

"I'm not saying it would be the same for you or Ernest. I'm not saying—"

"I understand. I do. It's perfectly all right. The thing is, no one else wants that boy either. But Sarah Anne does. Very much."

"Of course," June said, and wished she could take back what she'd told him.

Surely they were going to be interrupted any second. Surely this was all about to come to an end. Was this why June said what she said next?

She didn't know. It seemed to come out of nowhere when she declared, "I never loved Niall the way he loved me, not really, though the truth of it has never come to me before now, never fully formed, not like this, not until this moment of recalling how things had been for my father."

She had really said it out loud.

Jameson stared, his mouth slightly open.

"Mother of God," June said. "Every drunk knows it's better to purge when you're feeling sick than to try and hold it in."

Jameson was laughing, his head thrown back, when the first cars arrived.

28

How else to say it except the calm before the storm?

One minute Jameson was sitting with June having lemonade and sharing a string of confessions, and the next the world was coming to a halt.

The roofers pulled up in two separate sedans, both with loose mufflers. Behind them came a rusty flatbed truck full of shingles. The lumberyard truck was fourth in line, with the plywood, as if they'd all coordinated their arrival before heading up the hill.

Jameson stood as a third truck pulled out around the rest and went straight into the driveway to park behind Jameson's truck. Jameson shielded his eyes. He knew that truck. He knew the man getting out.

Van Hicks slammed the door and coughed.

"Quite a parade," June said.

Jameson pursed his lips. "I was hoping to be gone before he arrived."

Hicks stopped with hands on hips, looking around as if surveying the place. He walked up the driveway toward the bungalow's front porch, then he looked across and halted his step. It was clear he was looking at Jameson.

"I'm going to guess," June said. "Van Hicks?"

"The one and only."

Jameson excused himself and walked toward him just as Hicks was headed in his direction. Jameson held up his hand as a gesture for him not to take another step.

Hicks stopped.

When Jameson stood within a few feet of him, Hicks lifted his right hand forward, so slightly it could have been missed. Jameson stuck both hands in the front pockets of his jeans. No way in hell were they going to shake. "You enjoying this, Hicks?" he said. "Getting me back out here like this?"

"I know you didn't want to see me," Hicks said, "but I figured you to be gone from here already."

Jameson gripped his hips. Said nothing. Felt the small weight of the notebooks still in his back pocket.

"I was trying to help everybody out," Hicks said. "That's all."

"Everybody."

"Well, yes. You, Sarah Anne, this woman here." Jameson turned to see June walking toward them. "She's got no one at all, as I understand. I knew her grandparents. They were very fine folks."

Jameson's neck and face grew hot. "Why are you making our lives your business?" It sounded stupid, blustery, even to him. He couldn't help himself. The man's son had looked an awful lot like him. And that was just the start.

"She called me and I gave her your name. Nothing underhanded about it. You're hunting down the wrong path here, Winters."

June suddenly appeared. "What's going on?"

"I was asked to do a job," Hicks said.

Jameson took a step back, drew a large breath, and held the corner of his bottom lip between his teeth. *So help me God*, he thought.

June looked at Jameson as if she didn't recognize him. "Is there a problem?"

Jameson looked away, burning with rage.

"I had nothing to do with nothing," Hicks said.

"Double negative," June said, and Jameson wiped the smile from his face.

Then the sound of yet another car, the hum of an engine he recognized.

Sarah Anne was behind the wheel, craning her neck, searching for him through the windshield, ducking her head to see between the vehicles and the roofers walking up the drive with handfuls of tools.

Then a moment of recognition as their eyes met, a softening of their bodies as if a long-held discomfort could now be let go.

His wife got out of the car and opened the rear door, and as she lifted Ernest to her shoulder, Jameson turned to June.

"There you are, then," June said to him. "A good start is half the work, as Granddad used to say."

Before he could reply, June turned briskly for the backyard of the bungalow, motioning for Hicks. "Have a wonderful few days," June said, though she kept her back to Jameson, even as he thanked her and said he would see her soon.

29

SARAH ANNE WAS PETITE, BLOND, and lovely in ways June was not. She embodied a radiating warmth. She was exactly who June expected to see.

June turned away, asked Hicks if he would like some lemonade. But Hicks began coughing and shook his head no. "What do I need to haul out of here?" he asked, and June led him to the backyard. He told her he'd have get the drop box out here, and before he returned would she mind asking Jameson not to leave his truck in the drive so Hicks could pull in as close to the backyard as possible? June nodded. She didn't know what to think of this man aside from the awful crime his son had committed. Everything about him seemed pitiful.

"I hear it's supposed to rain," he said.

June looked up at the bright blue in every direction. "Says who?" she asked.

"My joints."

"I see."

"The radio, too. That hurricane down in Mexico is running off its edges up this way."

"What hurricane? In June?"

"It happens. We'll see in the next ten hours or so. Might be quite a wind. I'd like to get all of this cleared out of here today."

When June pushed back through the kissing gate, Sarah Anne was still there, holding Ernest to her shoulder next to her car in the driveway. His small arms were wrapped around her neck, his head on her shoulder as if he were still waking up. "Look who's here," she cooed to the boy. "Look who we've come to see."

Jameson reached for him, and the boy reached for Jameson, and they shared a hug, which lit up Sarah Anne's face. And then she saw June, and for a brief moment appeared startled. But then her smile returned and she walked toward June.

"It's nice to meet you," Sarah Anne said as they exchanged names and shook hands. Her look was tentative now, nervous, it seemed, a look June guessed she had brought about. "I've heard wonderful things about your place. All true from the looks of it. What a beautiful piece of property."

June glanced away in time to see the boy with his hand on Jameson's cheek, and Jameson smiling ear to ear.

Van Hicks reappeared from the backyard, and Sarah Anne looked stricken. She excused herself and went straight to Jameson, and they whispered heatedly while the boy appeared agitated, leaning back and away.

Jameson handed Sarah Anne the child, and she placed him in his seat while Jameson moved his truck. June stood watching the entire thing as the roofers stepped out around her.

She was about to go inside when Jameson opened the passenger-side door of the car. He turned and waved with a single rise and fall of his hand.

June lifted her palm halfway, like Grandmam, no higher than her ribs, and jiggled it side to side. Jameson acknowledged her with a sheepish sort of nod, and she could not help the hurt feelings in her chest, the sting of being dismissed, as if whatever was happening now canceled out June.

He got in the car and closed the door and Sarah Anne leaned over and kissed him so fast that June had no time to look away.

She was still staring when Jameson fastened his seat belt and shot her a glance she didn't know how to read.

June turned her back and then heard the car stop and a door open. She spun around to see Sarah Anne out of the car and re-trieving something from the trunk. She shut the trunk and then, instead of getting behind the wheel, she walked toward June in a hurry with something in her hands.

"It's a housewarming gift. I made it myself. It's been a while, but I like to offer up a vase for the new home, you know, for the show-ings after Jameson's work is done. This one would look beautiful with white lilies." She handed the vase to June.

Jameson sat sternly in his seat, watching.

"What a lovely gift," June said. "How incredibly thoughtful. Thank you. Lilies will indeed be perfect."

Sarah Anne said it was all her pleasure. She darted back to the car, which she turned around, and drove her family to the cabin on the river.

30

IT TURNED OUT TO BE as rustic as Jameson had hoped. No television, no cell service, no contact at all with the outside world, just a one-room cabin with wool blankets named for the national parks. Fishing poles leaned in the corner, tin cups lined the open wooden shelves. Out back a fire pit for roasting marshmallows, and beyond it, the river, though it was more a creek bed this time of year. It was enough for tossing rocks into with Ernest.

Sarah Anne had gotten a haircut. She had more color in her cheeks than he remembered. When Jameson brought their things in and set them down, she smiled at him in the cool shadows of the room.

"You look different," she said.

"So do you."

Ernest stood at the back screen door, looking out into the forest.

"The vase you gave June was beautiful. You're back at it. You dug the wheel out? I had no idea."

Sarah Anne came toward him, wrapped her arms around his shoulders. "I'm feeling like myself again for the first time in years."

Jameson pulled her in. He held her close and looked past her shoulder to the open front door, to the blue sky cutting through the endless stalks of trees.

"I am, too," he said, and it wasn't lost on him that they'd come to this place within themselves, while the other was not around.

"Big trees," Ernest said, and Jameson turned to see him pointing through the back screen door, smiling, though his smile appeared to be only for Sarah Anne. He seemed pacified, unknotted in the way that Sarah Anne seemed to be. They had both done well in his absence.

"He's speaking so plainly now," Jameson said. "It's only been a few weeks and so much has changed." He let go of Sarah Anne and crouched next to Ernest. A deepening ache struck his leg. "Let's go out there and see what we can see," he said.

He took the boy's hand, and Ernest turned to reach for Sarah Anne with the other. Their attachment had grown even deeper while Jameson was away. They stepped out in a line holding hands, with Ernest at the center, and looked up and around at the giant, ancient trees. Jameson drew in a deep, aromatic breath and felt the magnitude of the world, its vast forests and oceans and ranges of treacherous mountains and all that lived out there, and he imagined losing the boy in these woods, like a boy in a fairy tale with hard lessons to learn. For the second time in as many days, tears filled Jameson's eyes.

If the world worked the way it should, Ernest would keep on growing, well past the age of seven and into old age. He'd be around long after Jameson and Sarah Anne were gone, and the thought should have brought some measure of satisfaction, but Jameson found it best to not think such things, and said, "Let's take a walk in these big piney woods."

They followed a rough path and within minutes Ernest wanted to be carried, and he allowed Jameson to be the one to hold him, yet he remained a little shy, listening as Jameson pointed out the trees and fox trails and rabbit dens, and the sound of the river moving over rocks seemed to put them both at ease.

In the evening they warmed a can of refried beans and cheese and tortillas, and tossed together burritos, and everyone was acting a little shy. "He's grown," Jameson said, counting the days he'd been away. A month? It seemed longer. "You've grown, Ernest. You look like a big kid now."

Ernest raised both hands in the air and smiled, chewing his food. Sarah Anne smiled deeply at the boy, and then a little less so at Jameson.

An hour later, Ernest had fallen asleep in Sarah Anne's arms, and when she started to move him to the fold-out cot, Jameson stood to help. She shook her head to say he wasn't needed, and she laid the boy down and shushed him when he stirred. She whisper-sang a song Jameson had never heard, a new lullaby about snow-covered mountains and a baby swaddled in wool, and Ernest's eyes remained closed even as he gave her hand a single pat. His foot did not kick the wall. His fist did not slug the pillow. He was as still as a child who didn't know how cruel the world could be, a child drifting off with innocence.

The sun settled and the cabin shifted quickly into darkness amid the surrounding trees. It would still be light on the beach, and on the ridge where the bungalow and carriage house stood.

Jameson took Sarah Anne's hand, and he thought about the way he had taken June's the night before.

"What was Van doing there?" Sarah Anne whispered.

Jameson slid his hand away.

"What did he say to you?" she asked.

"He said he was trying to help everyone out."

"Everyone? Who's everyone?"

"You, me. June."

"What's he talking about?"

"I don't know exactly."

"It made me sick to see him. Especially here, on the coast."

It wasn't like Sarah Anne to refer to that other life. She glanced at the sleeping boy, slid a string of hair from his forehead, and sighed.

"How are you?" Jameson asked. "I mean, how are you really?"

Her face was half hidden in shadow, but he could make out the small curve of her smile. "I'm happy for the first time in a long time."

Jameson kissed the top of her head.

"I'm exhausted, too," she said, and what he heard was that she hoped he didn't want more from her tonight. The furtive glance, the lift of her hair from her neck, and quick drop of her hands. Signals he had learned over the years. "I wouldn't mind getting to sleep, if that's OK with you."

"Of course. It's been a long day. You go ahead. I might read a little and then I'll join you."

He leaned back in the dark, listening to the familiar sounds of his wife getting ready for bed on the other side of the bathroom door, the sigh before brushing her teeth, the tap-tap of the brush on the side of the sink, and the rustling of covers when she returned. Another deep breath as if releasing the day's troubles to make space inside herself for sleep.

They would not make love tonight, and they would not make love at all in the quiet cabin. There was one purpose here, a singular goal, and that was to take care not to wake the boy. To take care of the boy no matter what. The last time Jameson and Sarah Anne made love, they had reached for one another with a strange, apologetic greed, their pleasure overrun with guilt. And the time before that? Jameson had no memory of it.

He sat in the dim light, allowing his mind to follow through to the end of a road where a flurry of questions remained. Was there a place in this world where he and Sarah Anne could step across a border into some neutral land they could make their own? Did a place exist where they could free-fall back into the people they more closely resembled when the children were alive? If the answer was no, what then? Did it matter? Could they live in separate countries, side by side like good neighbors, like allies for a single cause? Could they do that for the rest of their lives?

The cabin was silent when Jameson opened June's novel. He

used a pocket flashlight to see the page, glancing first at June's photograph on the back flap. It must have been taken years ago: her smile appeared easy, relaxed, the author captured in a moment of unguarded happiness. Alongside the photo, the credit said *Niall Sullivan*. It was his face she would have been seeing. Was it true what she'd told him today about never really loving him the way he had loved her? Or was she, in the way of so many people, rewriting her own history?

Her novel was titled *London Orchard,* about an English botanist who survives World War II only to return home to find his beloved cottage has been destroyed by German bombs, his wife and child gone to live in America after thinking him dead, but his cherished orchard has thrived in his absence. As far as Jameson could tell, it was a story of missed chances and wrong turns. It was a story about grief.

Jameson read long into the night, falling asleep in the chair with the book in his hands. When he woke several hours later, he was confused by the shade of light in the room, by the wooden arms of the chair in which he sat. For a moment he did not know where he was. The sentences June had written still clung to the back of his throat, and in a dreamlike state it felt as if he were speaking them out loud, and then he understood that he was. Sarah Anne was propped on her elbow. "You're talking in your sleep," she said. "You nearly woke Ernest."

"What did I say?" he asked.

"Something about plums and hollyhocks and an ocean liner." She laughed a little in the dark.

Jameson apologized and crawled into bed next to her. He lay feeling the heat of her, the heavy weight of her returning to sleep while he stared at the strips of cedar ceiling he could barely see. Moments later came the first drops of rain.

31

JUNE CARRIED A UTILITY KNIFE upstairs to her father's room. Her limbs were drained of all energy, though it was only midafternoon and she had barely done a thing. By contrast, the air seemed charged, as if the storm that Hicks had mentioned was indeed on the way. But what June felt was more than tired. She had lived a fairly solitary life since childhood, and grew up to spend her working life alone, yet a sense of loneliness seemed attached to everything now. She felt small, vulnerable, as if the world had expanded without warning, everything overexposed and raw, distorted, like looking through a crooked aperture that was meant to remain closed.

The clamor next door had shifted into a harsh crash of wood and metal as loose slabs of what had once been the bungalow were being pulled from the heaps out back and thrown into the drop box, and June could not help feeling that she herself was being dismantled, torn apart in pieces, and stripped to the core.

She kneeled in her father's room and sliced the seal of tape on the box before her, reached in, and out came blankets and throws and yellow vintage pillows. The air trapped inside was from Ireland, its scent that of her other home, her other life. It smelled of Niall in the kitchen chopping carrots, the concrete floors, and the honeysuckle beneath the bedroom window. June sat back on her heels, squeezing the knife in her hand, feeling the ghosts of her past rising up and closing her in.

The second box was no different. Her waxed field jacket and knit caps and rubber boots and thick sweaters, every object attached to a memory, to a single hour or an entire season, artifacts of a life that had become nothing more than a place in history.

Then the familiar scent of books wafted through the air and landed her back in the present. Box after box was stuffed with her collection: stacks of poetry, novels, and short stories. Books on history, on how the brain works, biographies of painters and writers, tall crooked columns piling up around her like ancient ruins, and she thought of the piles next door that Jameson had made and set aside for someone else to haul away. Van Hicks, a man whose presence seemed to alter the way Jameson looked at the world. And how could it not? What had she seen in his face when she came upon the two of them in the yard? Fear? Disdain? What had they said to one another?

She pulled letters from a wooden keepsake box, warm sentiments from readers, and friends from whom she no longer heard. Eleanor Black used to be in touch, her letters purposely charming, meant to evoke a mood, an idea of who Eleanor was supposed to be. She'd married a Brit and lived in London. One of her letters had said something about June stealing the facts of Eleanor's life to use in her own work. *Have at it,* Eleanor had written, not trying to disguise her arrogance. June had done no such thing, and Eleanor should have known as much, being a writer herself. We find what we want to find in others' stories, see ourselves where we want to be seen, strolling through bright rooms of flattery, steering clear of the dark.

Eleanor was having a great run of success, but June hadn't spoken to her since the divorce. Their friends had mostly been Niall's, and the rest, she understood, had tired of her drinking. She'd been drinking when she packed these boxes and did not recall now what her reasoning had been. Two forks from the kitchen drawer. A clay bowl she never much cared for. To look at them in her hand was to look at the drunk who'd tossed all of this in a box. She was sentimental and sloppy. She was pathetic.

The vision of Jameson's hands returned, and June allowed this much, allowed herself to wonder if he was thinking about her in that cabin with his wife, wondering if she had made any sort of impression on him at all.

And here in a box was the violet sundress she'd worn the night she met Niall. She held it against her chest, expecting to feel some kind of loss, but what she felt was nothing at all. She *liked* the dress, even now; it was as simple as that. She would make a point of wearing it again.

The violent crack of shingles and plywood being torn away had begun in earnest, and in between the materials being ripped apart, the men yelled to one another while others whistled and sang. June stretched her neck side to side. It was a mistake for her to have stayed home. How perfect a cabin on the river would be.

And now her pillow, her mug, the Ulysses butterfly in the glass box frame she'd forgotten all about, its broad, Prussian-blue wings nearly painful to stare into, so electric and charged, as if chemically concocted in a man-made lab. It had been a birthday gift from Niall, the first he'd ever given her. It would look nice in the living room near her mother's drawings.

After June put away as many books as she could fit on the living room shelves, she removed the tape from the boxes and stomped all over them, jumping up and down with a great show of grunting that grew harder and louder as frustration built in her bones. What were they doing in their cabin on the river? How desperately had they wanted to get their hands on each other? She had seen the way Jameson smiled at the boy. How easily his heart could be won.

June tossed the flattened cardboard onto the front porch,

where the mess spilled out onto the lawn. She would ask that charmer Van Hicks to haul it away.

By dusk the roofers had gone, the ridge was empty of everyone except June, and the whispers began, telling her she would sleep much better tonight if she had a drink, if she had two, in fact, because everyone knew that a little vodka would loosen the shoulders and hands, and June's hands often clenched in her sleep. *You're a fabulist,* she said to her brain. *Full of wild notions. And lies.*

Clouds were beginning to roll in. The barometric pressure had dropped so quickly that June could feel it in her inner ear. It was going to storm, and summer rain would bring the rich aroma of lavender and grass and jasmine. It would fill the air with "Forest Pete."

She imagined the shelves of liquor down in Wheeler, all those beautiful glass bottles, such lovely works of art, every one filled with a promise, a story, gifts to be opened and shared in celebration of love and life, holidays filled with peace and joy. How pretty they were, how delightfully they kept company with each other in those colorful rows. The darker stories they housed, like genies, had not been let loose, and at first glance were nowhere to be seen. Where were the blackouts and bruises? Where was the infidelity and depression? Show me divorce and broken bones and lost careers, June thought. Show me the troubled children at the bottom of every bottle.

June didn't have to drive all the way to Wheeler. She could easily walk down the hill to the Little Grocer and buy wine. They carried a decent selection of deep reds with eloquent shapes, and they came with an actual cork. How she missed the sound of a cork, missed the waft of that old-world aroma, and the taste, that lingering sizzle on her tongue, heat filling her hands and cheeks and ears.

She was going to stay put in the carriage house. She was going to keep company with a bottle of red vitamin water, and the

campfires seen from afar like stars. She was going to watch for
the flash of green with the setting sun.

Then she recalled the evening her father put Nina Simone on
the record player. They had danced together at dusk, fingers en-
twined — "like this," he showed her, and their arms went up in an
arc over June's head as she spun. June remembered it that way.
She wanted to remember it that way. It was the way it came to
her, though she was old enough now to understand how memories could be unreliable. She knew the difference between truth
and lies, of course she did, the difference between fantasy and
fiction. She had known Jameson for several weeks, but already
she had forsworn herself, already abused what little trust in her
he might have had by not telling him the truth. We find what we
want to find in others' stories, just as we find what we want to
find in our own.

32

JAMESON SHOULD HAVE TOLD JUNE the truth: he may have found out more about her family than she knew herself. He should have given her the notebooks before he left, even as he could not yet bring himself to read them, and did not know how harmful or helpful they might turn out to be. It was none of his business. It was not his decision to make. This was what he was thinking, what he seemed to be dreaming, and then . . .

What he heard was a gunshot.

He leaped from the bed, not knowing where he was or who was moving in the dark. He did not recognize the voices in the room, the screams, he could not see his own hand in front of his face, could not understand where the cries were coming from, but he was certain that at least one had come from a child.

The other was a woman, shouting, begging for something to stop.

Jameson stumbled, caught his foot on something soft as he groped for balance, and finally grabbed hold of what felt like a table leg. Then a crash, and the child shrieking even louder.

He crawled toward a fissure of light shining beneath a door, snatched up a fishing rod next to it, and stood grasping the rod with both hands like a sword. He sliced the air, hitting someone or something, and the woman was now screaming his name.

A flashlight swirled into his eyes. Fragments of the room came into view — blankets, and tin cups on the shelves. Jameson dropped the fishing rod. He was in the cabin.

Another shot went off with a flash, and Jameson realized that it was not a gun he'd heard, but the crack of lightning.

Then the back door swung open and there was the shape of Sarah Anne holding the boy on the threshold, both looking terrified as they rushed into the downpour toward the river.

33

FIRST THE ROLL OF THUNDER, then rain like buckshot hitting the roof.

June vaulted out of bed toward the window. The roofers must have known it might rain. A blue tarp was fastened onto the exposed roof, but the corners flapped wildly in the wind.

She thought to call Jameson. To say what? She didn't know. The bungalow seemed to belong to him. He had been its truest, most loving caretaker since her grandparents died.

June pulled her robe over her peach pajamas, hurried downstairs to the living room, and turned on the TV. It was 3:42 a.m. A weather alert ran along the bottom of the screen. Forty-mile-an-hour winds, gusts up to sixty-five, with possible flash floods. June had lived through storms her entire life, and this one was mild by comparison. The battering of wind and rain, the groans of trees, an enormous crack that might follow when one snapped in half. She was used to landslides and sinkholes and flooding that could shut down Highway 101 within minutes. So why did she feel such crippling fear as she sat alone in her living room with a half-assed storm picking up all around her? Why did she feel as if she were hiding beneath that blanket in the Infirmary of Innocents again? Hiding even when she knew it would offer her no more safety than standing up and taking Claire's place might have done.

A thundering boom, the house went dark, and June pulled her knees to her chest and clutched her robe. She thought of the glass of chocolate milk on the table that day, the swirl of cocoa and fresh, toothy-yellow milk, that offering, that swallow of tangy and bitter and sweet, that moment of waiting to be told her father was gone forever. *Too-ra-loo-ra-loo-ral.* Her skin felt bristly, as if infested with mites, and she scratched her arms and legs, backed up on the sofa, turned sideways, and dug her heels into the cushions. And now she held her fists to her eyes and screamed to drown out the sounds inside her head, to drive away the images that followed.

34

JAMESON SLIPPED IN MUD, GRIPPED the trees and shrubs, and screamed Sarah Anne's name. He couldn't see where she'd gone, but he pleaded with her to come inside, unable to see or hear anything through the downpour and rumble of thunder. He fell near the car, got up, smeared clear the driver's-side window, and looked in, but Sarah was not behind the wheel. Ernest was not in his seat. The car was locked and empty.

She had gone into the woods with Ernest in the midst of a storm, had thought this safer than being in the cabin with him.

At the front door, he cursed and called her name. He was still wearing his flannel shirt, and it stuck to his ribs in the rain the way his shirt had stuck to him on his first date with Sarah Anne, when she'd said how glad she was that he had called, her words so carefree and warm, as trusted and true as any there would ever be between them.

He began to cry, swallowed it back with the bitterness and anger rising to his throat. He punched the front door with the side of his fist and regretted it immediately.

PART FOUR

35

IT WAS NEARLY NOON on the Oregon coast, the air damp and fifteen degrees cooler than the days leading up to this one, when June returned from Wheeler with two bottles of Irish whiskey. While out she'd seen a blue heron near the bay, brown rabbits flittering across the meadow, and a red-tailed hawk being chased by crows. Like watching someone else's life on a screen. She couldn't quite penetrate it, couldn't quite accept that it was real.

She arrived home and did not succumb to second-guessing or guilt. A flock of gulls squalled above the yard as she filled her favorite mug and stepped out onto the porch, set the bottle down, and screwed back the lid. The breeze was gentle, clear of tidal rot, the storm having washed everything out to sea. The sun was shining again, and June drank without ceremony. Like turning on the lights in the dead of night. Like opening windows after a season of cold rain. It was like that down the back of her throat, so sudden and clear.

She refilled her mug three times in the hour, listening to the blast of classic rock from the radio on the roof next door. Sometimes the men sang along, sometimes they switched stations. No one liked Steely Dan. One of them didn't like the Eagles and was told he could leave, to which he laughed and said they better be careful what they wished for.

Two hours passed in this way, mug after mug, the pummel of nail guns, the music, the laughter, those hard-working men accomplishing all they'd set out to do, the gulls busy above the house and shore in search of their next meal. June marveled at how smooth a day could be, how the roofers were likely to finish in two days as they'd promised, not four as Jameson had predicted, leaving two days of silence before he returned.

June drank.

She gazed into her beautiful mug from Ireland, held in both of her hands. She looked over at the grass, soaked like in Ireland, its parched color already turning a shade of green overnight. She was wearing her father's old cardigan over a T-shirt and jeans. When the roofers arrived at seven a.m. she'd been awake and dressed for hours, pacing, chewing her cuticles until they bled, thinking about Jameson.

The storm had scattered the empty cardboard boxes across the yard, catching several between the railings on the porch. June leaned over and tried pulling one loose, but it was heavy as a wet blanket and she lost her balance, slipping sideways down the steps. She landed in the grass below, looked down and saw the front of her T-shirt, soaked in whiskey. Her mug had rolled into the grass.

"You OK?" someone yelled.

June looked up. A man stood on the roof with what appeared to be a nail gun. She guessed he was the one who'd spoken.

She waved an arm and nodded. She was fine. She said she was fine.

A quick flash of memory that she'd started the washing machine at some point, though she could no longer remember what she'd put in there. Eyes closed, she listened now to the churning through the open front door. She got to her knees and felt the seat of her jeans, cold and damp from the grass.

"You sure?" the man called out.

June nodded, leaned forward, braced her hands in the grass, and rose onto all fours.

The men next door were laughing. At her? She didn't care. She put her weight on her left foot, and a pain, sharp and hot, struck her ankle. She fell back onto her rear and lifted her foot. More laughter from next door. Her ankle appeared to be swelling.

The euphorbia next to her head was in bloom, its tiny red dials of color reminding her of the ornamental yews. She closed her eyes and leaned her cheek against the bulbous shoots. She could hear bees floating near her throat and eyes and hands, and somewhere across the yard a squirrel was chirping, and she realized after a time that the men were singing again with the radio and blasting the roof with nails.

Then a car pulled into the bungalow's driveway. June tried once more to stand, mindful of her foot, bracing herself on the side of the steps. She glanced up to see Jameson getting out of the car; and it confused her. The driver's side door hung open as he went around for something in the trunk.

They had left only yesterday. Was that right?

"What on earth?" she said, feeling the full measure of her drunkenness, as if suddenly seeing it through Jameson's eyes. She knew enough to know that she could not stand on that ankle without damaging it further. She knew enough to know she was having trouble standing at all.

When she looked again, Sarah Anne was now behind the wheel, the car door still open.

June rubbed her forehead. Had she somehow missed a day?

Sarah Anne tried pulling the car door shut, but Jameson stepped up and put his hand out to stop it. Sarah Anne didn't look at him. She stared straight ahead.

June wanted to disappear.

She couldn't avert her eyes as Jameson leaned his arm on the top of the car's doorframe, dropped his head, and said something to Sarah Anne that June couldn't hear. Sarah Anne reached in front of him for the door, and this time Jameson stepped back and the door slammed shut while he stood there looking through the window at her. Then he glanced back at Ernest, and again at Sarah Anne.

June tried again to get up and into the house, sliding her rear onto the first step and placing her good foot on the ground. She heaved up and back to the next step, though it had taken more effort than she'd expected.

Now Jameson was headed across the lawn toward her.

"I was just going inside," June said.

"June," he said, his voice nearly cracking, his face puffy, as if he had not slept.

"You look like hell," she said. His hair had not been combed and his eyes were red and she wondered if he'd been crying. "Sorry."

"You don't look so great yourself," he said.

"Well."

Sarah Anne was driving away, and June raised her hand but could no longer see inside the car against the glare.

Jameson appeared to be examining the mug on the lawn. He picked it up and brought it to his nose.

"Listen," June said. "There's something I've been wanting to say to you."

Jameson set the mug on the porch. "How about you get inside?"

"It wasn't as if I haven't thought to offer you the spare room. It's occurred to me since you got here, and I just, you know. And now you're back and the roofers are still here, and my goodness, *what* is going *on?*"

"Let me help you get inside."

"Just this morning I was thinking: how many more times am I going to wonder if it's appropriate before I finally offer? How many times before the work is done and I no longer hear the racket, or, I mean, the very, very quiet of you next door? Or I no longer see you from the kitchen with your arms covered in sweat reaching for one thing or another?"

"June . . ."

"How soon before summer ends and you're gone from this place and the question is never asked?" She stood and put her foot down on the step. "Oh, that one smarts."

"Did you fall off the stairs?"

She glanced around the porch and lawn. "Your friend is supposed to get these boxes. Not your friend. I know he's not your *friend*."

"You're not sober, June."

"Oh, Jameson. Do you think I'm . . ." Laughter bubbled inside her. "Drunk? This is nothing," she said, trying to contain herself, suddenly recalling the stark, fierce sound of her scream last night, the feel of her skin. "This is nothing. You haven't seen anything yet."

36

"You haven't seen anything yet," she repeated, and it enraged him. He picked her up like some goddamn hero — this woman nearly as tall as he, picked her up and carried her laughing up the stairs and into her house.

He put her down on the sofa and asked if she'd mind if he had a look at her ankle.

"It's right there. What do you mean?"

"It's swollen," he said. "June," he said, and looked at her with a seriousness she couldn't bear. She squinted at the sun.

"Your day away didn't turn out so well," she said.

"Yours didn't either."

He thought she might cry. She bit her lip and sucked in a breath as if gathering resolve.

"I lied to you," she said.

"Hmn." Jameson lowered himself next to her. "Is that right."

"And not just to you. To everyone I've ever known in my life."

"Can I get you something? Some water or tea or something?"

"No."

"How much have you had to drink?"

June drew a long breath. "I was his favorite," she said. "Mr. Thornton liked me best of all the girls. I was the quietest and most compliant. I did everything I was told. I didn't trust myself after what I did to Heather. You understand?"

Jameson studied her. "How much?" he asked.

"I was seven years old, so what did I know about who I was or wasn't, but I certainly didn't know I could do something like that to Heather, so I made a point to try twice as hard to follow the rules when I was sent away."

June was shivering now. Jameson lifted the throw off the back of the sofa and wrapped it around her legs and up around her shoulders.

"My father was a bit mad. I get that. I always got that. Even as a child I understood that he wasn't right, but he was also just my dad, you know?"

Her teeth chattered.

"It's all right," Jameson said, wondering if there was someone he should call.

"And I understood that it was my fault that he killed himself. I mean, I *believed* it was, that I was the one who, you know, pushed him over the edge." June shoved her hands out in front. She grinned wildly. Jameson tried to smile.

"I made that glass of chocolate milk myself," she said. "I remembered in the middle of last night. I was awake. Were you awake? I got the feeling you were awake."

Jameson gripped his hips. "Yes."

"The wind was atrocious here, and the rain was crashing down and the electricity went out and I felt, I felt . . ."

"What?"

June looked at him closely. "Utterly helpless. You understand?" She gazed at the sofa. "I sat right here and I remembered. I allowed myself to remember that *I* was the one who made that glass of chocolate milk. *Me.*"

"I'm not sure I understand. Are you sure I can't get you something?"

"It was my little act of defiance." She was laughing now, eyes closed, chin to her chest, until her laughter quietly turned to tears. She lifted her head abruptly and went on.

"I asked my father for some chocolate milk and he turned on me and said, 'I hope you live long enough to regret what you've done,' and then he went next door. I suppose it was to say good-bye to his mum and dad, which was more than he had said to me, and then the bastard killed himself. So I made my own glass of chocolate milk. You understand? I made it myself."

"June, you're shaking. Let me get you another blanket."

"And I was sent away. Just like that. My grandparents didn't want me either. Well, that wasn't true. I've forgiven them every-thing. They were so torn up. Can you imagine? Their son, this *nut job*, jumping off a cliff, their granddaughter slicing open children at school. Jesus."

June laughed again and shook her head at her lap, then she held it in her hands and let out a wail that caused a burning ache in Jameson's chest and head.

"Another blanket?" she said. "Yes. In the top of the closet."

Jameson came back and wrapped a yellow quilt around her, tucking it tightly behind her shoulders and beneath her thighs. "I think you could use a rest, June."

"Don't tell me what I need."

"I didn't mean it like that."

"I'm sorry. That wasn't nice. I see you're trying to help. The thing is. The thing is . . ."

"Would you like me to help you upstairs?"

"The thing is, Mr. Thornton took me from my room, and I did what I was told. I don't remember all the sordid details, but I know that I did what I was told."

Jameson stared at her, gleaning what it was she meant.

"You understand?" she asked.

He said he did.

"He danced with me once." She looked across the floor, and he could see the troubled memories in her eyes.

"He had a record player in his office. He put on Nina Simone and made me dance like we were just going to dance, you understand? So then there was this time when Niall tried to dance with me and we were naked. He didn't know. I was drunk. What a mess. He didn't know."

"June. Listen to me." Jameson badly wanted to hold her. She looked at him with the innocence of a child.

"I was seven," she said.

He slid closer. "Is it all right if I sit here right next to you?"

She nodded. "*I* didn't even know," she said in hardly more than a whisper. "It's a very complicated thing. A crafty sort of evil."

She was experiencing some kind of shock. He told himself that if she couldn't calm down in the next few minutes he would call an ambulance.

"Is it all right if I hold on to you?" he asked, and she reached for him as best she could beneath the blanket as he wrapped his arms around her and pulled her closer.

He could feel her crying quietly against his chest. He rested his cheek on the top of her head. "It's good you told me," he said. "It's good you've said it out loud."

The roofers suddenly fired their nail guns into the plywood like a round of bullets, and Jameson startled and gripped June and she held him just as tightly and it went on like that until the men let up.

"May the roof over your head be always strong," Jameson said into her hair.

June looked up at him with only her eyes, her face so serious and close, close enough to kiss if he tried. "And may there always be work for your hands to do," she said.

It was only when the washing machine thunked to a stop that Jameson realized it had been running in another room. He looked up and finally saw the living room in which they sat — the botanical drawings and the hearth and the wool rug and the view of the sea through the front windows and open door. He glanced down at the copper streaks in June's hair. He had read her grandfather's notebooks in the back seat of the car, where he'd slept last night. He gave her a small squeeze, and he thought he had no right to the feelings in his chest, and he wasn't even sure if Sarah Anne was the reason.

37

JAMESON WAS STANDING IN JUNE'S KITCHEN when she came hobbling downstairs, riddled with pain. Her head weighed too much for her neck, and throbbed like her ankle. Worst of all, she was wrung out emotionally and didn't know what to say, where to begin. Jameson had helped her to bed yesterday, where she'd fallen asleep. He woke her in the early evening and fed her a few spoonfuls of lentil soup from Helen's. She'd fallen back asleep in the twilight, knowing he was at the end of the hall, listening to the old springs when he sat on her father's bed, the creak when he shut the door.

"Good morning." She didn't feel like drinking coffee, though the wondrous scent filled the kitchen. What she wanted was another drink.

Jameson stood before the sink, watching the roofers through the window. The bottles of whiskey she'd bought were where she'd left them on the counter. One nearly empty, the other still full.

Jameson looked at her and then at the bottles. He sipped his coffee. "How's your ankle?" he asked.

"Like my head," she said, balancing on one foot. "Thank you for making the coffee."

"Things didn't go so well at the cabin," he said to the window.

June hopped on one foot toward the table. "I sort of gathered that."

"I have night terrors," he said, still without looking at her. "It's gotten better over the years, but they still come for me every now and then. I don't know what's happening or where I am. I only know I have to save my children."

June had not yet sat at the table, and she considered going to him, wrapping her arms around him. "Here," she said. "Sit down with me."

"I can't save them, of course," he said, taking a seat across from her. "But in my dreams I'm willing to die trying."

"I'm sorry," she said, thinking she should take his hand, but did not.

He shook his head, glanced out to the backyard. "The thunder at the cabin was as loud as you can imagine. Lightning had to have hit a nearby tree. I thought it was a gunshot."

June held her hands together in her lap. She lifted her swollen ankle onto the empty chair to her right.

"I started screaming and whipping a fly rod through the dark. I didn't know where I was. I accidentally hit Sarah Anne in the side."

June gasped, and Jameson looked away, shook his head at the window.

"She ran out into the storm to get away from me. They were afraid of me. Her and the boy."

"Oh God. Jameson."

"I slept in the back seat of the car. Sarah Anne didn't want me in the cabin with them. I didn't want to be in there either. Everyone's nerves were shot. The boy flinched when he saw me coming."

"Oh, no."

"So this morning I told her to bring me here. The sooner I finish this job, the better off I'll be."

"I see." June crossed her arms. He had been so quiet in the

night, down the hall in her father's old room. How soundly she had slept knowing he was there. How soundly he, too, must have slept after the night he'd had.

"If you don't mind, I'll get back to work on the house today."

"Of course. I'm sorry about the trouble yesterday. It was the last thing you needed to deal with."

Jameson put up his hand. "Don't," he said. "That's not necessary. I'm glad I was here, and you weren't alone."

June brought her hand to the knot in her throat.

"So," he said, wiping the room clear of the subject, "I'll wear my earmuffs and get started on the downstairs bathroom. Shouldn't take me too long to replace those tiles."

"Sounds good."

"And June?" He turned to face her, and she looked right at him, waiting, though knowing what was coming before the words were said. "We can't. This is not. You understand, right?"

"Oh," she said, as if it had only now dawned on her. "There's no need." She held up her hand. "This place is . . ."

"This place is perfect, June. I'm not trying to pretend that what happened in this town didn't happen. But for all its faults and horrible memories, I don't hate it. In fact, I find myself needing it more than I ever have."

June glanced toward the window and the racket outside. It was day three, and the men had gotten far, all the tar paper laid, nearly all of the shingles fastened down. "They're going to be done today, aren't they?"

"It sure looks that way. Some of the guys are already packing up."

"I understand what you mean," she said. "I came back here from Ireland. It felt like — excuse me for saying it this way — but it felt like I was returning to the scene of the crime. I wanted to be here. I needed to be here. It pains me, and it also returns me to the person I was before anything ever went wrong."

Jameson nodded. "Yes," he said. "That's exactly it."

"Anyway, this other life of yours. A *new* life. You can't give up on it."

Jameson drew a long breath. He stood and rinsed his cup in the sink. "I should get back to work. I'm not getting paid to make conversation."

"Yes. I shouldn't like to dock you."

"I shouldn't like that either."

"I can keep to myself," June said. "I mean, I *will* keep to myself, until you leave."

Jameson nodded at the floor, the same way he'd done in the bungalow that day with the truth of something staring up at him, a look that said he'd like to explain things some other way, he'd like things to *be* another way. "Let me know what I can drop off for you from the store. I don't imagine you'll be getting around much with that ankle."

"I appreciate that. I'll leave a note and cash under the mat."

38

IT WAS EASY NOW TO IMAGINE — after the bedrock and hemlock compost were poured, and the plum trees were planted, and the dusty red hydrangeas with their giant balls of bloom appeared in the corners of the yard — that this place was about to become someone's dream. Jameson wondered who that someone would be, and he guessed whoever they were would have no idea how their life was about to change. He already envied them their existence, even as they remained unaware of the good fortune headed their way.

He had kept to himself while the place took on its final shape, walking the rooms, inspecting the fit and shine, doubling back. More than once he stood near a window just to feel the sash cord, or wrap his hand around a glass knob. There was comfort and pleasure in that, an aesthetic that went beyond the eyes. He could feel the harmony that had taken shape, and was grateful to leave behind this work, to put right this particular house in its highest order, for June.

He thought a lot, too, as he worked, of the things beyond this house and grounds: a young girl sent away to endure a punishment that did not fit the crime, a punishment that was itself a crime, and how death in exchange for justice seemed too

good for some. But that kind of thinking fueled a burning ven-
geance. It was good that Hicks's son was not alive when Jameson's children were dead. It was good that this Thornton character had died as well. Jameson might have gone looking for
him.

But here, this place was like a truce offered up to a world full
of heartache and regret. The season was bringing a well-groomed
close to these days, and soon he'd be home.

June had stayed off her ankle and sent word by text that it
was healing nicely. He didn't know if she was drinking, but he
kept himself from going over to see. He sensed she was doing all
right, that she would be OK, though his mind kept going back to
those bottles on the counter. He should have poured them out.
He shouldn't have said what he said when he was there that last
time, either, even though it was true.

He took the cash from the porch and bought what June
wrote on her list — coffee, yogurt, and bread on Tuesday; Dub-
liner cheese, strawberry jam, and pistachios on Friday — and the
weeks went on for them in this way, Jameson delivering the small
bag of groceries to her mat, and texting her afterward to make
sure she'd taken everything inside, out of the heat. June's replies
were always the same: *Thank you, Jameson, this is lovely.* He could
hear the sound of her voice in those simple words. Once he was
at his truck and saw her front door open and her arm reach out
to retrieve the bag. A rush of blood kicked his heart and filled his
face and he turned away so quickly he had no way of knowing if
she had seen him.

Then today she called.

"He never charged me," she said, referring to Hicks. "Called it
gratis and hung up." She sounded well. She sounded distant, too,
as if they'd never shared a personal word between them.

"Would you like to come over here?" Jameson asked. "I could
show you the house . . ."

June hesitated. "My foot is still a bit unstable . . ."

"Right. Right. Well, I'll come to you, then. I wanted to tell you some things about Hicks. Some things I've been thinking. I'll only be a minute."

Moments later he appeared at her door. "Hey," she said, so gently.

"Hey," he replied.

She didn't invite him in. Instead she stepped out with a small limp, and they sat on the first step, settling in with forearms on knees, their sights directed to the ocean.

"I know for certain that Hicks used to have money," Jameson started in. "He had a well-run construction business and a wife he cared about, so far as I could tell, and two kids. His daughter grew up and went to college in Seattle and never seemed to come back, but his son . . . he was younger, and troubled."

"Listen — you don't have to tell me if you don't want."

"No, no. I can tell you. I *want* to tell you."

June smiled with a hint of sadness.

"That boy, early on, it seemed to me, wasn't quite right. What happened to him, I don't know. What I do know is that his mother was cooking the books of the business, but I don't know if Hicks was in on it and let her take the fall. She went to jail."

"Wow."

"After that, Hicks's life pretty much went to hell. He lashed out at everyone who came near. I imagine his boy got the brunt of it. But the thing here is, the thing is, Hicks ran into Sarah Anne one morning, *the* morning I mean, the day everything . . . He ran into her at the Little Grocer. From the sound of it he'd been drinking. He seemed out of touch with reality, telling her I ripped him off on some job we'd done years before. She told him to go home, and he just sort of snapped, grabbing her by the shoulders and shoving her against the shelves of crackers and chips by the register. Grahame jumped in and got hold of him by the neck, I guess, and threw him out of the store. When Sarah Anne came home and told me, I got on my bike and took off after him. She begged me to leave it alone. So . . . yeah."

"That's when you got into the wreck?"

Jameson wiped his forehead of sweat. There was no need to answer.

"Well," June said, "that's simply awful. It's tragic. There is no other way to say it."

"I heard — and listen, I don't know, people talk, but I can easily imagine it's true — I heard Hicks went home and got into it with his boy. The boy picked up one of Hicks's guns and drove off. Seventeen years old. I don't know that he even had a plan so much as a deep hatred for the world, and that day he'd had about all he could take. Just a kid. A goddamn kid."

They fell into silence, and Jameson imagined June on the sofa where he'd held her, imagined her in the kitchen where he'd last seen her, the windowpanes behind her head, the old teacups on the wall shelf across from her, the apron on the copper hook. But she was right next to him, as lovely, if not more so, than the woman in his imaginings.

"And where is everyone now?" she asked. "I mean, his wife and daughter."

"His wife got out of jail and married a guy she'd worked with at an accounting office. His daughter, I don't know. I guess she's gone somewhere else to start over."

"If only it were that easy," June said.

After a moment he said, "I'll be leaving tomorrow."

"Oh?"

Jameson rubbed his palms down his thighs. "I'm finished. I finished yesterday, in fact."

June let out a long breath, propped her elbows on her knees, and cradled her forehead in her hands. "All right."

"The guy who'll paint the outside trim will be here in a few days. That's the last of it."

"You've finished in record time." She continued to look down at her feet.

"It was a pleasure."

"Well . . ."

"I mean that. The place came together pretty much in perfect order. I don't think I could have pictured it any better."

"Thank you." She looked up at him now. If he had touched her face just then, if he had kissed her like he wanted to, he believed she would have let him, he believed she was waiting for him to do just that. "For everything," she said, turning away.

"Thank *you*, June. For letting me come back like this. For being here again under these conditions. I think it was what I needed. I know it was. It's been good for me in ways I'd never expected."

"Then perhaps it's Van Hicks you need to thank."

"Perhaps you're right."

"It's done wonders for me too, you know, having you here, having the place returned to what it was. I'm going to get emotional here, so . . ."

"Yeah, that's all right then . . ."

"I don't plan to go over until you've gone. If there's anything . . . I don't expect there to be, but of course, if I have a question about anything I'll be in touch."

"All right."

"All right."

"So . . . I'll see you, or I won't."

"Yes. That's right. And Jameson?"

"Yes?"

"You know, don't you, that you can always come back."

"I suppose," he said. "In theory." He stood and brushed the seat of his jeans. "June," he said.

"Take care of yourself," she said.

He nodded at his feet. "You too."

"Goodbye, Jameson."

He looked directly at her, but she did not take her eyes away from the ocean. He thought of the way paint splatter and rust and the raw scent of turpentine struck him as the most beautiful things, and how he'd never said that out loud, but he wanted to say it to June.

"Goodbye, June," he said, and walked away.

39

THIS MORNING A BALD EAGLE snatched a seagull, a juvenile, right out of the sky, and June looked up from the beach in horror and wonder as the young bird's companions dive-bombed the powerful predator in vain. The eagle continued to fly gracefully with its prey, its wings streaking across the sky above June. What shocked her as much as seeing the capture in midair was how the eagle made a wide turn like a jetliner and swooped through the center of the frantic gulls with the juvenile dangling motionless in its talons. For a moment June had to look away. All her life she had witnessed how brutal nature could be, but she had never seen such calculated cruelty as this. The eagle headed north at what appeared to be full speed, and June watched until it disappeared into the trees along the cliff. She wondered if it had the capacity to feel pleased with itself, or if she had simply misunderstood what the bird had set out to do. She wondered what Jameson might have said had he been standing there with her.

It had been six months since he drove away, but June continued to see the world through his eyes, and in this way a part of him remained. She often wondered what he might say on any given day if she pointed out to him the things she saw, like the burst of yellow salmonberries on the ridge where she walked nearly every afternoon. She wondered what he might think if she baked a marionberry pie just to let the scent of buttery crust fill the kitchen before giving the pie away.

Days ago she had come upon a baby seal, white with black spots, sleeping on the shore. She kneeled in the sand several yards back, far enough so as not to disturb it, yet close enough to warn tourists to keep their distance. This wasn't the first time. They would think it was injured or beached and try to "rescue" it, somehow lift it back into the water. She knew that its mother had left it for safekeeping while off on a hunt. June waited for the sun to lower and the tourists to stop coming, and that's when the tide lapped at the sleeping pup, and it woke at the movement. Its eyes, round and black and unblinking, fixed immediately on June. The tide rocked the pup harder, and the rocking became a swaying that buoyed its body up, until suddenly its head snapped around as if a loud noise in the ocean had caught its attention. June heard nothing, but sensed the mother must be nearby. She watched as the pup hobbled into the water, struggling at first when the tide pulled away, until finally it was deep enough to dive into the curl of a wave where the pup disappeared. *Jameson,* June thought. *You would have loved this. Your children would have loved this. Jameson,* she thought, all through the day.

Six months since they had said goodbye, a mild winter come and gone, and here it was the start of another spring. They hadn't had any contact at all. The days were beginning to get longer, the sun traveling farther from the horizon, the shadows shortened across the lawn and kitchen and porch. In all these months, June recalled, often, the words that came to her the day she first saw Jameson.

Long after the sky lowered its gray blanket onto her skull and the rain fell without end and the air turned to thin, stringy wool in her lungs, long after her body became heavy upon rising and her mind slipped into dark, familiar places, she would recall his fluid

shape in the sun on the hill exactly as it was in this moment, and
the memory would take over like branches rupturing her heart,
sprouting stems of white heat, and she would welcome the pain,
all she had left of him, even as her ribs seemed to crack with every
breath, she would smile while drinking her morning coffee, and she
would smile at the unrelenting rain.

The morning Jameson left, June had slipped out before dawn and placed a blank postcard on his windshield. The photograph was of the beach, taken from atop Neahkahnie Mountain. Where June's house was located she'd drawn a tiny red circle, the way her father had done on the maps. After that she remained inside the carriage house behind closed blinds, sitting very still on the sofa in her robe, kneading the hem, remembering to breathe, and she listened to the sounds of Jameson in reverse of that first day, until finally the truck door closed, he backed out of the drive, and the sound of his engine faded. She had gone on sitting there long afterward, afraid to move, feeling the threat that whatever was holding her together might suddenly tear loose.

It wasn't until later that afternoon that she'd gathered the courage to step inside the bungalow.

The rooms still held his presence, the feel of his body cut the air, and she recognized the scent of his hair and the coffee he had drunk that morning. The spaces shone beyond the reflection of the wood, everything plumb and square and warm in the way of memory, of something known and true, and to stand there was to be wrapped in the arms of someone who loved her.

The garden was sprouting with color, and the front porch, with its bright strips of pine, took her breath away: it was where she and Jameson had shared a picnic, and where she had sat between Grandmam's knees while Grandmam braided her hair. To stand in the house was to be filled with a belief that a world full of sorrow was also a world full of grace.

But it was the manila envelope on the kitchen counter that changed everything that day. Across the front, Jameson had written: *I found these in your grandfather's work shed, tucked inside a false drawer. They are something you may have been looking for all your life.*

Inside the envelope were two field notebooks that June had never seen.

On this 21st day of April, the world, our world, is bursting with spring and rain alike, the primroses spreading color was our first sight of the day, mine and Maeve's, and it gave us hope for all things, including that our Finn would someday find his way to being well. He's been slipping so far so fast. Even I am willing to admit that this is true.

It is now after the fact, the 25th day of April. It has taken several days to comprehend how one is supposed to hold a pen in hand, how to write down words, how to breathe. Maeve asks where I find the wherewithal, and she says it like she's cross with me, as if I don't feel what she feels, as if I have somehow escaped being ravaged by the loss. I tell her I write because I do not want this time to pass unnoted. I do not want to behave as if these days were not the most grave and perilous of our lives. It's just, poor Maeve. If I could take her pain and add it to mine, the entire world would feel a little lighter. She was the last person Finn spoke to. "Promise me that you and Da will take care of her. Promise me you won't let June grow up to be like me. She's her mother through and through, Ma. Please keep her that way."

June felt lightheaded, the room a little hazy when she glanced up and took hold of the counter. She closed the notebook, in need of air. She walked out and sat on the back steps and stared across the yard into the white trees, feeling her father nearby, feeling Jameson looking over her shoulder.

June turned the page.

Maeve said she could see in his eyes what he planned to do and she just kept calling for me, but I was out of earshot in the work shed. "I cannot bear the love mixed so deeply with the loss," that poor boy told his ma. "She looks just like her mother. What a gift. What a beautiful, heartbreak of a gift."

June gasped.

Maeve called for me once more and I believe this was the time I heard her, her frightened tone, calling me Cronin when she had only ever called me "Love," but by then Finn had already walked out the front door with Maeve racing at his back, begging him to stay, even as he crossed the road, Maeve screaming his name, screaming for me, and causing a ruckus with the crows. It was there in the road where I found her, crouched and wailing the way a mother wails when she's lost a child, a sight no one should ever have to see.

June's tears fell quickly. How she longed for Grandmam in this moment. How she longed for them all with an ache that doubled her over.

Still she read.

He was never as happy as the day Izzy went into labor. I recall it here as I recalled it then. Finn running around the house, saying she was on the way, on the way, on the way, and though he meant both midwife and baby, it was clear to us that the baby was the one who made him run and shout like that. Poor Izzy. In between labor pains she found the strength to laugh at him, and he wiped the sweat from her forehead and told her so tenderly how sorry he was for the pain.

June was in the room with them, feeling the love, feeling the weight of so much possibility.

Then the awful seizures, the quick collapse before the doctor arrived, and the last word she ever spoke was JUNE.

June's hands shook so badly she could barely read the words before her. She wiped her eyes and set the notebook on her knees and she read through the blur of tears.

We'll never know if she was just calling out the month in a delirium or if she'd meant to name her daughter June, and it never would matter one whit because it was the last thing she ever said, and from that day forward we would all continue to speak her final word, day after day, year after year, June, June, June.

June stood, feeling something like anger. She'd had no idea she was born at home. Born in the bungalow just like her father. Her birth certificate has Nestucca Beach as the place, and the midwife's name and signature, but June had always assumed she was born at the clinic several miles south on the highway. Why hadn't anyone ever told her? Did they think she would blame them for her mother's death? Did they feel responsible because June had not been born in a hospital? June knew enough to know it wouldn't have made a difference. Not if her mother hadn't been diagnosed beforehand. Not if what had happened came on as suddenly as it appeared to.

June wiped her face and drew a breath that smelled faintly of fall, of something brittle on the wind, and when she glanced inside the other notebook she saw the date of her birth and the outline of the same story, written there as it was remembered by her grandfather in the days after her father's death.

June immediately returned to the carriage house and packed up her belongings. Several days later she moved into the bungalow, the place where she was born, among the people who had loved her, who had wanted her so much, the place where all had spent their final moments on earth. June felt their presence around her, not as ghosts but as threads here and there, as lively and real and true as a bird knowing where her springtime nest lay, even when returning from thousands of miles away.

A steady stream of writing followed in the bungalow, and June finished the novel within weeks of moving in. Leigh, the sister who'd needed love the most, found it, as love is so often found in books.

June had not taken another drink since the day Jameson wrapped her in a blanket and let her say the thing she needed to say. It helped, too, to have a neighbor who'd become such a good friend to June. Elin was her name, and June had liked her from the minute she saw her standing in the center of the wool rug with a grin on her face. With a single clap of her hands, her accent softly Floridian, she said, "Let me make an offer you can agree to right now."

She bought the carriage house the week it went on the market, and a kinship wove between them, as June could sense that Elin, too, had been shellshocked by this world, and had found that here, among the Pacific evergreens and rain and the brightest summer sun, was her true-north home.

Now, six months and two weeks after June had placed the blank postcard on Jameson's windshield, it was returned. Elin walked it over with a lopsided smile, fanning the card as if to ward off its heat.

June recognized the card and snatched it up. She held it to her chest and went inside the bungalow and shut the door before she read what was written on the back.

A long and strange tale for another time. Love, Jameson.

June propped the card on the mantel, where she could see it when she crossed the room, the small red circle a reminder of who she was, where she was, the place she was meant to be.

That same evening, Elin began telling June stories about her sister and mother back in Florida. It was as if the postcard, arriving by mistake at the carriage house, where Jameson believed June to be, had broken through another dimension, and each was able to step across and speak her truth. Elin told June about her nieces and their father, and how everyone's life had been shaped again and again by tragedy. They made the best of what they had, she said, and she also told June about her divorce. Then slowly June revealed pieces of her own life, sitting next to her friend in the Adirondack chairs, feeling part of a life she could not have imagined months ago, or ever — watching the waves, drinking Elin's sweet iced tea. "You can steal my story if you want," Elin told her, and June smiled and said how people often said this to writers, believing novels were based on somebody's real life, as if only the names were changed and the rest was laid out, ready for the taking, like that. "But all right," June said. "I just might."

40

His DREAMS WERE NO LONGER about the children. Mostly they were not. Mostly they were about June, and he would wake in the night feeling her watching, feeling her somewhere behind him, the slightness of her, the feel of her, the smell of her cutting the air like a fragrance. Then he would turn to find Sarah Anne dozing beside him. Sometimes she patted his shoulder. Most times she slept right through, exhausted by her days at the wheel and all the hours with Ernest — the pedagogic play that Jameson neither fully understood nor fully became a part of, the favored meals, the cheese melted in the way he liked. The boy deserved all of this and more, and yet Jameson could not help feeling like an interloper in his own house. He could not watch the two of them without his mind filling with thoughts he could not seem to drive away. Was she ever this tender with Nate and Piper? Did she adore them in just this way? Take possession over them in a way that squeezed Jameson out?

He believed he could take it. He wanted to believe it was true, that he could go on this way, now that he had become a father again, now that Sarah Anne was back at her wheel and selling her work in shops around the country. He watched her move through the world with purpose in a way he had not seen since the twins were alive. For as heavy as Jameson felt with the passing of time, Sarah Anne appeared lighter, less complicated. He still could not look at her without feeling the loss of the children. His love for her in one hand, his loss in the other. He could not pick up Ernest without feeling as if he were betraying his own children, and in turn failing the real-life boy in his arms.

He'd catch himself, at the sink or in the shower or in his workshop thinking about June falling on the front lawn, the sound of the washing machine churning in the other room, the way he had held her on the sofa, his cheek against her soft hair. Then he'd close his eyes and listen to Sarah Anne's bare feet on the hardwood, her sighs, her hands shifting jars through cupboards, returning foil to the drawer. Sarah Anne teaching Ernest to sing the alphabet. To tie his shoes and make a bowl out of clay.

June's postcard arrived last week in response to the one he'd sent her six months ago, an entire year gone by, and the only communication they had had were these two cards six months apart, with so little written on them. And yet it was enough. Everything that lay beneath it felt fixed and understood.

The card was similar to the one she'd left on his windshield, another aerial view of Nestucca Beach with her home somewhere down in the trees, circled in red. Jameson kept the card in his shop without showing it to Sarah Anne. A small and simple act that filled him with a terrible guilt. He went out there when he didn't need to, just to take it from the drawer and stare at the circle and read again and again what she had written, and he had to force the smile from his face when he locked up the shop and returned to the house, to a woman and a child who no longer seemed to want or need him near.

> *May those who love us love us.*
> *And those that don't love us,*
> *May God turn their hearts.*
> *And if He doesn't turn their hearts,*
> *May he turn their ankles,*
> *So we'll know them by their limping.*

41

A YEAR AND A HALF AFTER they had said goodbye, and still they laughed about those cards, now placed side by side on the mantel in the bungalow.

They laughed about the way he came upon her in the back garden that day, and stood in the same place she had stood the first time she came to see him. She had turned in the same startled way, nervous as he'd been nervous, and when it started to sink in that he was not part of her imagination, she felt herself smile, and he came toward her with his arms out, and my God, how long did they stand there holding on to each other for dear life?

Now, most mornings June watched from bed while he dressed. He liked to make breakfast before she came downstairs, to be alone in the kitchen first thing, with the birds and the quiet and the chance to watch the elk undisturbed. It was summer, and they ate yogurt with granola on the front porch in their pajamas. June liked to pick blackberries by herself, off along the edges of the forest, collecting them in the white pail she'd given to Jameson that day for the birdbath. She'd return with a calm mind and her pail half full, her fingers the stained colors of her dreams.

Some days June accompanied Jameson at work. She'd read in the yard or she'd write by hand in her notebook beneath the shade of a tree. When the rain returned she'd take cover on a porch or in a living room, and they would share a picnic lunch inside, and she would read to him from the things she wrote and ask what rang true to his ear and what hadn't yet hit the mark, and he understood the history of words in a way she did not, the paths they'd followed to arrive where she could use them, and she found it strange that he knew such things, and that he'd known just when to come back, and she wondered how it was that they had found each other at all, in a world so large and grievous.

ACKNOWLEDGMENTS

Grateful thanks to my agent, Larry Kirshbaum, for his continued support, counsel, and much-needed sense of humor. And to everyone at Houghton Mifflin Harcourt for guiding and championing this book with kindness, acuity, and patience: Nicole Angeloro, Larry Cooper, Liz Anderson, and especially Bruce Nichols for opening the door and welcoming me in.

Thanks to Mary and Robert White of County Carlow, Ireland, for opening their lovely home and sharing their knowledge and friendship and appreciation for all living things.

Thanks also to Sharon Harrigan, Holly Lorincz, and Nancy (this is our life!) Rommelmann for the whip-smart writing advice on very short notice, and for the wholehearted, enduring friendships that stretch far beyond the small circle of the work we do.

Much appreciation to Amy Pulitzer for the gift that allowed this book to be written, and a life to be lived with imagination, grace, and goodwill. And Kerry Allen for planting the seed of this story shortly after my arrival in this beautiful haven.

And to Robert Kelleher, whose tenderness and love for the world and for me inspires my work and life every single day.